DANIEL G. MILLER

The Orphanage By The Lake

HOUNDSTOOTH
BOOKS

First edition

ISBN: 978-1-7376463-9-6

Editing by Elyse Lyon
Cover art by Damonza
Advisor: Siobhan Jones

This book was professionally typeset on Reedsy.
Find out more at reedsy.com

To the missing girls.

Acknowledgement

Reed Soeffker for teaching me the ins and outs of a missing person investigation. Hazel wouldn't be half the investigator she is without your patient instruction. All mistakes are mine alone.

Daniel Maya for showing me a day in the life of a private investigator. I can't thank you enough for how generous you were with your time and for answering my rookie questions.

Christina Kang, Phil Lee, and Sung Cho for providing me with a window into Korean culture through your friendship, kindness, and advice. Hopefully, I did you proud.

Siobhan Jones for delivering the perfect developmental edit. Your ability to zero in on the changes that take a novel from good to great is a marvel.

Elyse Lyon for trudging through my sloppy grammar and editing, and carrying this book over the finish line in fine form.

My wife, Lexi, for listening to my off-the-wall story ideas at all hours of the day, always with an open heart and an open mind.

My family and friends for serving as the ultimate alpha reading posse and softening the rough edges of my first draft.

My beta readers, particularly Anne B., for your enthusiasm and determination in coaxing this novel to reach its potential.

And finally, the team at Damonza for your creativity and inventiveness in designing the cover and supporting art for this novel. You brought *The Orphanage By The Lake* to life.

Chapter 1

Ah, the morning...

Is there anything worse?

I've always envied people who spring out of bed and jog around the neighborhood with a broad smile on their face. Unfortunately, I am not that person. My standard routine is to be woken from a deep sleep by a song from my Totally '80s mix. The sound of "Bette Davis Eyes" usually points me in the right direction. Then I snooze my phone alarm once on a good day, three times on most days. At this point, my roommate, Kenny, barks from the other room, telling me to get up and turn my damn alarm off. This is when I heave myself out of my squeaky bed and, with one eye open, stumble into the shower. Because my brain is only partly functional, I stand there under the hot water singing "Bette Davis Eyes" for the next five minutes before I embark on the whole soap-and-shampoo process.

Today is no different. I go through my routine and throw on a white blouse and navy pencil skirt. Once I've applied my makeup—a touch of bronzer, a dab of mascara, and a streak of highlighter to make those cheekbones pop—I enter the living room of our firetrap Chinatown apartment. The room doubles as our kitchen and dining room. It was open concept before people knew what open concept was. Kenny lounges at the folding-card-table-slash-dining-table and works his way through a trough of Froot Loops while he reads. He's studying for his police officer's exam. The thought of him as a police officer is slightly horrifying. There isn't an object in our place that Kenny Shum hasn't dropped, toppled, or flat-out obliterated since he arrived. I'm sure that will go down swimmingly at the New York City Police Department.

My phone's calendar notification pings. Ugh, I'm going to be late for my meeting. I reach into the fridge and grab a sugar-free Red Bull. I know what you're going to say...What am I doing drinking Red Bull in the morning? Well, I don't like coffee, and when you're as tired of your job as I am, you do what it takes to get you through. Plus, it's sugar-free. You've got to give me credit for that. This day-old mochi doughnut I'm eating isn't going to wash itself down.

Kenny observes me and gives me a smile and a nod. He's witnessed my panicked late-for-work routine before.

"Good morning," he says.

He sports black hair, kind brown eyes, a tight haircut that feels like a tennis ball when you rub it, and a face as flat and round as a pancake. He reminds me of an Asian Stay Puft Marshmallow Man, except without the sailor hat. I suspect he might have a crush on me, but I do my best to make it clear that's not happening.

"Good morning. How many days till your exam?" I say with doughnut crumbs hanging from my lips.

"Five. I can't wait to be done."

"Don't worry. You'll crush it. I'll quiz you when I get back tonight."

Kenny's eyes light up.

"Thanks, Hazel. That would be great. I'll cook us some

bibimbap."

Kenny and I bond over food, especially Korean food. It reminds us of home.

"Yum. That's a deal. All right, Special K, I'm off to the office. Good luck with your studying."

I run out the door with my doughnut and Red Bull in hand. Kenny says something back to me as I leave, but I don't hear it because I'm already rocketing down the stairs of our walk-up building. We live on the fifth floor, which makes for a soul-crushing slog up the stairs at the end of a tough workday.

I hustle down the steps and launch myself out the front door and onto Mulberry Street. The sidewalk is bustling with a bunch of those smiley early risers I can't understand. It's a cloudy fall day in Manhattan, cool enough to keep the less pleasant smells at bay but warm enough to take a long stroll. Aromas from the Chinese vendor stands float through the air. An enchanting mixture of fish, fruit, and flowers. I wish I had time to stop and smell the proverbial roses, but I'm already late, and this is not a client I want to keep waiting.

Fortunately, my office stands just a few blocks from my apartment. I power walk down Mulberry and then hook a left on Canal. My agency sits on the third floor of a weathered brick building on Cortlandt Alley, which oddly isn't an alley but a tiny street. When I signed my lease on this building, I was the only tenant. But in the intervening years, it's somehow become trendy, with various designers and fashion start-ups moving in. I think it's the first and last trend that I'll start. Not a day goes by when I don't stumble over a self-important fashion shoot when I pop out for lunch. Still, it fits what I do. Close enough to walk, but far enough away that the shady characters who hire me can't find where I live.

Speaking of shady characters, time to meet with my client. I wave my key card at the keypad of the building and scamper up the worn wooden stairs. More stairs. Keeps the glutes tight. I turn the corner of the stairwell, and an unwelcome sight greets me.

"You're late," says Gene Strauss.

Gene slouches on the bench outside my office, beads of sweat gathering about the slicked black hairs on his receding hairline. He's wearing a brown-and-yellow-striped shirt, buttoned about two buttons too low and revealing a rash of chest hair. The knuckles of his thick, meaty, gold-ringed fingers crack before he rests his hands on his oversized gut. He's here to find out about his wife, and I can't stop thinking to myself, *Who in their right mind would marry this man?*

I take a moment to catch my breath.

"I'm sorry about that, Mr. Strauss. How did you get into the building?"

He stands and smiles, showing unnaturally large canine teeth on a face that's sloped forward like a rat's.

"Never mind how I got here. You got something for me?"

I don't know how I feel about the fact that anyone can access my supposedly secure office building, but I decide to dismiss it for now. I don't want to spend more time with him than necessary. Unfortunately, right now he's my only client, so it is necessary.

"Yes, Mr. Strauss, I have the report you requested. Why don't we discuss it in my office?"

I pull out my key and unlock the door. As I open it, I look at the engraving in the frosted glass: "Hazel Cho – Private Investigator." It sounds so official, so badass. When I was a kid, my dad and I used to watch old Humphrey Bogart movies, and I fell in love with Detective Sam Spade in *The Maltese Falcon*. "The cheaper the crook, the gaudier the patter." Someday I'm going to deliver a line like that. If only my clients knew I live blocks away, in a building that the city should condemn.

"Why don't you have a seat, Mr. Strauss?" I say, closing the door behind him and gesturing to one of the two leather chairs that sit across from my desk. I don't have many things that I'm proud of, but my office is one of them. My sister, Christina, and I decorated it during the early days of my private investigation business, when I thought I would be like Veronica Mars, Thomas Magnum, or someone similar. I raided my savings and bought beautiful white chairs and a glass desk with gold trim. We installed built-in bookshelves and stuffed them with a bunch of books I still aspire to read. My dad and I painted the walls a calming dark blue gray, while Christina looked at her phone and pretended to help. My detective license hangs behind my desk in a frame that would be more suitable for a Van Gogh. Little did I know then that my private investigation business would be less *Magnum, P.I.* and more *To Catch an Insurance Swindle*.

"Before we start, can I get you anything? A coffee, water, soda?" I say.

My news for him isn't good, so I'm hoping the coffee might help it go down smoother. Maybe I should slip in a sedative while I'm at it.

"Nah. Just give me the report."

He has a thick South Philly accent and the charm to match.

"Okay, your call."

I pull a manila folder from my canvas work bag and put it on the desk in front of me. I used to show clients the reports and pictures on my computer or via email, but I've found that they're less likely to be in denial if I show them the hard copies. It makes it more real.

"Mr. Strauss, you hired me because you wanted to know if your wife was having an affair. In short, the answer is yes. Per your instructions, I followed Emily last Thursday and Friday when you were out of town. On both occasions, she ate dinner with another man. The dinner was clearly personal in nature. No laptops, documents, or other work paraphernalia. She and that man then left dinner. I followed their cars, which traveled the same direction, and they eventually returned to his house."

I open the folder and hand him the report. He flips past the text and skips to the pictures. They always skip to the pictures. As his thick, hairy fingers flip through the images of his wife in the arms of another man, I watch the rage building. He clenches the photos harder. His face turns a dangerous shade of purple, and his legs bounce violently up and down like a washing machine on full tilt. Then his eyes rise from the pictures to me.

The eyes of a demon.

"You fuckin' bitch," he says to me, savoring every word. A malevolent smile crawls across his face.

"I'm sorry, what?"

At first, I think I misheard him. He must have said *That fuckin' bitch.* I replay it in my mind. Nope, he said *You fuckin' bitch.*

He rises from his seat and hurls the pictures in my face. A vein protrudes from his forehead. "These pictures are fakes. What, you think you can give me a few fake photos and I'm going to just say thank you and pay you my hard-earned money? You think I'm an idiot?"

When I followed Mrs. Strauss, I thought I saw bruises on her

6

wrists, but I couldn't be sure.

Now, I'm certain.

I ease up from my chair and raise my palms to calm him. This isn't the first time one of my clients has tried to shoot the messenger. Of course, none have been as big as Gene Strauss.

"I assure you those pictures are real. Now, I'm sorry to be the bearer of bad news, but it's the truth."

He points a thick finger in my face. Loud, fast breaths rush from his nose.

"Don't you lie to me."

"I'm not lying to you. I've seen many of these cases, and it might take time, but you can f—"

He heaves one of the desk chairs, and it crashes against the bookshelf. Private investigation handbooks tumble to the floor. I glance back at him. Sweat pours from his hairline. I search his eyes. They remind me of a wounded dog I found once in the woods by my parent's house: hurt, scared, angry, unpredictable. I glance over at my bag. My Taser sits inside it just a few feet away.

"I want my deposit back."

I stiffen my spine and shake my head.

"I can't do that, Mr. Strauss."

What I don't tell him is that his fifty percent deposit has already been spent and I was banking on his second payment to cover this month's rent.

His fists clench, and he takes a step closer, lumbering around my desk. An artery pulses in his neck. He's coming for me.

I keep my eyes locked on him, but my hand slides toward my Taser. I've seen this look before. It's the look of a predator searching for his advantage.

A door slams on the first floor, interrupting our stare-down.

Strauss takes a step backward and listens. A woman's heels click and clack up the stairs. The only other sound is our breathing. I want to run, but if you want to be a female private investigator, you don't have that luxury. That's what they want. They want you to run. They want you to be afraid. They want you to quit. They want you to cry. I hear the entrance to my hallway squeak open, and then a rap against my office door. I release a breath. I don't know who it is, but they can't be worse than being alone with this animal.

"Who is it?" I say. My voice catches in my throat.

"It's Madeline Hemsley," says a haughty voice through the door.

I rack my brain to put a face to the name, but I don't remember any Madeline Hemsley.

"Who?"

The door opens and she glides into the room, the scent of expensive perfume wafting around her. She is the inverse of Gene Strauss: lithe and immaculate, dressed in a tailored suit that screams money—something I desperately need. She's young but has clearly had several rounds of Botox. The pale skin on her forehead shines beneath a waterfall of blonde hair. Everything about her is pointed. Her nose, her cheekbones, her speech, her gaze. But what distinguishes her are her eyes, an icy shade of green that penetrates. Relief washes over me at having another woman in the room.

She shoots a dismissive look at Gene Strauss, oblivious to what she's walked into.

"I'm sorry to interrupt, but I really must speak with you." She looks like she's in her midthirties, but she speaks like a middle-aged countess.

Madeline's disdain only fuels Gene's rage. I watch his pupils pulse back and forth to me and then Madeline, calculating whether he should take out his anger on both of us. I squint at him and shake my head, silently telling him it's not worth it. After a few interminable seconds, his shoulders slouch and his face cools. He's not smart, but he's smart enough to know this doesn't end well for him. He'll have to fight another day. Still, he can't walk away without a parting shot. He points at me.

"This isn't over."

He trains his stubby finger on me for a beat, letting the threat sink in, then brushes past Madeline and slams the door behind him.

Chapter 2

"What a hideous man," says Madeline. She extends her hand for a shake, but with her palm down, as though I'm meant to kiss it.

I stare at her in disbelief. A man just trashed my office and was pretty clearly about to attack me, and she acts like we're having tea at the country club. I look at the ceiling while I try to find my breath, pushing the exasperation down. A mash-up of emotions rips through my chest. Anger at Gene Strauss for what he tried to do to me. Disappointment in myself for how I wasn't more prepared. Frustration with the fact that every day I feel like I'm one wrong move away from being throttled by an impotent man and his insecurity. But none of those thoughts are going to do me any good right now. Right now I need to deal with this porcelain doll in front of me.

I reach out to shake her hand. My hand trembles, and my palm is sweaty, and I can tell by the look on Madeline's face that she notices. I lean on my desk to steady myself.

"I'm sorry, Ms.—?" In my distress, I've forgotten her name already.

"Hemsley."

"Ms. Hemsley. I'm going to have to ask you to come back later. As you can probably see, you've caught me at a bad time."

I feel tears welling in my eyes, so I turn toward the window. I'm still trying to process what just happened, and I can tell this woman isn't going to offer a sympathetic ear.

She glances at her watch. "I must insist that we meet now."

I snap back around and watch as she picks up the chair that Strauss tipped over and sets it upright before sitting down. She shows no care or concern for why the chair is toppled; she simply knows she needs a seat, and that's all that matters. Her lack of empathy is unnerving. I've seen this type of rich person before. They almost enjoy inconveniencing you. It makes them feel special, important. I remember when I was a teenager waitressing at the local country club and a woman made me mix tartar sauce from scratch just because she could.

"Have we met?" I ask.

She scoffs at the suggestion, as though I'd asked her if she'd like to smoke crack with me.

"No, Ms. Cho, we have not met."

An awkward silence hangs in the room, and I realize that there is no way I'm getting this woman out of my office without listening to whatever sob story she's got for me about a cheating husband or duplicitous mother-in-law. I bend over and pick up the pictures Strauss tossed on the floor. Then I grab a tissue and wipe the edges of my eyes, but I can't erase the tremor from my hands. She doesn't seem to care.

"You can call me Hazel. What can I do for you, Ms. Hemsley?"

"Of course, Hazel."

I notice she does not offer for me to call her Madeline. Shocker.

"Hazel, I'm here because I require your assistance. My goddaughter has gone missing."

I sit back in my chair. I didn't see that one coming. You don't see a lot of godparent casework when you're a private investigator.

"Your goddaughter? When did she go missing?"

She pulls a picture from her supple black leather purse and hands it to me with both hands like a priceless piece of jewelry. The girl in the picture is about thirteen or fourteen. She has dark irises, soft brown skin, a spring of kinked hair, and an electric smile suffused with the joy and energy of youth. My first thought is astonishment that Madeline has a Black friend, let alone one who likes her enough to make her a godparent. A dazzling floral dress accentuates the girl's face. Her smile is bright and innocent, but there's a wisdom in her eyes, as though she's seen things but keeps her own counsel.

"She went missing six months ago," says Madeline.

"Six months ago?" My eyebrows jump up my forehead. "Ms. Hemsley, the most important hours in finding a missing person are the first forty-eight. After that, it's a needle in a haystack. After six months, there's nothing left to investigate."

Madeline's lips pinch, and she looks right through me. She picks at her nails like I'm boring her.

"I'm aware. Yet here we are."

"What about the parents?"

She flicks a piece of lint off her suit pants.

"They're dead. She's an orphan."

"How did they die, if you don't mind me asking?"

"A car accident, when she was an infant."

I feel like I'm cross-examining a hostile witness on the stand. "I'm sorry. Were you related?"

"No, just close friends."

12

"Is there a godfather?"

"No."

"So you're her sole guardian?"

Her neck tightens. "No. She was staying at an orphanage, or I guess they call it a children's home now, but it serves children who have lost their parents or had other family issues."

She shifts in her seat, anticipating the question I'm going to ask next.

"Why was she at a children's home? Why doesn't she live with you?"

Madeline's gaze drifts away from me and out the window as she loses herself in memory. She agonizes over her words.

"My lifestyle isn't suited for a child. Besides, she has a better life there than I could ever give her, and I've ensured she receives the absolute best care. It's the premier home upstate."

When I hear the word *upstate* I stand up from my desk. I've had enough of this woman who's too cool to care for her poor orphan goddaughter.

"Well, they're not giving her very good care if she's gone missing, are they? I'm sorry, but you're going to have to find someone else for this. I strictly work in the city, not upstate. And given the time that's passed, I doubt there's much I could do for you, anyway. I don't even have a car."

For a moment, the mask breaks, and I glimpse a quiver cross her lips. She swallows hard and stands with me. She grabs my hand with both of hers and bends at the waist toward me. These hands have never done manual labor, but the grip suggests resolve.

"Please, Hazel. I'll pay for your car and all your expenses. I understand it's a long shot, but it's all I have left."

She digs into her purse and takes out an envelope filled with cash. I don't know how much it contains, but it's significantly more than I have in my bank account, which is approximately $172. Kenny saw my bank statement the other day and literally laughed out loud.

"This should get you started. I'll have my assistant drop off another five thousand today or tomorrow. If you find her by the end of next week, I'll give you one hundred thousand dollars."

I have to work to keep my jaw from dropping open. A hundred thousand dollars would change everything for me. I could pay off my debt, pay my rent, refurbish my office, take out some ads, take better cases, turn down the Gene Strausses of the world, become the private investigator I always wanted to be. But only if I find her by the end of next week, which isn't enough time.

"What if I don't find her?"

"Then I hire another private investigator. You're not the first and won't be the last unless you find her."

"Ms. Hemsley, that's not nearly enough time for a case as complicated as this, particularly when so much time has passed. This could take weeks. Months, even. And even then I can't guarantee I'd find her."

"I'm sorry. Those are my terms. My dad used to say a ticking clock focuses the mind. And judging by your office, if that's not enough, the money should be sufficient motivation."

I reappraise her, and I catch red around the edges of her eyes and the bloodshot whites within. She's been crying. Then my gaze flicks to the stack of unpaid bills on my desk. I can't afford to decline this offer, or any offer, for that matter. I'm guessing that Gene Strauss will be less than timely with his final payment. But I still need to know more.

"What about the police?"

"I reported it to the police. They did a thorough investigation but, frankly, I don't think it was their top priority. They told me she probably ran away and would come back soon enough. That was months ago."

"What about another private investigator? You mentioned I wasn't the first."

"I've tried other investigators. They're all incompetent and have failed."

"Regardless, talking to them might save me some time. I'll need their names and contact information."

"I'm afraid I can't do that. I want a fresh pair of eyes."

Her words hang heavy, punctuated by the distant wail of a siren from outside my window. In my experience, when someone has hired multiple private investigators, one of two things is going on, or both: the case is impossible to solve, or the client is impossible to work with. I'm guessing this is both. Everything about this situation tells me I should walk away, but the thought of this beautiful little orphan girl tugs at me. Plus, let's be honest: I've got an envelope full of cash in my hand, and I really could use the money. I place my phone in front of her.

"Do you consent to being recorded?" New York law requires that I ask.

"Yes, I do."

"Okay, tell me everything you know."

As I open my laptop and prepare to take notes, I see the corners of Madeline's mouth drift upward. She places her purse down in the chair next to her like she's placing a ring on a pillow and takes a deep breath.

"Unfortunately, I don't know much. I was at home on a Monday morning. I had just finished my morning HIIT class and was making my usual espresso when I received a call from Saint Agnes—that's the name of the children's home—where Mia was staying. That's her name, Mia. Mia Ross."

For a moment, Madeline's voice falters, but she quickly steels herself.

"Go on."

"The head of the home, Thomas Mackenzie, who's an old family friend, informed me that Mia had gone missing and asked if she had contacted me."

"Had she?"

"No. As you can imagine, I found the news quite distressing and told him I would come over right away. He rejected the idea out of hand and tried to calm me down. He told me it wasn't necessary for me to visit and that she was most likely out exploring the campus, and they'd track her down in short order. He said he would call once they found her. I waited at home holding my phone, staring out the window for the rest of the day, but the phone never rang."

"What did you do then?"

Madeline rolls her eyes, as though telling her story yet again is exhausting. "I called Saint Agnes, of course. Thomas told me they were still searching the grounds, and in contact with the neighbors. I asked him if we should call the police and he told me not yet, that we should at least wait forty-eight hours."

I type a note in bold. Strange that they resisted bringing in the police.

"Okay. What happened after forty-eight hours?"

"Nothing. That was what was so infuriating. My goddaughter is missing, and after forty-eight hours, Thomas doesn't even have the decency to call me with an update. I said enough is enough and called the police."

I peck away on the keyboard, darting my eyes back and forth from the computer screen to Madeline so that she knows I'm listening. Most private detectives are men, and men don't always listen. This is one of my few competitive advantages.

"Tell me about your interaction with the police."

Madeline digs back into her purse and pulls a card from her wallet. She hands it to me. The card says *Detective Robert Riether.*

"I called the police, and they directed me to this detective, Detective Riether. He took down my information and told me they would begin an investigation."

"And did they?"

"Yes. To his credit, he went to the home and visited Mia's room, talked to the staff, and walked the grounds."

I raise an eyebrow. "He told you this? Normally, police don't comment on an active investigation."

Madeline sneers like my questions are an inconvenience. "Actually, no. I found that out from the home. Thomas called me in a huff the next day. He told me it was premature to involve the police and that he would have appreciated it if I had told him they would be coming. I told him if he knew where the girls in his care were, we wouldn't have to involve the police. Since then, he hasn't returned my calls."

I underline the name *Thomas Mackenzie* in my notes. "He sounds like a real gem."

Madeline's eyes crinkle in agreement. Her version of a laugh.

"He's not all bad. He's just a bit of a curmudgeon and takes a great deal of pride in Saint Agnes."

"And did Detective Riether ever call you?"

"Yes. At first he was very helpful, calling me to let me know the police were investigating. Of course, he couldn't share any details, but he seemed genuinely interested in finding Mia and to be working on resolving it. He asked the right questions and was throwing himself into the case, but—"

"Go on."

"But then he just sort of...faded out. He stopped calling me, and when I called him, he would take days to return the call or just not call back at all. When I did speak to him, he would say they were still actively investigating, but the department had limited resources and they had reallocated those resources to 'more pressing matters.' What could be more important than a missing little girl?"

I pivot my chair from the computer screen and look directly at Madeline. Her brow creases with genuine concern, and I feel for her. One of the toughest aspects of missing persons investigations is the fact that the police can't share information because they don't want to compromise the investigation. And you don't want to pester them to the point where they stop wanting to help you. That leaves you in the position of just hoping and waiting. Of course, I don't have these limitations, so if nothing else, I might give Madeline peace of mind by sharing what I find. But first, I need to know more about this girl.

I lean forward in my chair.

"Tell me about Mia."

Madeline's face softens, her emerald eyes clouded with memories. She smiles a pained smile.

"She's the most beautiful girl, Hazel. She has this big mischievous grin and brings joy into every room she's in. The staff tells me she's quite the prankster too. You know, putting fake bugs in girls' cereal, plastic wrap on the sink faucet, et cetera. She loves music and is the biggest Olivia Rodrigo fan, or at least she thinks she is. I don't get it. Too angry for my taste. And there's no game or sport she won't play. She loves tennis. She would spend all day outside if she could."

She pulls her phone from her purse and scrolls through her gallery. Each tap of the phone is performed with the delicacy of a seamstress.

"She wants to be a singer. She has such a beautiful voice, and there's a presence to her when she's onstage."

Madeline presses play on a video and hands me the phone.

Mia stands alone at the center of an old wooden stage in what I can only assume is the auditorium of the children's home. Behind her, plush royal purple velvet curtains pour from the rafters. The video is grainy, but even through the blur, I can see what Madeline means. Mia holds her head high and stands with assurance, like she belongs there. Her hair springs from a bright-pink headband as though powered by her energy. The spotlight highlights the sparkle in her eyes and her bright-white smile of big teeth. Unlike at my nieces' recitals, where parents chatter and fall over themselves to get a better video angle of their "special" child, the audience sits silent and at full attention, as if they know they're about to see something special. She begins to croon, and I smile because it is one of my favorites: "Time after Time" by Cyndi Lauper. She sings it a cappella, rendering the words poignant and moving.

Her voice carries through the hushed space, beautiful and haunting. A soprano with an echo of depth. Maybe it's what I just went through with Gene Strauss, but as I hear this girl's voice, I can't help getting choked up. If I don't pull it together,

Madeline's going to think I'm a mess.

I glance at Madeline and can tell it's getting to her as well. I clear my throat and try to steer us back on track.

"How old is she?"

"She's thirteen. She'll turn fourteen in a month."

"How often did you visit her."

"About quarterly. I'd take her out to the movies or we'd grab ice cream."

"Did she have a boyfriend or crush? Someone she might have run off with?"

"Not that I know of."

The song continues in the background. Mia sings those famous lyrics: about being lost; about how if you look, you can find her.

If that isn't a sign, I don't know what is. I bite my lip and extend my hand.

"All right, Ms. Hemsley, I'll do it."

An ecstatic smile flashes across her face before she catches herself. She jumps up from her seat and straightens her jacket. She extends her hand and I shake it, feeling like I've just done a deal with the devil herself.

"Thank you, Hazel," she says as she gathers her purse and heads toward the door. It seems like she's trying to escape before I reconsider. "By the end of the day, you'll have a car and additional funds for expenses."

"Thank you. I appreciate that. And please send me that video and any other pictures or videos you have of her."

She grabs the doorknob, straightens her back, and regains her dictatorial tone.

"Of course, but I will expect a report in forty-eight hours."

I nod. Nothing comes easy with this woman.

She shuts the door behind her, and I collapse into my chair. My mind speeds, thoughts colliding with one another as I consider the case. There's something about Madeline that sets me on edge, and I can't shake the feeling that I've been drawn into something more complex than what she's shared with me. Still, it's that very niggling that intrigues me. I became a private investigator to crack cases like this.

"Forty-eight hours," I whisper to myself.

Time to get to work.

Chapter 3

I try to work, but I can't. I'm still absorbing what just happened. For the next ten minutes, I stare at my computer's desktop. There's a picture of me from about ten years and fifteen pounds ago looking back at me. You know how people say "That woman's got a body that won't quit"? Well, mine does, and it quit right after I graduated from college. It's not that I'm unattractive, it's just that when you used to be better, everything about you feels worse. In the picture I'm with my friends at a Las Vegas pool party, wearing a horrifyingly small bikini, my black hair shining in the sun, my charcoal almond eyes full of confidence, tan, a little too skinny and bursting with optimism.

Oh, how the mighty have fallen.

But I don't really absorb the picture. I don't absorb anything. I'm shaken from my brief visit with Strauss. Every time I consider this fresh case, I'm distracted by a creak on the steps or the whistle of wind through my underinsulated windows. The words *This isn't over* ring in my ears.

It reminds me of a time when I was less prepared. And that's the thing you can't understand unless you've been assaulted. It's something my parents and my sister never understood. The assault doesn't end when the attack ends. It stays with you, hiding behind every door you open, every corner you turn, even haunting your dreams. It's happened to me before. It's why I got into this business, and it's why I won't stop now or ever.

My mentor, Perry Johnson, used to always say to me "The second you stop learning is the second you stop being a good private investigator," so I decide to stop dwelling and to start learning about Madeline to distract myself. From some quick internet research, I learn she is exactly who I expected her to be. She's thirty-six and hails from a wealthy family from upstate. Her great-grandfather made his fortune in bootlegging, and her grandfather proceeded to engage in the time-honored rich-man tradition of whitewashing dirty money with respectable businesses like real estate, which Madeline's father continued, eventually becoming one of the largest property owners in the Lake George area. Her mother is a homemaker, and Madeline's main profession appears to be New York socialite. There's not a gala or benefit that she doesn't attend, and she makes regular appearances on Page Six. She never married and has no kids, which is a bit of a surprise until you consider her personality. Her dating life seems to be the only aspect of her life Page Six hasn't covered. While she's not exactly a paragon of virtue, there's nothing illicit in Madeline's background that hints at her being anything more than a concerned godparent. Maybe the police can tell me something different.

I grab my phone and pick up the cop's business card. I catch a whiff of Madeline's perfume on it, an unpleasant reminder. In these situations, dealing with the police is a delicate dance that varies by department and by officer. Official police protocol is usually not to comment on an open investigation or share information with private investigators. However, in certain situations—say, where you have a relationship with an officer or they need additional assistance—they'll provide relevant details or, if you're really lucky, share the case file with you. Of course, I have zero relationships in Lake George, but I hope that since it's a small-town force they will welcome the help. With that in mind, I dial the number.

I close my eyes to steady myself. I've made a million of these calls, and I've never gotten comfortable making them. My mom says that's the millennial in me.

"Sheriff's office, how can I help you?" says a kind voice on the other end. It's a pleasant surprise. I'm used to dealing with the NYPD, who you might describe as brusque on the phone.

"Hello, could I please speak with Detective Riether?" I say.

"Yes, I'll put you through."

The phone purrs twice before someone answers.

"Detective Riether," says a voice on the other end. I hear the smack of food in the detective's mouth.

"Yes, hello, Detective, my name is Hazel Cho. I'm a private investigator who is working with Madeline Hemsley on the Mia Ross missing person case."

I allow him a moment to respond, but he greets me with silence. Not exactly the warm welcome I was hoping for. That's another reason I hate phone calls. In a face-to-face interview, when someone gives you silence, you give it right back to them until they break. On the phone that doesn't work. They just think there's a bad connection.

"Anyway, it's my understanding that you were the detective assigned to the case, so I wanted to touch base with you in the spirit of collaboration."

"Mm-hmm." I hear the crunch of an apple. "I'm sorry, but you know we can't discuss an active investigation."

I feel creases burrowing into my forehead. "Wait, so you're still investigating? Madeline gave me the impression that the investigation was closed."

"Nope, it's still active."

This detective is talking like he's being charged by the word. It reminds me of when we called my mom's parents in Korea. They could never get it out of their head that international calls didn't cost five dollars a minute anymore. I take another swig of Red Bull, hoping the caffeine will catalyze some way of cracking this sphinx.

"Look, Detective, I'm not trying to get in your way. I'm sure you've investigated Mia's disappearance thoroughly. I just want to ensure I'm not duplicating efforts or stepping on toes. Is there any information you can share regarding the investigation or any leads?"

He pauses, and for a moment I think I might have found a gap in the brick wall. Then he says, "I'm sorry. We can't comment on an active investigation."

The way he says it gives me the creeps. It's robotic, re-hearsed, as though he's hiding something. That they haven't closed the investigation only adds to the sketchiness of the situation. I wonder what they've found. Regardless, this guy isn't going to tell me. But where there's smoke, there's fire.

"Thank you for your time, Detective."

Detective Riether hangs up without saying a word. Apparently, he hit his word limit.

Chapter 4

I put down the phone and evaluate my office. It's still charming but, like my life, has fallen into a state of disrepair. Dust decorates the shelves. The corners of the chairs have torn through their covering, exposing cheap fabric beneath. Stains and signs of wear mark the heather carpet. When I see what's happened to my office, it feels like I'm looking in a mirror. I'm thirty years old, I'm broke, I have no clients, and I'm alone. Other than that, I'm crushing it.

Things weren't always this way. I return to the picture on my desktop and remember when I was an honor list college student with a seemingly limitless future in front of her. I led the Legal Eagles club and dominated mock trial. The world seemed simple and filled with promise. But the world tends to take our hopes and dreams and steadily beat them down until they become something else entirely. Maybe this case will give me an opportunity to punch back.

Given what happened with Strauss this morning, I'm not eager to leave my office, but if I spend another minute in here, my rising sense of claustrophobia will become unbearable. I gather my purse and prepare to head downstairs. I grab my Taser out of my bag just in case Strauss is sitting outside waiting for me. A gun is locked away at my apartment, but New

York City makes it such a pain in the ass to carry that I rarely use it. As I head down the stairs, each step fills me with dread. The Taser rests in my left hand, and I grab the doorknob with my right. I take a deep breath and brace myself.

I fling the door open.

Nobody's there.

The street to my right sits empty, except for two trash containers and a couple of loose beer bottles. Gene Strauss is nowhere to be seen. He's probably off sulking in some bar somewhere, wondering where he went wrong. The abusers always blame everyone and everything but themselves.

To my left, the sidewalk hums with pedestrians enjoying one of the last beautiful days of autumn. The strange noises of New York—the honking of horns, the chatter of friends, the tapping of footsteps—wash over me. I raise my eyes skyward and see the sun peeking out from behind the clouds, providing a welcome warmth against the underlying chill of the city. I feel like I can breathe again.

On the corner I see Yanush, the hot dog vendor with whom I've built far too close a relationship. He's a wily-looking Persian man with six kids and a wife he adores. They say that the key to retail is location, location, location, and Yanush knows that the closer he is to me, the better his location. I'd hate for the man's efforts to go to waste, so I stop at his cart and grab a dog.

Yanush shoots me a nod and a knowing grin. He's missing a tooth, but somehow it suits him.

"You want the usual, Hazel?" he asks with a hand-rolled cigarette dangling from his mouth.

I smile and nod back but steal a glance around to confirm that nobody heard the hot dog man ask if I want "the usual."

"Somebody has to support Darya and the kids."

Yanush unleashes a smoker's chuckle and sets about his work.

A few seconds later, he hands me the perfect hot dog, steaming in the cool air. Ketchup, mustard, chili, cheese, onions, and relish piled high. I like to think of it as brain food. And I've got thinking to do. The smell of warm pretzels tantalizes me, but at some point, you've got to say enough is enough. I'm still young enough where the calories mostly don't stick to me, but that time is rapidly coming to an end.

I hand Yanush a five and take my hot dog along with a couple of napkins. With my free hand, I insert my earbuds and stroll the sidewalk, soaking in the day. I know it's a little weird, but I enjoy walking while I'm eating. Somehow it makes me feel like I'm doing something productive instead of sitting around tossing back junk food. Of course, I'd probably have to walk to Harlem to burn off the hot dog, but I don't like to get bogged down in those details.

I turn right down Walker Street and stride toward the West Side. I enjoy walking through Tribeca, people-watching, and envisioning the life I could have had. Married to some white dude in finance, eating croissants while we walk our baby stroller around town. It's a pleasant escape from my current existence of doomscrolling Tinder while Kenny plays *Call of Duty* on his Xbox. Truth is, I would probably hate that life, but from the outside, it sure looks tempting. I take another couple of bites of my hot dog. Chili runs down my face just as a cute guy passes me with a look of mixed curiosity and disgust. That pretty much sums up my luck with men.

As I make my way west and polish off Yanush's wonder dog, I steer my mind back to the Hemsley case. I don't specialize in missing person work, but this situation still mystifies me. That this girl just straight-up vanished in the middle of the night and the children's home didn't seem that worried about it? There has to be something more.

Something Madeline's not telling me.

Walking is getting the blood flowing to my brain. I pull out my phone and search for Saint Agnes Children's Home and dial the main number. I navigate the automated phone tree to child services and then connect with a receptionist who transfers me again. After a few rings, a kind voice with a hint of a Latin accent answers.

"Thank you for calling Saint Agnes. This is Sonia Barreto. How can I help you?"

She says *Barreto* with that nice rolling *r* I can never quite pull off. I repeat the standard intro that I gave Detective Riether and prepare for another curt response. To my surprise, I receive the opposite.

"Ms. Hazel, I'm so happy to hear that someone else will be working to find Mia. Those other private investigators were no good. It will be nice to have a woman on the job."

"Thanks. I'm happy to be involved."

"I must tell you, Hazel, we've been worried sick here, and the police seem to have lost interest. I've done what I could to reach out to friends and family, but I'm no expert detective like you."

As I turn onto Varick Street, I smile to myself at Sonia's overestimation of my abilities. I'm no Sherlock Holmes. I like to think of myself as slightly above average at what I do. If I've got one thing going for me, it's that I never give up.

"Well, I wouldn't call myself an expert, and I can't make any promises, but I will do my best to find her."

"I'm so pleased to hear that. What can I do to assist you, Ms. Hazel?"

"If it's all right with you, I'd like to visit and tour the property. See Mia's room, walk the grounds, talk with people who spent time with her the night she went missing."

"Of course! We'd love to have you come to Saint Agnes. I can tour you around, and I'm sure our headmaster, Dr. Mackenzie, would like to meet you as well. How about tomorrow?"

"Tomorrow?"

I pause because I'm uncertain if Madeline's going to deliver my car by then and I like to take more time to do research before conducting interviews. But time is of the essence.

"Yes, tomorrow," she says. "It's like I tell the girls. There's no time like the present."

I beam. I think I want Sonia to be my mom.

"Okay. Tomorrow it is."

Cars roar by me on the West Side Highway. Maybe not the best time for a phone call.

"You can probably hear from the background noise, but I'm in the city, so I've got a bit of a drive ahead of me in the morning. How about we say noon?"

"Noon is perfect. The girls will be eating lunch, so you should have the run of the place."

"Great, I'll see you then."

As I hang up the phone, I reach Hudson River Park. The water glitters with light, and a whisper of a breeze floats off the river. Joggers and bikers roll by in every direction. It's one of those beautiful fall New York days when anything seems possible. In a month, I'll be slogging through slush, cursing myself and wondering why I live here, but today it's breathtaking.

It's funny, I talked to Sonia Barreto for five minutes, but

in brief conversation she reinforced me, made me remember the confident Hazel I used to be. I wish my mom had been like that, but she took the tiger-mom approach to parenting. Those piano lessons still give me night terrors.

Unconsciously, I start humming "Time after Time" to myself. I hear Mia's voice in my head, and her words pour through me, singing about being lost and how if I look I can find her. She's out there somewhere. This girl who never knew her family and now has lost whatever human connection she did have.

I can't let her down.

Chapter 5

I amble along the Hudson for a few hours, typing notes about the case on my phone and plotting my strategy for the investigation. Normally, a missing person investigation is pretty straightforward. You first gather as much information as you can about the missing person from the reporting party, including physical description, last known whereabouts, proclivities, risks, and anything else that can give you a sense of what could have happened. Then you interview family, friends, and acquaintances. Then you check with local hospitals, hotels, motels, and gas stations to see if anyone's seen her. Then you run a skip trace and review any public records and electronic, social media, or personal records you can find to see if you can track their cell phone or if they used a credit card. But this case is odd in that the reporting party, Madeline, doesn't know her goddaughter that well, and because Mia's an only child and an orphan, she doesn't have any family. Not to mention that since she's thirteen and lives at a children's home, there's no electronic data to go on either. The cops have probably already checked the hospitals and motels. This whole investigation hinges on Saint Agnes and the people inside it.

I just hope they'll open up.

Another key part of a missing person investigation is re-searching the family. Obviously, Mia doesn't have any immediate family, but Madeline warrants additional research. Who is she? She's beautiful, alluring, but unattached, and the gossip columns gave me nothing. Where does her money come from? Most people don't drop thousands in cash without blinking. Does she still receive money from Dad? And who is her family? How did she know Mia's parents? She seemed evasive when I asked her earlier. One of the first rules of being a private investigator is don't trust your client. Half of what they tell you is a lie and the other half is half-true.

As I'm lost in thought, the sun slinks behind the clouds and the temperature drops. The caws of crows grow louder, signaling that late afternoon is here. I tap my phone and start my EDM playlist—that's electronic dance music, if you're not in the loop—and begin my power walk back home. The funniest thing about listening to music while you're walking is it somehow makes everything you're doing seem much more important. Like you're the star of your own action movie. It doesn't hurt that I'm now powered by a newfound responsibility for this little girl I've never met.

As I head back home along the river, a prickling sensation crawls up the back of my neck. I can't shake the feeling that someone is watching me. My mind flashes to Gene Strauss, to the fury in his eyes. I glance around, searching for any signs of danger, but nothing appears out of the ordinary. Joggers gallop by, red faced and out of breath. Happy-hour professionals enjoy wine and a view of the river, red faced for an entirely different reason.

Am I just being paranoid?

I did just get threatened by a lunatic a few hours ago, so

it wouldn't surprise me if I'm seeing ghosts. I pick up the pace and head down Canal toward Chinatown. I weave my way through the crowds. Tourists gawk and stop abruptly, oblivious to the pedestrians behind them. The ultimate New Yorker pet peeve is the tourist who goes from full stride to full stop in the middle of foot traffic. We need special prisons for these people.

Vendors clutter the sidewalk, selling fake Prada bags, and steam flies up through the grates, providing a useful cover. But the feeling of being watched gnaws at me as I hurry toward my office. I remove my earbuds and replace the music with the cacophony of Chinatown's bustling streets. It's probably nothing, but inside, my mind sparks, calculating escape routes and backup plans. Part of me almost hopes it is Gene Strauss so I can deliver payback.

The sun dips lower, and shadows stretch across the pavement, obscuring faces and making everyone look like a potential threat. A taxi slams on the horn behind me, and I flinch. I can't shake the feeling of being watched. It crawls up my spine and then rests there.

My fears are confirmed as I look into the reflection of a shop window and my gaze locks onto a dark-gray Tesla SUV creeping behind me. It crawls the right-hand lane of Canal at less than five miles per hour. The driver's face remains hidden in the setting sun's glare, but I can't help wondering if it's Strauss, back to finish the job. He doesn't seem like he would drive a Tesla, though. If it's not him, then who is it?

I quicken my pace, trying to put distance between us. I bump into a woman selling bobbleheads, and she curses at me in Chinese. My thoughts run alongside me. Can I make it to my office before he catches up? If not, what then? Is he even following me, or is this just a lost tourist navigating the narrows of Chinatown? I search the streets for a cop. The Tesla accelerates slightly, and the distance between us shrinks. My breath sprints. I assess the surrounding storefronts: a noodle shop, a bakery, a dimly lit bar. None of them feel like safe havens, just traps.

Keep moving, I think, pushing myself to walk even faster. The office is a few blocks away.

Sweat trickles down my back as my legs pump harder, each step propelling me closer to safety. The Tesla shadows me, never too far behind, easing forward like a cat. Horns honk behind it, but the driver remains unfazed. That's what makes it so unnerving. The car moves at exactly my pace, oblivious to the world around it, like a shadow. I cross the intersection, the rich red brick of my building in sight. Unfortunately, Yanush has gone home for the day. I suppress the urge to break into a run.

The tires screech.

My heart lurches.

The man pulls over and exits the vehicle. The slam of the car door echoes through the street. I glance back, pulse pounding.

It's not Strauss.

It's somebody else.

A younger man in a black leather jacket. His snowy-blond hair and eyebrows shape a ruddy, determined face.

Keep walking, my mind screams. *Faster.*

I'm five steps from Cortlandt Alley. Four. Three.

Even through the New York din, I can hear his footsteps growing louder, matching my pace.

Two. One.

I hook a right down the alley. Fear rises in my chest. I bolt toward the entrance.

"Ms. Cho!"

His voice cuts through the air, but I don't stop. The sound of his shoes against the pavement grows closer, thundering behind me. How does he know my name?

"Ms. Cho, wait!"

Sweat beads on my brow. I'm almost at the door.

"Ms. Cho, please!"

"Leave me alone!" I shout, breathless.

"Stop!"

I ignore him. I don't know who he is or what he wants, but given what I've been through today, I can't risk it. Just as my hand reaches for the door handle, the man grabs my arm. I yank away, eyes wide with fear.

"Please, wait! I'm not going to hurt you."

His voice is not what I expected. It's high pitched and kind. More Mr. Rogers than Freddy Krueger.

"Who are you? Why are you following me?"

"Madeline Hemsley sent me. I'm Patrick, her personal assistant," he pants, raising his hands in a nonthreatening gesture. "She asked me to drop off this Tesla for you to use during your investigation. She said it was urgent. I stopped by your office, but you were gone, and the hot dog guy that was here earlier said you had gone walking, so I was driving around looking for you. The car's right here."

He points to the car he just double-parked.

"Madeline...sent you?" My mind stutters, trying to absorb my change in fortunes. It's not every day you're granted a car by a mysterious man you thought was chasing you.

"Yes," he says, a warm smile spreading across his face. "And I also have this." He pulls an envelope from his jacket pocket and hands it to me.

"Go ahead, open it."

I take a moment to inhale. Five seconds of sprinting and I'm winded. Sad. My shaky fingers tear open the envelope. Inside, I find a stack of crisp bills totaling $5,000.

"Expenses," he says, still catching his breath. I guess we're both out of shape. "This should tide you over, and then you can bill us for the rest."

I let out a single sharp laugh and place a hand on his forearm.

"I'm so sorry. I thought you were someone else."

"Don't worry about it. I can see how my approach might've been a bit...startling, especially given your line of work. Normally, I would have just waited at your office, but Madeline insisted it was urgent. I'm probably more scared of her than you were of me. You know how she gets."

I don't know how she gets, but I can imagine, so I nod in agreement. I wave the envelope in the air.

"Thank you. For the car and the money."

"Just doing my job. Here's the key card. Just tap it on the driver's side door." He looks at his watch. "I've got to run and catch the train. Stay safe."

With that, he turns and saunters away, leaving me standing in front of my office door, pulse still pounding from the encounter. When I can breathe again, I turn my attention to the sleek gray Tesla parked by the curb. Cars honk, irritated by the double-parked SUV, but I ignore them. They can wait. I approach the car and awkwardly tap the key card against the doorframe until the door handles glide out smoothly, inviting me to take the wheel. My eyes widen at the thought of taking it out for a spin.

I slide into the driver's seat. The interior is pristine, with supple seats hugging my body comfortably. I grip the steering wheel, admiring the minimalist design and futuristic dash-board. I've lived in the city so long that I can't remember the last time I drove a car. It brings me back to the days when Christina and I would cruise around town with the windows down, singing Beyoncé songs at the top of our lungs.

"Mama's home," I say aloud, feeling a surge of gratitude for Madeline's largesse, but also a lingering curiosity concerning the source.

Now I just need to figure out how to drive this thing.

Chapter 6

ine days left

NThe next day, I slide into the driver's seat of the Tesla that Madeline lent me, gripping the steering wheel as the car flashes to life. It only took me about two hours last night to find a parking spot, but eventually I got the job done. This is a major step up from my last car, a broken-down Mercury Sable I bought with the money I earned working at Jamba Juice near campus. I swing into the morning Manhattan traffic, and the hum of the electric motor sends a thrill down my spine. I haven't driven since I graduated from college and moved to the city, and now I'm behind the wheel of this luxurious beast. I wonder if I look a little ridiculous. It's a big car for a small woman. I work my way through downtown bumper to bumper, only garnering two honks and one middle finger, which I consider a minor victory.

I've barely started this case, and I'm already regretting it. Normally, in a scenario like this, I would spend days researching every angle before I started talking to people. That way you're in the power position, having full information when you're conducting interviews. You can ask questions that you know the answer to, and if you find a liar, you can pull on the thread. But Madeline's deadline—combined with how much time has already passed—means I've only had one night of research. I'm flying blind.

After forty-five minutes, the cityscape gives way to the natural beauty of upstate New York. Trees envelop the winding road, their leaves a vibrant symphony of oranges, reds, and yellows. But I notice dark clouds gathering and crashing over the trees. A storm is coming.

Despite the looming weather, I realize how much I missed this: the fresh air, nature, the energy of motion. An exhilarating sense of freedom fills me, one that I haven't felt since moving to the city. My fingers slide along the steering wheel as I navigate the twists and turns. I fire up my '80s playlist and belt out Whitney Houston's "I Wanna Dance with Somebody." At one point, the connection cuts out, and I'm reminded what singing off key sounds like. Fortunately, the music starts up again, and I watch Manhattan fade into the distance in the rearview mirror. It feels like a metaphor: leaving home for a new adventure.

As the city shrinks behind me and the roads grow wider and trees thicken, memories of my childhood in Palisades Park flood my mind. Palisades Park is a small Korean community in New Jersey just across the Hudson from Harlem, and the neighborhood operates like one big extended family. I remember my mom cooking bulgogi or galbi jjim for my aunts, uncles, cousins, and friends. My dad, who ran the local market, would hold court at a table with his buddies, playing gin or some other card game. Christina and I would dutifully toil on homework until Mom said it was time to eat—we all had to be doctors or lawyers, after all. I can't help but laugh, thinking about how sheltered I was. When I was really little, I was surrounded by so many Korean people that the first time I met a white man with a prominent bridge on his nose, I asked him "Why is your nose like that?" I still remember the look on my dad's face: half-amused, half-mortified.

The sudden buzzing of my phone startles me, pulling me back into the present. Glancing at the screen, I see my mother's name flashing before me. She must have felt me thinking about her. I take a deep breath and answer, readying myself for the inevitable questions about my life choices.

"Umma, hello," I say in Korean, trying to keep my voice light and cheerful.

"Hazel, my girl, how are you?" She responds in Korean as well.

"I'm good. I just got a new case."

"Hmm, that's nice," my mom says with skepticism.

I don't know what I was expecting her to say. My parents have never approved of me being a private investigator, so to them, me saying I have a fresh case is like a gambling addict saying I just won a bet. The best thing I could say to her is I've decided to return to law school.

"I got a new Tesla," I say, trying to find another avenue to impress her.

"Hazel! You can't afford that."

"No, Mom, it's fine. My client gave it to me to use for the case." My pitch rises an octave, reverting to my teenage years.

"Oh, that's nice of him. Is he single?"

My eyes roll so hard I can barely see the road.

"No, Mom, the client is a woman."

I hear a sigh on the other end.

"Oh, that's a shame."

"How's Dad?" I say, trying to steer Mom away from my personal life.

"Your father is fine. You know how he is. Obsessed with his golf and cards. I hardly ever see him. He wakes up, goes to the golf course, plays cards all afternoon, and then is only home for dinner. They're like boys playing in their tree house."

It was strange growing up with my father. He was the life of the party. Everyone loved him. I swear half the people that shopped at our market just showed up to chat with him or hear one of his jokes. But the problem with having a father like that is you share him with the rest of the world, and that doesn't leave much time for you. To me, he always seemed more like a fun uncle than a father.

And he never showed weakness. Ever. I remember one time he told us he was leaving on a business trip and then returned with a bandage on his neck. I later learned he had surgery to remove a tumor. It was benign, but it would have been nice to know.

"Are you coming over for family dinner next week? I have exciting news," my mom says, interrupting my thoughts.

We have family dinners every other Sunday. Fortunately, this weekend's my week off. But there's a mischievous tone in her voice, and dread fills my stomach. My mom and I do not share the same definition of the word *exciting*. I hit the accelerator as if I can drive past the destination of this conversation.

"Yes, Mom, I'm coming over for dinner next Sunday, as always. What's the exciting news?"

"Dr. Lee will be joining us."

Ah, the famous Dr. Lee. I can feel Mom beaming through the phone. Phil Lee is a guy I grew up with who just finished his residency, so now everyone must refer to him as Dr. Lee. My mom and dad have been trying to set me up with him for years. It doesn't help that my sister's a doctor and married a doctor as well. Unfortunately for Dr. Lee, I'm partial to white guys. Another disappointment to my family.

My GPS shows that I'm five miles from the children's home, so soon I'll have a convenient excuse to end this conversation. As I round a curve, a flash of white and blue catches my eye in the rearview mirror: a police car pulling out from a side road behind me. My heart skips a beat as I glance down at the Tesla's speedometer—I'm speeding.

I'm definitely speeding.

"Great," I mutter under my breath, watching as the cruiser draws closer. The weight of Madeline's deadline bears down on me; I don't have time for this. As the police car continues to tail me, the knot in my stomach tightens. "Mom, I'll call you back. There's a police car behind me."

My eyes jump between the rearview mirror and the road ahead. The cruiser lurks behind me, inching closer with each passing minute.

"Hazel, when are you going to give up this dangerous job and settle down?" My mom never misses an opportunity. "You could find a nice man like Dr. Lee and get married."

I feel my voice rising and the blood rushing to my face.

"Mom, I can't do this right now. I'll call you back."

I hang up the phone, and my eyes laser in on the rearview mirror. The sweat beads on my palms as the police car edges even closer. I grip the wheel tighter, knuckles white, trying to steady my breathing. My heart pounds, and I can't shake the nagging suspicion that this isn't just a routine patrol.

But even as I try to reassure myself, doubt lingers. This car isn't mine, after all. The police car continues to tail me, uncomfortably close. I wish he would just decide already.

Either pull me over or back off.

I curse as the sirens blare and red and blue lights flash in my rearview mirror. Misfortune never arrives alone. I ease the car onto the shoulder and roll down my window.

"License and registration, please," the officer says, peering into the car. He wears gold-rimmed aviator glasses, and his face shows no emotion. His mustache barely moves when he speaks. If I didn't know better, I would think he was in a Halloween costume.

"Of course," I reply, fumbling for my wallet and handing over my driver's license. I glance at the glove compartment, praying Madeline left the car's registration inside. First, I need to figure out how to open the glove compartment. It doesn't have a latch. That would be too easy.

"Is there a problem, Officer?" I ask, stalling for time.

"Do you know how fast you were going?" he responds, thick, dark eyebrows furrowed. His voice grates on me.

"Uh, no. I didn't. I'm not used to driving this. It's not my car, you see. A friend lent it to me."

He pulls his sunglasses down his nose.

"I see."

Finally, I find the button on the screen that opens the glove compartment. It pops open, and thankfully, the registration is front and center.

"Your friend should teach you how to follow the speed limit," the officer says, studying my license. "You're a long way from home. What's your business in Lake George?"

"Um," I say, trying to collect my thoughts. I'm used to doing the questioning, not being questioned.

"I'm here for work."

"What work do you do?"

I consider telling him it's none of his business, but I don't think that will get me the result I'm looking for. "I'm a private investigator. I'm working on a case involving a missing girl from Saint Agnes Children's Home."

"Ah. That place has quite the reputation for missing girls."

"Really?" In my research, I had found that other girls had gone missing. It's not uncommon in children's homes. But something about the way he says it is just...off.

"Yep." The officer leans against the car, crossing his arms. He's chewing a small piece of gum in that disinterested way that men in dangerous jobs often do. "It's almost like they vanish into thin air." His lips curl.

"Have there been any leads?"

"Not that I know of, but that's not really my department. You'd have to talk to Detective Riether about that. But I'm sure you'll have no problem solving the case, being a PI and all."

"I hope so."

I clench the steering wheel tighter. He takes another long look at my license and clears something from his teeth with his tongue. Something about this cop isn't right.

"All right, Miss Cho. You're free to go. Just be careful out there. You never know what might be lurking around the corner."

He bangs on the roof of my car twice and then walks away.

"Thank you."

As he walks back to his cruiser, I shift into drive and roll toward Saint Agnes, the air around me growing colder with each passing mile. I drive for five more minutes. Then I see it: Saint Agnes atop a hill in the distance, a giant gray structure rising over the tree line like an apparition.

From one glance, I can see this is a place of history. A place of tradition.

A place of secrets.

Chapter 7

I pull up to the gates of Saint Agnes Children's Home, steady myself, and absorb the scene. I'm still rattled from that unscheduled stop, but I slow my breathing and shift my attention to the job at hand.

The first thing I notice about Saint Agnes is that it looks like it's been transported from another era. Two massive black, barred wrought iron gates guard the entrance, with a crest in the middle that says *Saint Agnes Children's Home*. A security booth stands outside the gates, attached to a brick wall protecting a sprawling, forest-lined property that backs up to Lake George. Nestled in the center of the grounds, amid perfectly manicured lawns, looms what I can only describe as a castle. Made of dark-gray stone, with a pitched roof and cross-paned windows, Saint Agnes at first resembles a traditional English boarding school, but as I look closer through the windshield, I see that something is missing. The main building sits atop a slope, cold and defiant, as though daring the visitor to enter. The lawns and the building itself lack any decoration. No emblems. No signs welcoming visitors. No banners or logos. It's monastic.

The wind whips across the hill, and the trees have shed some of their colored leaves. It is as though they've stripped the place of any excess, any color, any joy. I try to imagine growing up here as a little girl. It seems a lonely place.

I pull my car up to the gate and roll down the window. The security guard does nothing to brighten my perception of the place. He's dressed in an all-black security uniform with black combat boots. He's built like a brick house, but there's something about him that reeks of ill health. His skin is a waxy yellow and covered in perspiration, though he's been sitting in a booth all day. Even outside, I can smell the tobacco on him, and when he smiles at me, his teeth show the effects as well. And that smile. There's a hollowness to it. All the attributes of a smile are on display. The eyes squint, the cheeks move up, the teeth show, but it's unnatural, like clay molded into shape.

"Welcome to Saint Agnes, ma'am. How can I help you today?" says the guard through his dead smile mask. His words carry a southern lilt, and his voice is much higher than I imagined, which only adds to the effect. I do my best to hide my disgust.

"Hello, I have an appointment to meet with Ms. Barreto."

The security guard grabs his clipboard and pages through the guest log. I notice there's a patch of scabbed skin on his left hand, a scratch mark.

"Can I get your name?" he says.

"Yes, it's Hazel Cho." I hand him my driver's license.

He looks at my ID and then down at his clipboard and nods. He grabs a small badge that says *Visitor* and hands it to me along with my license.

"Welcome to Saint Agnes, Ms. Cho. Visitors' parking is to the right. You can just go on in, and the receptionist will point you to Ms. Barreto's office."

"Thank you. I'm sorry, what's your name?" I ask. I know

nothing about this guy, but I definitely want to talk to him about Mia's disappearance later.

"Neil. Neil Paver. It's a pleasure to meet you."

"Nice to meet you, Neil."

The security guard opens the gates. The hinges whine so loud I half expect Vincent Price to jump out of the booth. I squint at the sky. The clouds are darkening, black as smoke. The rain is coming, and I didn't bring an umbrella. Perfect. As I pull forward, a tree branch slams against the passenger-side window, and I jump halfway out of my seat. The branch falls harmlessly to the ground. Another casualty of the wind. I need to pull it together. Nobody wants to talk to a private investigator who gets freaked out by a storm.

I hit the accelerator and peel down the gravel entrance road to Saint Agnes. I've had my fill of alone time with Neil for now. I pull into the visitors' parking, grab my work bag, and head toward the office. I hear the crunch of gravel under my feet and thank God I didn't wear heels today. I'm wearing gray pants, brown loafers, and a kelly green sweater. I wanted to look professional but not blow them away.

Before I go in the main building, I take pictures of the campus: tracks on the road coming in, the forest guarding the perimeter, the grand lawn, and the various buildings: the main hall, chapel, gymnasium, athletic fields, and residences. Pictures are crucial in a small-scale investigation like this. Even though Mia went missing months ago, you never know when you'll spot something you missed in real life. Once I was taking a picture of a guy's house for an insurance fraud case. He had supposedly ruined his back, so I was snapping pictures of where he lived and waiting for him to leave the house. He never came out, but later, when I reviewed the pictures, I caught him running in the reflection of his window. Often I can lean on photos taken by the cops, but given my abbreviated call with Detective Riether, I don't think that's happening in this case.

I open the front entrance door of the main building and am immediately struck by the solidity of Saint Agnes. The door is made of ancient hickory and weighs a ton. A tasteful woven rug leads from the entrance right to the receptionist's desk like someone designed it specifically for that purpose, and an original stone fireplace rests to reception's right, complete with roaring fire—something I appreciate on this frigid fall day. The clicks and cracks of the fire remind me of Christmas at my grandpa and grandma's house. Yet I experience the same feeling that I did outside: that something is missing here.

A chirpy receptionist with a smile so warm it could bake cookies guides me down a long hallway to the left of the entrance. Doors line the way, and I sneak peeks as I pass. This is clearly the administrative part of Saint Agnes. I pass one shoebox-size office after another with bookkeepers and guidance counselors tapping away at their keyboards or hunched over paperwork. Yet nothing adorns the walls. No pictures of student artwork. No announcements on a corkboard. Nothing.

The receptionist stops at a closed office. She gives the door a gentle knock, pops it open, and peeks her head around the corner.

"Ms. Barreto, Hazel Cho is here to see you."

From the other side of the door, I hear Sonia Barreto's familiar accent.

"Of course. Send her in, please."

I enter the room, and the receptionist scurries back to the

front desk. Sonia raises her head from her paperwork, stands, and gives me a gentle smile. She's middle aged, probably in her fifties, but still stunning. Her shining auburn hair tumbles off her head with just the right amount of curl. Her skin is immaculate, not a blemish to be found, and set off perfectly against a deep-red lipstick. A minuscule cleft rests in the center of her chin, strong and stubborn. She wears a bright-green dress with a big stand-up collar that accentuates her small waist and wide hips. I look at Sonia Barreto and I say to myself, *I am still a girl; this is a woman.*

She shakes my hand and gestures to a chair, inviting me to sit down.

"It's a pleasure to meet you, Hazel," says Sonia. She smiles, and her espresso eyes twinkle, making me feel like a coconspirator.

"It's a pleasure to meet you as well, Sonia," I say, mimicking her formal tone.

She leans back in her chair and appraises me. Her plump lips curve slightly upward by default.

"I must say, I was very pleased when you called."

I pop up in my chair at this piece of information. Nobody is ever pleased when I call.

"Is that right? Why's that?"

"Mia is very special to me. She's one of my favorite students. But for the police and these other private investigators, she's just another girl. Girls run away all the time, they say. I'm hoping that as a woman, you understand that this isn't just a girl, it's Mia."

She holds her eyes on mine, and I feel the weight of her expectations. I wipe the stupid smile off my face and clear my throat.

"Yes, that's one of the reasons I took this case. I saw that video of her singing at the recital, and it reminded me of me when I was a little girl."

"Oh, did you sing?"

"No, I played piano. It's basically a requirement for Korean kids. But I remember those piano recitals, all those eyes on you. I dreaded it, but she was phenomenal."

"She is unquestionably the most talented girl we've had here at Saint Agnes. And a lot of girls have come through these doors. Her voice stops a room. But regardless of her talent as a singer, she's just a sweet, lovely girl. We must find her."

Her hands dance as she speaks, and I notice she uses the present tense when she talks about Mia. She hasn't given up yet.

"We will. That's why I'm here. Do you mind if I record our conversation?"

Sonia recoils for a moment, but then nods.

I snatch my phone from my bag and place it on the table.

"What is your role at Saint Agnes?"

"I'm the director of child services. Essentially, I ensure that all of the girls are getting the proper care and support they need to be successful. I oversee the residence program as well as our private school. We believe in a holistic approach at Saint Agnes. Unlike most children's homes, we don't just provide food and shelter. We provide educational, athletic, and spiritual enrichment as well."

"You've got a lot on your plate, but it sounds like you know Mia very well."

"Oh, yes. As I said, she's one of my favorites."

"Tell me, does Mia have any friends?"

"Yes and no. Mia is well liked, but she keeps to herself for the most part. I think the other girls are intimidated by her."

"Really? How so?"

"It's hard to explain. She's so beautiful and talented. She seems too big for this place. Like she doesn't belong here. You understand?"

I remember how I felt growing up. I didn't belong there either. Not because I was talented but because I was different.

"Has she had any mental health issues? Medical issues?"

Sonia laughs. It's a deep, throaty chortle.

"No, she is the happiest girl you've ever met."

"Any discipline issues? Interactions with police?"

Sonia chuckles louder and shakes her head.

"How about her routine? Did she ever leave campus or participate in outside activities?"

"Not really. The girls mostly stay here twelve months a year. Occasionally, we'll take a field trip to a museum or something, but that's as a group. We would never let Mia go alone. Dr. Mackenzie likes to keep the girls sheltered. He believes we need to build them up before releasing them out into the real world."

My head aches. It's not her fault, but Sonia's shutting down all the investigative trails I would normally follow. It's possible that Mia made contact with someone on one of her field trips, but I doubt it. I shift gears to Sonia.

"What about you? How did you end up at Saint Agnes?"

"It was quite simple. I needed a job. I married a man who lived in Lake George. He told me I didn't need to work, that he would take care of me. But he was a drunk, and when he lost his job, he left town and left me with nothing. Nothing. No savings, no job, no options." When she speaks, the bracelets on her wrists clink and clank. "I told myself that would never happen again. I would never rely on a man for my livelihood. So, I found a job working here as a cleaner and fell in love with the place...well, fell in love with the girls."

She beams, and I catch the memories reflecting in her eyes.

"Eventually, Dr. Mackenzie asked me if I would like to move into administration, and I jumped at the chance. And here I am twenty-five years later. Time flies. That's probably longer than you've been alive."

"Not quite, but close. Tell me about the day Mia went missing."

She grabs a pen from her desk and turns her chair ninety degrees to look out the window, searching for the memory. She clicks the cap on and off: click, click, like a metronome. I follow her eyes out the window. The clouds are spitting now, and tiny raindrops tap against the window. She speaks but continues to look outside.

"It was a Monday morning. I remember because I had been in the city for the weekend and drove back early in the morning for work."

"Really? I live in the city. Do you go to Manhattan a lot?" I ask.

Sonia's eyebrow jabs for a moment. Like me, she's used to doing the questioning, not being questioned.

"Whenever I get a chance. Things up here in Lake George can get a little stale, so it's nice to escape to the city every so often."

I nod along in agreement. I'd probably lose my mind if I was out here for more than a week.

"So, what did you do when you got back here in the morning?"

"I grabbed my notebook from my office and then went to

the dining hall to check on the girls at breakfast. I like to say hello every morning to encourage them for the day."

I warm at the thought. There wasn't much encouragement at my house. Just demands.

Sonia's face drops into a frown, thick creases emerging in her forehead, as she recalls that morning. "As I walked along the dining tables, Mia's roommate, Penny, approached me and asked if I had seen Mia. I told her I hadn't and asked her why she was asking. Penny explained to me that Mia was gone when she woke up this morning. At first, she just assumed that Mia had woken up early to go to breakfast, but when Penny arrived at the dining hall and noticed Mia wasn't there, either, she informed me."

"And what did you do then?"

Sonia looks at me indignantly. "I informed Dr. Mackenzie, of course."

"And what did Dr. Mackenzie do?"

"He initiated a full search of the campus. But I should let him speak for himself. I've booked time on his calendar for you to speak with him in a little over an hour."

"That's very kind of you," I say with a forced smile.

I know Sonia's only trying to be helpful, but I prefer to run my process without assistance. You can't truly investigate if someone is just giving you the dog and pony show. You need to dig beneath the surface to understand the truth. I get the sense that Sonia's used to having order and control. I'll need to work on softening her up as we go along.

"I assume you have security cameras."

"Yes, we do."

"And as part of your search, did you review the footage from the night that Mia went missing?"

55

"Yes. And that's what makes it so vexing. The footage shows that nobody came onto the property or left the property that evening."

My forehead scrunches. "How is that possible? We know she left somehow."

"I'm sure Mr. Paver could tell you more about this than I can, but the cameras are only stationed along the gate and the tree line. There are no cameras by the lake."

"Why is that?" I ask, shaking my head at this oversight—although, based on my interaction with Paver at the security gate, I can't say I'm surprised that trusting him with security hasn't worked out well.

"Again, Mr. Paver would be much better equipped to answer your question, but I believe it would have been an additional cost, and the presumption was that no girl is going to jump into a forty-degree lake. Dr. Mackenzie has since corrected that and installed cameras at the lake."

That seems like one hell of a presumption to me. The teenage girls I remember from school would walk through fire to get where they wanted to go. Especially if a boy was involved.

"What about internal cameras?"

"No internal cameras. Dr. Mackenzie feels that Saint Agnes should be like a church, free of technological intrusion. No cameras. No cell phones. No social media. No video games." She raps her knuckles on the table in reciting each rule. "We've convinced him to let the girls use computers, but with strict limitations on websites and email usage. It took us years to convince him to get the external cameras we do have."

I lean back in my chair and run my fingers through my hair.

"So, if I'm understanding you correctly, we have no visibility into anything on campus. Just if someone leaves either through the main gate or the tree line?"

"That's correct."

"So, do we know for sure that Mia was in bed the night before she went missing?"

"Yes, Penny saw Mia in their room before she fell asleep."

"Was Mia asleep at that time?"

"I'm not positive, but I believe Penny said Mia was reading a book when she fell asleep. Yes, I remember, she was reading a book called *The Inheritance Games*."

"So, someone took her after Penny went to sleep?"

"Not right after. We do a bedtime check every evening to make sure the girls are in their rooms. Lights-out at nine o'clock."

"Who does these checks? You were out of town, correct?"

I spot a glimmer in Sonia's eye, and her back straightens in her chair.

"That's correct that I was out of town, but to answer your first question, the staff that live on campus rotate who checks that the girls are in bed."

She nods as she anticipates my next question.

"And who was the staff member assigned to Mia's hall that night?"

Sonia's eyebrows rise.

"That would be Gregory Goolsbee, the choir teacher. He was also the last person to see her out of her room, as they had evening lessons."

"The girls have evening choir lessons?" I say, my eyes widening.

Sonia laughs. "No, the girls don't have evening lessons. Only Mia. Mr. Goolsbee believes Mia is a unique vocalist and would benefit from having additional attention."

As she speaks, Sonia squints her eyes as though she's trying to tell me something without telling me something. I turn the recording off and stand up from my chair.

"I'd like to speak with Mr. Goolsbee, now if possible."

Sonia nods and gives me a knowing stare.

"I think that's a wise decision. He's in between classes, so I'll take you to him right now."

Chapter 8

The choir room at Saint Agnes matches the chill of the campus. A lone, ancient grand piano sits at the front of the room. Behind it, to the right, a giant soft-green chalkboard stands watch, covered in musical notes and illegible scribbles. On the left, risers lead upward in stair steps. Each step on the warped blond wood floorboards echoes through the space.

As Sonia and I enter, Mr. Goolsbee slouches on the piano bench, plump fingers plunking out a gloomy tune. He's a round little man with a sizable potbelly straining against his sweater-vest. A thick gray broom mustache droops over his small mouth. Beady eyes peer out through wire-rimmed spectacles perched on a bulbous nose. He covers his bald spot with a comb-over of gray hair, revealing a sheen of sweat across his forehead despite the chill in the room.

Sonia ushers me in and clears her throat to gain Goolsbee's attention.

He stops playing and looks up. He glances at me first and then Sonia, and I think I spy alarm in his eyes. He scribbles a note on his music sheet.

"Sorry to interrupt, Mr. Goolsbee, but I'd like to introduce you to Hazel Cho. She's the new private investigator hired by the Hemsley family to track down Mia."

I give Goolsbee a polite acknowledgment.

"Hello, Hazel," he says in a deep bass with a faint lisp. He remains seated at the piano bench, and his eyes dart back and forth between me and Sonia like he's a dog in a kennel.

I grab a metal folding chair and drop it next to him at the piano. The chair screeches as I open it, metal on metal, making us both wince. I extend my arm to shake his hand: my standard shortcut for assessing an interviewee. Criminals are often reluctant to shake hands, viewing you as a threat more than an ally. After a quick glance at Sonia, Goolsbee shakes my hand with a clammy palm. I settle into my seat with my notebook and start gently.

"Mr. Goolsbee, thank you for taking the time to speak with me today." He blinks, and then his brown-gray irises dart over my shoulder. I turn and see that Sonia is still standing there watching us. From her face, I see she dislikes this man. "Sonia, would you mind giving us the room for a few minutes?"

She nods. "Of course. I'll go take care of some work and fetch you when it's time for your appointment with Dr. Mackenzie. Mr. Goolsbee, please give Hazel everything she needs."

Goolsbee clears his throat and crosses his arms over his belly. "Yes, Ms. Barreto, I will."

I can't get used to how everyone here refers to each other as *Mr.* and *Mrs.* It's giving me flashbacks to junior high. Sonia leaves the room, and Goolsbee lets out a breath. She intimidates him.

"No need to be nervous, Mr. Goolsbee. I'm just trying to get some background information on Mia and her disappearance. Tell me about Mia. How long have you known her?"

He relaxes on the piano bench.

"Oh, let's see, I've been teaching her since she was eight. That's when music classes start here."

"What was she like? What were her hopes and dreams?"

His eyes twinkle as he thinks of her. "She was wonderful. The kind of student that made me go into teaching. She was smart, eager to learn, respectful, mostly. She was a big practical joker. I remember one time she put a fake snake under the piano cover, and I nearly peed myself when I opened it to start class."

I laugh. I like this girl more every minute. Goolsbee rubs his hand over the piano and speaks wistfully.

"You know when people talk about celebrities having that 'it factor'? I never really got that phrase until I met her. She had 'it.' I think her classmates sensed it, too, because nobody ever got that close to her. They were more in awe of her. She dreamed of singing on Broadway. And she had the flair to do it. The best singer that's passed through these halls, and it's not even close. And I've been here for decades. I thought with my help and training we could make her a star."

"Yes, I've seen video of her. She's incredible. You taught her well." He offers a proud grin. "And she had training with you that night, correct? Walk me through Mia's last choir practice before she disappeared."

Goolsbee's sausage fingers wrestle and twitch on his stomach. "N-not much to tell, really. We had a typical practice session. I'm trying to teach Mia to sing more from her chest, so we did a lot of breathing work. Mia sang beautifully, as always. Then, around eight p.m., she packed up her things and left."

"And you didn't notice anything unusual about her behavior that night?"

He shakes his head, the flesh under his chin wobbling. "No, Mia was a good girl. Focused at practice, never caused any fuss."

When he speaks, there's an odd juxtaposition between the depth of the octave and the lilt in his speech. It's like a lumberjack singing show tunes. I can't get a good read on him.

"I'm told you have evening lessons only with Mia and not the other girls. Is that true?"

Goolsbee's lip curls, and he snatches his glasses from his face. He rubs his eyes and removes a handkerchief from his pocket to wipe his forehead. The skin on his cheeks hangs loose and moves like putty.

"Who told you that?"

"That's not important."

"Humph. I'm sure it was Ms. Barreto."

I look at him stone faced and say nothing. After a brief pause, he continues.

"Yes, that's technically true. But I've given extra lessons to other girls over the years as well. You must understand, Mia was an extraordinary singer. She could have been a star."

"I notice you used the past tense, Mr. Goolsbee. 'She could have been a star.' She still could be a star if we find her, unless you know something different?"

"No, no, of course not. I hope you find her. It's just...just."

"What was your relationship with Mia outside of choir practice?"

Goolsbee's already drooping cheeks seem to sink even deeper into his face. He avoids meeting my eye. "I told you. I gave her...private lessons sometimes. To nurture her genius."

I lean forward. "What did those private lessons entail?"

"Just singing techniques. Breathing exercises. I was grooming her for a solo career." He tugs at his collar.

"The two of you, together late into the evening?"

I let the implication hang.

Mr. Goolsbee finally drags his gaze to mine, eyes wide and fierce. "I don't like what you're insinuating."

He half rises from the bench.

"Please, sit. I only want to understand your relationship with Mia."

He sinks back down, smoothing his rumpled sweater-vest with sweaty palms.

"Did you two ever spend time alone outside of lessons?"

"Occasionally. She needed a mentor, someone she could confide in. I tried to provide that guidance."

"So you filled an almost paternal role in her life?"

Something dark crosses his features. "I...suppose you could say that. I wanted what was best for her."

"Did Mia have close friendships with other students?"

"Not especially. She got along with everyone well enough, but kept to herself."

"Any romantic relationships that you were aware of?"

Mr. Goolsbee tugs at his collar again, even though the room is frigid. "None that I know of. Mia was devoted to her music. Of course, I'm a teacher. I don't know the detailed personal lives of my students."

I decide to confront him directly. Sometimes you need to shake the tree.

"Mr. Goolsbee, did you have romantic feelings for Mia?"

His reaction is instantaneous. He leaps up from the piano bench so quickly it clatters to the floor behind him. The tree has definitely been shaken.

"How dare you!" he says, face purpling. "I cared deeply for that girl, but only as a teacher, as a mentor, for God's sake!"

He stomps around the room, movements stiff and agitated. His musky aftershave ripples through the air. He massages his giant cheeks with his hand. I remain seated.

"Please, sit back down. I had to ask. I didn't mean to offend you. I'm just doing my job."

He whirls to face me, eyes bulging. "Offense taken. Who do you think you are? You don't know the first thing about Mia, about this place. About what goes on here. You're just another private investigator. The fifth one, by my count. And none of you have done a damn thing to bring Mia back."

"I'm sorry. Now please sit down. If you help me, maybe we can bring her back together."

I retrieve the fallen bench, and after a long hesitation, Goolsbee slouches back down. Mopping his brow with a handkerchief, he seems to have spent his outrage.

I flip to a new page in the notebook and soften my tone. "I understand you were in charge of bed check on Mia's hall. Is that correct?"

"Yes. I was filling in for Ms. Barreto."

"When you checked on her and Penny the night she went missing, they were both in their room?"

"Yes. I checked on them at ten p.m., and both girls were in bed."

"You're positive? There's no way that she pulled the old two-pillows-under-a-blanket trick?" That was a staple for Christina and me when we'd sneak out the back door while our parents were sleeping.

Goolsbee snorts.

"No, there's no chance. I've been at this a long time, and

I've seen every trick in the book. Both girls were in bed and said good night. I'm certain. Whoever took her, took her after I left."

He lays a hand gently on the piano, as if remembering Mia singing while he played. I feel a twinge of sympathy for this strange man. But the nagging questions remain. He was invested in this girl. Too invested, in my estimation.

"Mr. Goolsbee, do you have any idea what happened to Mia that night? Any suspicions at all?"

He rubs his temples and then opens his mouth like he's going to say something. Then looks down and plays with his handkerchief. I let him gather himself. He starts to speak, but before he can form a word, Sonia pops into the room to collect me.

"Sorry to interrupt, but Hazel, it's time for you to meet with Dr. Mackenzie. He's on a tight schedule, so I don't want you to be late."

I put a finger in the air. "Just give me one moment, Sonia."

I turn back to Goolsbee. "I'm sorry, you were saying?"

His shoulders slump. Gazing down at his hands, he whispers, "No, it's nothing. She sang like an angel, then disappeared. That's all I know."

I watch him closely but detect no deception. Glancing at my watch, I decide to wrap things up for now. I've squeezed all I can out of the jittery choir teacher. But as I rise to leave, I hand him my business card.

"If you remember anything we could use to find Mia, please don't hesitate to call."

He bows, still avoiding my gaze. As I turn to go, I notice the sheaf of music resting on the piano stand. It's a solo piece titled "Mia's Song" in what must be Mr. Goolsbee's cramped handwriting. The song he was working on before we interrupted him.

He knows more than he's letting on. I can feel it.

Chapter 9

Thomas Mackenzie's office looks like it should be on the cover of *Headmasters Quarterly* magazine. A worn square Persian-style rug covers a wood floor that moans with each step. A bookshelf that would make most libraries jealous lines the wall, mahogany shelves stuffed with early editions of the classics, *Crime and Punishment*, *The Grapes of Wrath*, Dante's *Inferno*. And these books aren't just for show, like in my office. The spines are cracked and worn from caring hands reading and revisiting their pages. On the left wall hang two paintings that I fail to recognize but that appear quite old. One depicts a Greek or Roman soldier standing proud, bow and arrow in hand, looking into the distance. The other shows a mischievous-looking man wearing a toga and a crown of grapes, drinking from a golden goblet and surrounded by fawning half-clothed women. A man definitely painted that one.

At the center of the room sits Thomas Mackenzie, reviewing and signing documents. A beautiful tri-paned window hovers behind him, overlooking the sprawling lawn and campus that I saw on the way in. Stained glass frames the windows and shows what looks like a series of angels and demons.

Mackenzie sits at an ornate carved wood desk, but even when

he's sitting you can tell that he's well over six feet tall. His face is long and thin and his cheeks sunken. The man reeks of dour seriousness.

Sonia gives a knock on the doorframe and introduces me.

"Dr. Mackenzie, this is—"

He raises a long bony pointer finger to silence her and continues writing.

I roll my eyes and look at Sonia, whose round cheeks fill with a light flush. Who does this guy think he is?

After we've stood in silence for an interminable minute, Mackenzie finally raises his head.

His face looks like it was carved from granite. A proud forehead rolls into a prominent nose and sharp cheekbones, which descend into a strong but narrow jaw. And at the center float two fierce eyes the color of sky. His skin carries a ruddy tint caused by microscopic burst blood vessels in his cheeks and nose. Thomas Mackenzie probably enjoys a scotch or three at the end of a hard workday. As his eyes meet mine, he forces a smile, but it's obligatory. There's no joy behind it.

"You were saying, Ms. Barreto," says Mackenzie, reverting his eyes back to Sonia.

I notice that Sonia, who exuded such strength and command in her office, shrinks in front of this man. She proffers an obsequious smile and continues.

"Dr. Mackenzie, this is Hazel Cho. She's the new private investigator hired by Madeline Hemsley to assist with finding Mia."

Mackenzie nods and clears his throat but says nothing. He closes the leather-bound notepad he was writing in and rises from his desk, every movement completed with the utmost care. I was right. He's at least six feet six. I feel about two feet shorter than I did when I walked in here. He moves from behind his desk toward the middle of the room. His steps are slow, showing his age—I would guess he's in his late seventies or early eighties—but there's a power lurking in his lithe frame. I approach him with my hand out to break the awkward silence.

"Mr. Mackenzie, it's a pleasure to meet you. You have a beautiful off—"

"Doctor."

"I'm sorry?"

He extends his hand and shakes mine. His hand is all bone, no warmth.

"It's Dr. Mackenzie, Ms. Cho. I didn't spend ten years studying education at Harvard to be called mister. We use formal titles here at Saint Agnes. We believe it instills the girls with a respect for tradition and authority, which sadly seems so lacking in the modern world. Thank you, Ms. Barreto, that will be all."

Sonia shows a flicker of resentment at his dismissal but swallows it and exits the room.

"I'm sorry, Doctor," I say. I don't have time to get into a pissing contest with this fossil, especially without Sonia's support.

Mackenzie continues to stare into my eyes as though I'm a girl in his children's home and he's debating whether to give me detention. I try to get on his good side.

"This is a gorgeous office. May I ask, what are these paintings depicting?"

Mackenzie gives a knowing grin as though he senses what I'm doing, but he goes along with it. When he's thinking, he purses his lips, like he's sucking on a lozenge.

"Yes, they're quite beautiful. You must read the classics, Ms.

Cho. Homer, Hesiod, Sophocles. Look no further. All of life's questions and answers can be found there."

He points a wiry arm at the picture on the right.

"This painting depicts the Greek god Apollo, and the painting on the left is of the god Dionysus. I like these watching over the girls when they're in my office as a reminder of what we stand for at Saint Agnes."

"I'm not sure I'm following."

"Apollo represents all that we strive for: strength, rationality, order, selflessness. Dionysus represents the outside world: weakness, emotion, disorder, selfishness, hedonism, intoxication. I've been here twenty-five years, and in every one of those years at Saint Agnes, we've taught our girls to be Apollos. No cell phones. No social media. No corruption of the mind."

I welcome the message behind Mackenzie's words, but I'm not sure centuries-old paintings of Greek gods looking down on these girls is the best way to deliver it.

"Very interesting," I say, nodding along noncommittally. "Dr. Mackenzie, I'm wondering if you have time to answer a few questions about Mia's disappearance."

Mackenzie continues to look at the paintings, but his jaw clenches.

"Yes, Ms. Cho, I'll answer your questions, but I only have thirty minutes, so it will have to be brief. We've already had the police and your predecessors here asking questions, and I have a children's home to run. Why don't we walk the grounds so you can familiarize yourself with the place and I can show you Mia's room."

He grabs a brown houndstooth blazer off the coatrack in the corner and ushers me out the door. I've had ice water warmer than this guy.

We walk back down the hallways of the ancient building. He moves at a brisk pace. As we walk, I remove my pad and pen from my purse to take notes. As my neighbor Mrs. Yu says, "The palest ink is clearer than the strongest memory." That and I'm pretty sure Thomas Mackenzie will not be down with being recorded.

"Well, Ms. Cho, proceed with your questions."

"Okay. First, can you tell me about Mia?"

He looks down, and I think I see a flash of regret on his stone face.

"Mia was the model Saint Agnes girl. If every girl was like her, I'd be out of a job. She was an A student, popular with her classmates. And a marvel of a singer. She had a boundless curiosity about everything around her. She wanted to know the history of Saint Agnes, the size of the lake, the name of each bird in the trees. In many ways, this place was too small to hold her. What I hope for all these girls is that I can mold them to be like Mia. She hoped to be on Broadway someday."

We walk into the lobby, and the girls flood out of classrooms for lunch. There's a wide range of ages, from elementary schoolers to high schoolers. The hum of chatter, laughter, and footsteps echoes through the building. The girls wear a traditional private school uniform: plaid skirts and white shirts. Mia's peers, the adolescent girls, buzz around, awkward and giggly. However, at the sight of Mackenzie, they all immediately cease their talking, wipe the smiles off their faces, and put their heads to the ground.

They're afraid of this man.

The silence hovers in the high-ceilinged lobby. The only sound comes from the logs crackling in the fireplace. I have to lower my voice to barely above a whisper not to be overheard as we move through the lobby toward the outside.

"What ages of girls do you serve here, Doctor?"

"We start as early as five and go through high school, although we've taken in a few four-year-olds as exceptions."

"And where do the girls come from?"

"A variety of places. Saint Agnes was founded in 1908 as an orphanage. But over time, as society has changed, both the services we offer and the girls we serve have broadened. Now we care for children who have lost parents, or been abused, or whose parents are unfit to care for them."

"I'd like to speak to some of these girls later today, if that's all right."

Mackenzie releases a long breath through his nostrils and rubs his temples.

"No, Ms. Cho. That's not all right. The police have already questioned these girls with one of those specialists."

"A child forensic interviewer?"

"Yes, that sounds right. Anyway, it's distracting them from their studies and, frankly, scaring them. I won't have it."

"But, Dr. Mackenzie, the first step in any investigation is to question the people who were close to the victim. If I can't do that, how am I supposed to investigate?"

The truth is, I don't actually need to question the girls. Interviewing kids more than once is rarely a good idea, and the police have already trod that ground. Children often say whatever they think will please the interviewer and are susceptible to memory implantation. What I want to see is how Thomas will react to me requesting to interview the girls.

"You aren't supposed to investigate, Ms. Cho. I don't know why Madeline thought you would be of service in this case.

Leave this to us and the police. We don't need another private investigator. The only reason we're having this meeting is as a courtesy to Madeline."

We walk outside, and after a long silence, Mackenzie gives me the lay of the land. The property sits on a hill overlooking Lake George, looking black and ominous in the gray mist. Surrounding the main building are single-story family-style residences where the younger girls stay and larger multilevels where the older girls reside. On the other side is the entrance and security gate. The brick wall guards only the front quarter of the grounds. Dense forest protects the rest. It wouldn't be easy, but anyone could access the property through the forest on foot.

"Did Mia have any visitors?" I ask.

Mackenzie thinks as we walk from the front of the main building around toward one of the dormitories. The air is cool and damp. A light drizzle falls and pitter-patters on the gravel parking lot.

"Only one visitor that I can recall. Madeline would visit about twice a year. Maybe quarterly."

My eyebrows rise as we walk. We're following signs to Mia's dormitory. The building resembles a scaled-down version of a 1950s mental hospital. The structure is a perfect rectangle made of dark brick with four-paned windows with white trim.

"Only one visitor? No one else? No cousins. No friends. Boyfriends. Prospective parents?"

Mackenzie shoots me a glare that rips through me. He scans a key card, pulls open the door of the dormitory, and holds it for me to enter.

"She's an orphan, Ms. Cho. She is lucky to have one visitor. Some of these girls have no visitors. And I'd remind you that she has us. We're her family."

For the second time, this man makes me feel three feet tall. I step through the entrance to the dormitory, which looks like a college dorm, but cleaner. The white-and-gray linoleum floors are shining; the white walls are spotless. But spartan, like everything else here. Nothing on the walls; no evidence that anyone is, or ever was, here. It's hard for me to imagine the girls having much fun in this sterile institution. It's one step away from *One Flew over the Cuckoo's Nest.*

"Did Madeline and Mia ever leave the grounds when she visited?" I ask.

"Yes, but I don't know where they went. I'm sure Madeline could answer that question for you."

"Who has access to these dorms?"

"The only people who have access, other than the girls, are me, Ms. Barreto, and the staff members who live on campus."

I jot that down in my notebook.

"How many staff members live on campus?"

"Twenty. Four dorms. One for each floor of the dorm."

"How about friends? You mentioned she was popular. Could you tell me who she hung out with?"

Mackenzie frowns as he leads me down the hallway.

"Ms. Cho. I'm the headmaster of a children's home, not head of the social committee."

"Of course. I understand she had a roommate?"

"Yes. Her name is Penny Besser."

"May I speak with her after we're done talking?"

"No, I don't think that would be appropriate. These are children, after all. This has given them quite the scare. And she's already spoken with the police. You can speak with them about this matter."

He stops at the last door on the right of the dorm room hallway and scans his key card to open it, revealing Mia's room.

Chapter 10

Mia's room is tiny but spotless. The space is a rectangle, about twelve feet wide and twenty feet deep. Tan oak closets stand next to each side of the entrance, and twin beds rest against the right and left walls. Nothing hangs from the walls, and a sickly yellowed cream paint covers every inch. A spare metal desk sits against the far side, facing a tall window overlooking the lawn. A raven sits on a tree outside the room like a sentry.

It reminds me of my dorm room in college, but with no personality. There are no colorful blankets or comforters. No posters of boy bands. No lava lamps. No fun decorations. If it weren't for the textbooks perched on the desk and a retainer lying on the nightstand, I would assume school was out for summer. The only reminder of young girls is the smell of fruity shampoo. This place feels less like a children's home and more like a prison.

I step into the room and then look back at Mackenzie for his reaction to this depressing cell. He's beaming and for the first time gives me a smile. His teeth are crooked and stained with age.

"This is a Saint Agnes room," he says. "Order, cleanliness, modesty. As I told you, Mia was a model student. Her closet and bed are on the left."

There's something sadistic about him, taking such pleasure in the lack of joy. I swallow my tongue and continue to investigate the room while Mackenzie's treelike frame stands in the doorway, watching my every move. A feeling of claustrophobia and oppression hangs in the air, as though Mackenzie's presence is pressing down on me.

I open Mia's closet door slowly, dreading what I might find. But it's quite ordinary. The closet holds a few uniforms and some personal clothes. Nothing much. It surprises me, and I make a note. I would have expected Madeline to be the type to buy her goddaughter lots of fancy clothes to compensate for her guilt at not doing more. I open her roommate Penny's closet for comparison. It's bursting with clothes packed so tight you can barely move the hangers in any direction.

I turn back to Mia's side of the room. A mirror hangs to the right of her closet over a built-in dresser. Mia's blow-dryer and toiletry bag remain atop the dresser. I peer inside the bag but find only a few items: some lotion, a few hair clips, and scrunchies. No toothbrush. No toothpaste. No deodorant. All the essentials are missing. I snap back to Mackenzie.

"Do you know if the police took Mia's personal items into evidence?"

Mackenzie sighs and stares out the window as if the question is beneath him.

"I'm sure I don't. That would be another question for the police."

I'm squeezing water from a stone. Does he even want to find this girl? "Was an Amber Alert issued once it was determined she was missing?"

"No. The police felt that there was insufficient evidence that

Mia has been abducted to justify an Amber Alert."

I make my way over to Mia's bed. Like her roommate's, Mia's is perfectly made. The sheets are tucked into hospital corners, and the crimson comforter hangs evenly on both sides. If she had been snatched in the night, the bed would be disheveled. I'm reminded of what my old boss, Perry, used to say: "If you see a turtle on a fence post, you know it had some help." I can't fight the feeling that the police were probably right. When Mia left, wherever she was going, she knew she was going there for good, and she likely had help. I hear Mia's voice in my head, singing "Time after Time," about a suitcase of memories she left behind.

"Was Mia's bed made the morning she went missing?"

Mackenzie squints, trying to glean the meaning behind the question, but then relents.

"Yes. I would notice if one of our girls had failed to make their bed."

I let out a breath. It's still early, but wherever Mia went, she seems to have gone willingly.

"Did Mia swim?"

"I'm sorry?"

"Could she swim?"

"Oh, yes, of course. All the girls are taught how to swim."

"Would you describe her as an excellent swimmer?"

"I couldn't say, but she didn't swim on a team or anything like that."

Interesting. So, Mia could have swum away in the night. It's cold water and a long swim, though, particularly at night. Something to keep in mind.

I spend the next ten minutes inspecting every inch of the room but find nothing. There's nothing under the bed or the mattress. Nothing significant on the desk besides a picture of Mia and her roommate in uniforms, smiling. No hiding spots or secret compartments. If there ever was any evidence, the police have it now. I have to find a cop who will work with me.

Mackenzie clears his throat and looks at his watch.

"I really must be getting back to my work. Are we done here?"

I want to say *No, we're not done here. I want to interview every staff member in this damn place and dig through every record they have of Mia.* But part of being a young woman in an older man's world is picking your battles, and this is one I won't win. Sometimes you have to eat shit.

"Yeah, we're done here, for now," I say as I exit.

Mackenzie raises an eyebrow and then guides me out of the dormitory. I can barely keep up with his long, quick strides. It's obvious he can't wait to get me out of here. But why? I can't be that much of a threat. Is he protecting someone? Himself?

We step outside the dormitory, and the rain pelts the awning above us. Out of habit, I check the doorway for security cameras, but then I remember what Sonia told me.

"Ms. Barreto mentioned that you have security cameras, but only on the perimeter. Is that correct?"

Mackenzie points to a security camera attached to a post facing the woods across the parking lot.

"Yes, we had them installed a while back, after..."

He stops himself.

"After what?"

"Nothing you need to concern yourself with. Anyway, we placed cameras all around the perimeter to ensure that no one could enter or leave the property without being seen."

"But you didn't place cameras at the lake? Is that correct?"

Mackenzie grunts, sensing where I'm going with this.

"At the time of Mia's disappearance? No. Our security man didn't think it was necessary. And given the size of the lake and the rough terrain surrounding it, I agreed. However, after Mia's disappearance, we all decided that, out of an abundance of caution, we should have cameras on the entire perimeter. Ah, speak of the devil."

In the distance, I hear the soft hum of a motor and see the security guard, Neil Paver, rumbling toward us in a golf cart. He's here to run interference for Mackenzie. But I need to know more about these cameras.

"Why not have cameras on the interior as well?"

He scratches the thinning gray hairs atop his liver-spotted head and purses his lips again.

"Look around you." He waves his long thin arm at the buildings, the grounds, and the lake. "Where do you think you are?"

I squint my eyes as if I could see what he's driving at if I look hard enough.

"A children's home?"

"A church, Ms. Cho. A church. This is a church of shelter, learning, and growth. These women come from the outside world, a world that has abandoned them, abused them, distracted them, poisoned them. Saint Agnes houses them, feeds them, protects them, builds them back up. Now, how do you think they would feel if they had cameras pointed at them all the time? What would that say to them? That we don't trust them? That we're watching them? No, no, this won't do. This is a church."

Neil, the security guard, has arrived, and Mackenzie extends his gargantuan hand to signal that this is the end of the tour.

"Thank you for coming, Ms. Cho. Mr. Paver will take you around and see you home."

I shake his hand and give a polite smile, but I can barely mask my frustration with this man. A girl under his charge is missing, and he acts as though looking for her is an inconvenience. I can't resist. I must ask.

"One last question, Dr. Mackenzie." I emphasize the word *doctor*. "What do you think happened to Mia?"

Mackenzie looks at me matter-of-factly and says, "I think she ran away." His face is rock.

"Doesn't that bother you? Don't—"

"It doesn't bother me. It disappoints me. Here at Saint Agnes, we are in the business of taking girls from broken homes and fixing them. Most of the time, we succeed in doing that. But sometimes the expectations are too much. For Mia, it may have been too much. She may have felt the weight of her potential. I hope she will realize the error of her ways and return to us, but there's nothing more I can do. All I can do is focus on giving the proper attention to the ladies that are here."

He turns and walks back to his office, but as he walks, he stares at the ground and kicks pebbles, lost in thought.

He's hiding something.

Chapter 11

"All right, ma'am, you ready to roll?" says Neil Paver as I pull my eyes away from Mackenzie.

"That's the second time you've called me ma'am, Neil. Do I look that old?"

Neil smiles his plastic smile, and I can see what unnerved me the first time he grinned. It's his eyes. They stay dead. The lips and cheeks mold upward, but the eyes stay flat.

"Apologies, ma'am. It's an old navy habit. Happy to call you Hazel if you'd like."

"Yes, Hazel would definitely be better."

I hop into the golf cart, and Neil hits the accelerator. The golf cart is gas, so it lurches and spurts fumes into the air as we roll.

"So, where are we headed?" I ask. I notice he fails to ask me where I'd like to go or what I'd like to see. Everything at Saint Agnes has to be controlled.

A light mist filters into the cart, spritzing our faces. Neil licks his cracked, dry lips.

"I thought I'd take you down to the part of the lake that's on Saint Agnes grounds so you could look around there, if that's all right?"

"Seems like a good place to start." I find myself mimicking

Neil's southern accent. It was one of my dad's tricks with the customers. Whoever you were, he met you on your level. "So, you mentioned you were in the navy, and I'm guessing from your accent you're not from around here."

Neil slows the cart down as we approach the shore of the lake. In the summer, I imagine this spot would be quite beautiful. A small beach hugs the shore, a rope swing hangs from a tree, a series of large polished rocks lead into the water. I wonder if Mackenzie allows the girls to enjoy this spot or if it's too much of the "outside world." He probably makes them swim laps until their arms fall off and then sends them back to their studies. Regardless, today is not so beautiful. The beach sand is more like mud. The rope swing reminds me of a noose. The rocks disappear into the fall mist. I look over at Neil, but his cheery demeanor is unfazed.

"Yeah, I grew up down in Texas, but they stationed me up in Saratoga Springs. During the time I was up here, I got to liking the seasons and decided I'd hang around."

He licks his lips again. They have a ring of dark chapping around their edges.

I step out of the golf cart and inspect the ground. The rain has matted the grass and compressed the sand, so at first glance there isn't much to see.

"How long have you been working security at Saint Agnes?" I ask.

Neil scratches his chin, and I notice the jagged scabs on his hand.

"I've been here going on ten years now."

"Not bad. And do you do security for the whole place or just the front gate?"

He frowns and puts his hands on his hips.

"Oh, no, I do security for the whole place. I just work out of the front gate station. We don't have a lot of visitors, so one of the first things I did when I got here was axe that bum of a security guard we had before. Saves Saint Agnes money so we can spend it on the girls."

"Sorry, I didn't mean to offend you. Dr. Mackenzie says you installed all the security cameras?"

"Yep, managed the whole process. Took me forever to convince him to install those things."

"And you personally reviewed the camera footage when Mia went missing?"

The drizzle comes down harder now, so Neil grabs an umbrella from the rear of the golf cart, opens it, and hands it to me, leaving himself in the rain. I offer to share, but he declines.

"Yeah, me, Dr. Mackenzie, and Ms. Barreto checked it out. Went through the whole evening. But there was nothing. That's why we installed the camera here." He points to a security camera in a tree. "We figured Mia had to have gone into the lake."

I stare into his eyes, looking for deception, but they seem earnest. Walking along the beach, I notice impressions in the sand and bare spots where the grass along the lake has been torn away. I snap some more pictures and point.

"Does Saint Agnes have a boat?"

Neil puts his hands in his pockets and kicks at the sand.

"No, I have a boat back home that Dr. Mackenzie lets me take out sometimes, but Saint Agnes? No."

"Are these marks from your boat?"

Neil shrugs his shoulders. "I'm no boat track expert, but it sure as heck looks like mine. Who else's could it be?" His tongue slithers across his lips, and I'm questioning this *aww, shucks* routine. But right now, I need Neil on my side.

"So, if I'm Mia and I wanted to avoid the cameras, I could just walk down to the beach, swim out, and then double back to the shore a hundred meters in either direction?"

Neil hangs his head.

"That's right. But that's tough terrain out there. Lot of jagged rocks. Lot of thorny bushes."

"What about the staff? Where do they stay?"

"Ms. Barreto and the staff members who are house parents live on campus. Most of the other folks live in town. Dr. Mackenzie and some of the other teachers live on Scholar's Way off campus right over there."

Neil points up the hill off campus, and I can spy a row of beautiful Victorians.

"See that dark-blue one with the yellow shutters? That's Dr. Mackenzie's house."

"And how about you? Where do you live?"

"Oh, I'm over in Chestertown. Got me a nice little cabin. Real secluded. Got a nice little fishing hole next door. Besides, the homes around here are out of my price range."

I shudder to think what Neil's "secluded" cabin looks like, but regardless, I've seen what I need to see here, and something about him makes me crave having other people around.

"All right, let's get out of this rain. Can you show me the rest of the campus?"

"Yes, ma'am."

We pile into the golf cart, and for the next fifteen minutes, Neil takes me around the perimeter of the property, to the athletic fields, and even to the maintenance shed. But there's nothing of interest there. This entire case revolves around what happened at the lakeshore. Neil drops me off at the parking lot and wishes me well. He gives me one final plastic smile and drives off in his golf cart. As he drives away, I notice his shoulders slump in relief, like he just got out of an interview. I second-guess whether I let him off too easily.

I run through the rain out to the parking lot, my new Tesla still glistening. The one bright spot in this dour place. I open the driver's side door and am about to jump in the car when I hear a voice behind me and the crunch of footsteps on gravel drifting through the rain. I turn my head, and there's a girl running toward me. It's the girl from the picture in Mia's room, her roommate, Penny Besser.

She's a tall, pale, homely-looking girl. She has a thick body and broad shoulders, and acne dots her face. Her eyes spark with shrewdness. She's carrying something in her hand and running so fast that she's out of breath when she reaches me.

"Are...you...the private detective?" she says, trying to find her air. Her lips vibrate with fear.

"Yes, hi, I'm Hazel," I say and give a soft wave so as not to intimidate her.

"I don't have much time. I have to get back to class, but I wanted you to have this."

With shaking hands, she hands me a picture of Mia that looks like something you'd find in a yearbook. She's wearing a chunky, oversize red sweater and leaning up against a tree next to the lake, smiling. You can see the glint of sunshine bouncing off her round cheeks, and there's a flash of optimism in her eyes. I scan the picture for something revealing, but I come up empty.

"Flip it over," says Penny as she hurries back inside.

I flip the picture over. There's a bright-blue stamp on the

back that resembles a logo with simple strokes meant to convey a feeling rather than an accurate rendering. In the middle of the logo is a bearded man with an enormous grin on his face. A bunch of grapes floats in the space on either side of him.

"Wait, Penny," I shout to the girl.

But she races away with long strides, her head turning left, then right to ensure that no one has been watching her.

I look back down at the card. The face in the logo appears to be laughing at me, taunting me. I don't know what it is, but I'll take anything that might help me find Mia. The rain is rolling down hard now, and I'm shivering. I jump back in the Tesla and blast the heat.

I want to go home. There's something about this place, something eerie that slithers inside you. But I can't leave Lake George yet. Not before I talk to the police and find out what they know.

Chapter 12

Being the crack detective that I am, I did some preliminary research before I hauled my ass out to Lake George. I soon realized that Lake George doesn't actually have its own police department. Apparently, there's not enough crime here to justify a stand-alone police force, so they just lean on the Warren County Sheriff's Office, which keeps a small station in Lake George inside the volunteer fire department. I don't mean to be a snobby New Yorker, but I'm not confident that this elite squad is going to find Mia.

I pull up to the volunteer fire department building, which is nestled in a modest neighborhood a few blocks off the lake and main street. On a summer's day, this would be a quaint little municipal building, but now in the cold and rain it merely seems lonely and sad.

I sit in my car for a minute watching the rain. I can't escape the look on Penny's face when she handed me that card.

Raw fear.

Eventually, I brave the rain, and as I step into the building, I find the "sheriff's office" consists of a front desk with a receptionist and three tiny offices with cops stuffed in them. Pictures of the various cops on the Warren County Sheriff's Office hang from the periwinkle wall. I introduce myself and ask for Detective Riether. A surly, waifish teenage girl who seems more interested in her phone than my presence reluctantly heaves herself from her seat to grab the detective. Teenagers could make breathing look exhausting.

Detective Riether steps out from his office and greets me. He's different from what I pictured. Based on his truculence on the phone, I expected an older man with a hard, stubborn cop's mug. But Riether is young, probably in his midthirties, and has kind eyes and a sharp hawk's face with a five o'clock shadow. His hair is buzzed like he's about to enlist. He's not traditionally handsome and carries a little extra around the midsection, but he's appealing, nonetheless.

"Yes, can I help you?" he says. His high-pitched voice is tight, like he needs to clear his throat.

"Hi, Detective, I'm Hazel Cho. We spoke on the phone yesterday about the Mia Ross investigation."

The small, quiet office somehow gets smaller and quieter as my words hang in the air. The assistant looks up from her phone, and the other cops pause what they're doing in their offices. It's only for a moment, and then everyone adopts careless poses, but it strikes me.

At first, Riether grimaces, and I think I've made a mistake coming here. But then his eyes brighten, and he takes a step toward me.

"You hungry, Hazel?"

Is this guy asking me out on a date? I mean, I'm not saying I'd say no, but you got to warm me up a little. Then again, I am hungry.

"Yeah, I could eat," I say, trying to give off the vibe that I don't think about food twenty-four hours a day.

His mouth breaks into a wry smile, and I notice he has a small chip on his right front tooth and a priceless set of dimples.

"Good. I'm starving. Let's get something to eat."

The two of us walk out the front door and onto Amherst Street. The rain has subsided, but a damp chill lurks behind it. It's a shame Madeline didn't reach out to me in the summer. This would be the perfect mix of business and pleasure. Now, it's drudgery. As if sensing my hesitation, Detective Riether points to the lake a few blocks away, and we walk.

He pulls out a cigarette with a white filter and lights it with a Zippo. I notice that his hands have a slight shake. Normally, I'm not a big fan of smoking, but Riether somehow makes it look cool and sexy, like in the old movies my dad and I used to watch. As he walks, he scratches the stubble on his chin and looks up at the sky. He opens his mouth to speak, but then stops. He opens it again, then closes it around his cigarette, takes a drag, and releases.

"Sorry if that was a little weird in there," he says. "That office is a little too small, if you know what I mean."

I recall the eerie silence when I mentioned Mia.

"Yeah, I know what you mean."

Sweat gathers on Riether's upper lip, and a pallor seeps through his skin. He hasn't been taking very good care of himself.

"Is there something you wanted to tell me, Detective, or do you just not like to eat alone?"

His coffee-colored eyes crinkle, and he takes another drag, blowing the smoke up into the air so as not to hit me with it. It rides the damp fall wind.

"You can call me Bobby, Hazel. And the reason I wanted to grab food was because I don't trust anyone in that office to keep their mouth shut. You probably noticed I was a little curt with you on the phone earlier."

I perk up at this information but don't want to seem too eager. The easiest way to spook somebody about to give you information is to show them how badly you need it.

"I understand."

We turn onto the main street of Lake George. It's stunning. A large deep-blue lake is backed by a rich, colorful rolling hill. Quaint shops and restaurants line the quiet street by the water, selling lake-themed tchotchkes and sweets. But Bobby doesn't look at any of it. He's just staring into an infinite distance, searching.

He stamps out his cigarette, throws open the door of a sleepy diner, and holds it for me. He's more of a gentleman than most of my Tinder dates.

"Hey, Carol," says Bobby to an overly made up server behind the counter as he slumps into a booth along the window.

The diner is 1950s themed and boasts aqua vinyl booths that look like the interiors of cars. A collection of older couples rest in the booths in each corner, watched over by pictures of Elvis and Marilyn Monroe, but other than that, the diner is empty. The smell of eggs and grease wafts through the air. "Wake Up Little Susie" plays on a soft pink jukebox.

"Hey, Bobby. You brought yourself a date today, I see," says Carol as she approaches our booth and drops two plastic menus the size of catalogs on the table. Lipstick spots her teeth.

Bobby blushes a little, and so do I. He rubs a hand back and forth through his buzz cut and acts like he's looking at his menu, but his mind is elsewhere. Sensing the awkwardness, Carol trundles back to the kitchen and pretends to be busy.

"So, how long have you been on the force?" I say, trying to break the ice.

Bobby peers into my eyes and raises an eyebrow.

"You trying to soften me up, Hazel?"

"No, I just figured if I didn't start talking, it was going to be a quiet lunch."

He bites his bottom lip, and a corner of his mouth slides upward. One dimple comes out of hiding.

"I've been on the force for fourteen years. Man, has it been that long?"

"So you're one of those guys who wanted to be a cop since he was a kid, huh?"

"Sort of. I wanted to be a football player, but with this frame"—he points to his scrawny body and tiny paunch—"and after a couple of concussions, I quickly realized that pro football wasn't in the cards. My dad was a cop. My grandpa was a cop. My two brothers are cops. I'm the youngest, so I guess I never considered being anything else. It's fine. I try to do good work, but it's not my dream or anything."

"Yeah, I thought being a PI was my dream, but now I'm not so sure."

"Tired of dealing with scumbags?"

"Something like that."

"Well, I'm not sure this case is going to make you feel a whole lot better."

"Yeah, I'm getting that feeling. But I'm hoping you're going to make it a little easier on me?"

He leans in closer to the counter and lowers his voice.

"All right, let's talk. But first, a couple of ground rules. Number one, I can't show you the case file. This is still an active investigation, and my superiors have made it clear in no uncertain terms that we are not allowed to discuss an active investigation."

"Okay," I say. But in my head, I'm dying. How am I supposed to dig into this thing without the case file? First Mackenzie gives me the runaround, and now this. I might as well visit a fortune teller to solve this case.

"Number two, I cannot discuss the case with you."

I lean back in my booth and cross my arms.

"This *is* going to be a quiet lunch. Then what are we even doing here, Bobby?"

"We're just two friends having lunch." He gives me a wink. I've never been able to wink, so I'm immediately jealous and intrigued.

"Aah, so if I were to ask my friend how life is at work, he might tell me what he's been up to."

"He might, if you were to be open about what you've been up to."

Carol comes back to the table and takes our orders. I order a garden salad as though this is my standard meal. Bobby orders a double bacon cheeseburger. I'll have to live off the free smells. I wait for Carol to move out of earshot—she seems like a nosy one—and then I dive back in with Bobby.

"Okay, since we're friends, Bobby, why don't you tell me how work's been?"

Bobby looks around to make sure no one is eavesdropping.

"Thanks for asking, Hazel," he says mockingly. "It's been pretty frustrating, now that you mention it. A few months ago, we got a report from a local children's home that a girl had gone missing. My partner and I were assigned to investigate the case. So, we investigated."

"And what did you find?"

"We found that the girl almost certainly left on her own accord. Her backpack and toiletries were gone. She'd made

93

her bed. There was no sign of a struggle. Her roommate said she was in bed at lights-out and didn't hear her leave in the night."

I nod along with him. Bobby's voice rises an octave when he gets excited, like it might crack. A taut string vibrating. It's endearing.

"Yeah, and her closet was half-empty," I say.

"Exactly. So, once we knew that, the obvious question was, Who did she go with?"

"I assume you looked into the faculty and staff?"

"Of course. No criminal records. Cell phone records show that all the staff that live on campus were on campus the whole evening, with the exception of Sonia Barreto."

"Yeah, she said she was in the city. I assume you confirmed that?"

"Correct. Got her at the restaurant and the hotel in Manhattan, so she's out."

"What about the staff that lived off campus?"

"We checked the cell phone tower, and nothing pinged that tower other than the phones on campus."

"Did you review the security camera footage? Mackenzie and his people said they did, but I just wanted to verify with you that there's nothing on it."

He takes a sip of his water and crunches ice in his teeth while he talks.

"We checked the security cameras. No vehicles on the roads, no people on the ground. There was nothing, but as the saying goes, you can learn something from nothing."

"You mean, if there's nothing on the cameras, then whatever happened had to happen off camera?"

"Yep. The only cameras on the grounds point to the front

and sides of the building, presumably because those are the only points of entry by car or by foot. And it's a pretty solid system. Not a lot of blind spots and pretty good resolution."

"So, if she left the grounds, it would have to be from the rear?"

"You got it."

"But that leaves just the lake. It's fifty-degree water. I just don't buy that she swam and crawled through a mile of rock and scrub brush. Unless she had access to a boat."

"That was what was interesting. When we went down to the water with the bloodhounds, they tracked her right to the shore. At that location on the shore, we noticed an impression in the sand and grass."

"Yeah, I was down there this morning. And I noticed an impression. Probably not the same one, but definitely a sign that boats have been there. Neil, the security guy, seemed to think that was from his boat."

Carol arrives with Bobby's steaming-hot burger and my sad garden salad. The smell of cheese and ground beef tantalizes my nose, and I immediately regret my order.

"I don't buy that. Nothing about that Neil guy sits right with me."

I nod my agreement as I force down a bite of my cold salad drenched in ranch, and try to picture this thirteen-year-old girl running out in the middle of the night and getting into a boat with someone.

"Neil said there aren't any boats on campus. Is that true?"

"That's correct."

"So, for a staff member to take Mia by boat alone, they would have to leave the campus without being caught on camera, get a boat, and then return to pick Mia up?"

"That's right."

"Any cameras on neighboring properties on the lake?"

Bobby takes a massive bite of his burger and talks with a chunk wedged in his cheek, as though he's taunting me about my poor lunch choice.

"No, and that's where things get weird."

"What do you mean?"

He looks behind him again, and he wipes his forehead with a napkin.

"I presented what I found to my boss and requested more resources so that we could reach out to homeowners on the lake and get access to their security cameras to see if they caught anything. I figured we might get lucky and see a boat pass by a house and maybe get a shot of the make of the boat or the name of the boat."

"Yeah, probably not a lot of boats on the lake in the middle of the night, so if a camera catches it, you at least know where they're headed. It's not a lot, but it's something."

Bobby takes another big bite of his burger and says, "That's what I said. But my boss said no way."

"What? Why?"

"He said we're a small department and we don't have the resources to chase after an orphan girl who's clearly just run away and hasn't been abducted. And it's hard to argue when your office is wedged in the corner of the volunteer fire department."

I've been around long enough to know that there's a sad truth to what the sheriff says. Unlike in the TV shows, police departments, especially small-town ones like this, don't have unlimited resources. And in a world with murders, rapes, drug deals, and worse, a teen runaway doesn't top the list. It would almost be better if Mia had been snatched out of her room screaming in the night.

If only Madeline had come to me sooner. Most of these home security systems only store footage for a day or two, maybe thirty if you're lucky. If she had reached out to me right away, I could have knocked on every door in the area and been certain to find footage.

"What about hospitals, hotels, or gas stations?"

"We checked the ones in the area, and they had nothing. We also checked the cell phone towers, and the only pings on the tower were from people at the children's home or in the neighborhood nearby."

"So, either Mia left alone, went with someone from the children's home, or whoever she did go with is smart enough not to bring a phone and not to stop at a hotel?"

"That's right."

Something that cop who pulled me over on the way up here said to me echoes in my mind.

"Bobby, do you know if any other girls have gone missing from Saint Agnes recently?"

He puts down his burger and wipes his hands on a napkin.

"Yeah, there's been runaways, but that's not uncommon when you're dealing with kids from broken homes. In fact, it's a big part of the reason my boss doesn't want to put any more resources toward this investigation. In the past, half of the runaways eventually come back or are found, and the other half cause some sort of trouble in the community on their way out. You know, petty theft, hitchhiking, graffiti, et cetera. Why?"

"Nothing. Just something I heard. Did you get a chance to talk to the girls at Saint Agnes? Mackenzie didn't want me talking to them."

"Yeah, we interviewed all the girls who had regular interactions with Mia. They didn't have much. They liked Mia. Said she was a great singer. Wanted to be in the theater. She didn't tell anyone she was leaving. Nobody saw her or heard her leave. The roommate might know more than she's letting on. But I think Mackenzie's got that place run pretty tight, so I'm not sure any of those girls are going to say much, regardless."

I think back to the look on Penny Besser's face. He's right. If the girls know anything, they're not going to tell me. The answer to this case lies elsewhere. Maybe in the picture Penny gave me?

Bobby checks his watch.

"Oh shit. I've got a briefing in five minutes. I gotta get running."

He slams another bite of his burger and then pulls out a twenty and tosses it on the table.

I've still got a mouthful of salad and ranch dressing dripping down my chin, but I can't let him get away that easily.

"Wait, one more question. Does this mean anything to you?"

I show him the picture with Mia on the front and the logo with the smiling bearded man on the back.

Bobby squints and rubs his tongue along his chipped front tooth, then shakes his head.

"Nah. I don't recognize it."

"Yeah, it was a long shot. Okay. Well, thanks for taking the time. This was really helpful. Call me if you hear anything or change your mind about showing me that case file," I say as he gets up from the table.

He laughs, but then concern rolls across his face. "Probably best we don't talk anymore, Hazel. I've already said more than

I should, but I wanted you to have a fighting chance picking up where I left off. Good luck."

And with that, Bobby Riether hurries out the door.

Not my worst first date.

Chapter 13

I spend the few remaining hours of daylight I have left canvassing the neighborhood, knocking on doors of houses on the lake to see if I can catch a break and get camera footage from the night Mia went missing. But it's October in Lake George, so most of the houses have been abandoned for the season. The few people I do get have cameras that reset every week. I'll have to hit the phones later, but now I need to get home.

By the time I arrive back in the city, I'm starving. It took me about four hours to navigate the bumper-to-bumper traffic on I-87, another thirty minutes and a brief chat with a couple on a road trip to figure out how to charge the Tesla, and then another hour to find a parking spot for the car. This is exactly why I didn't want to take a case upstate. You spend too much time with your feet on the pedal and not enough time with them on the ground. Fortunately, as I climb the endless stairway to my apartment, I'm greeted by the familiar smell of spice and soba noodles. Kenny must be cooking.

I open the door, and Kenny's at the stove, swirling steaming noodles in a pot. He's wearing earbuds and singing to one of the K-pop songs he listens to. His round frame sways side to side in a pair of joggers and a police academy T-shirt.

The smell in the apartment is delightful: the perfect blend of grease, salt, soy, and gochujang. My stomach barks at me to do something about it.

I slam the door closed so as not to sneak up on him. He turns, at first surprised, and then a sheepish smile rises on his face. He removes his earbuds and stops dancing.

"Don't stop the show on my account," I say, stifling laughter.

"Hazel, you're home."

"I am. The food smells delicious."

"Good. I made it just for you. I figured you probably had a long day and would be hungry when you got back."

"How did you know when I'd be home?"

"Oh, I was watching you on Find My Friends."

I squint at him. I've known Kenny since we were kids, and he dances on that fine line between protective and stalkerish. Just when I think I know which one he is, he throws me a curveball.

"That's not creepy at all," I say.

I grab one of the mismatched forks from our utensil drawer and steal a couple of noodles. They nearly burn my tongue off, but they taste perfect. A divine blend of spice and carbs.

"I was right that you'd be hungry, wasn't I?" says Kenny, watching me steal more noodles from the pot.

"Yes, you were," I say through a mouthful of noodles. "I made the rookie mistake of ordering salad today at lunch."

He grins and looks at me again for several seconds too long.

I run back into my room and change into my apartment clothes: red sweatpants and my old gray Union College sweatshirt. I've found that if you want to enjoy a meal, it's nice to have pants with little to no waistband. Tight elastic is your enemy.

The two of us sit down at our wobbly card table with two bowls of noodles. I inhale my food, and Kenny gives me side-eye like he's watching a rabid raccoon. It's a pleasant distraction from the day I just had. Kenny eats so slowly, sometimes I finish my meal before he's done preparing his. Luckily, he doesn't seem to mind.

"So, how'd it go today?" he asks.

He's just asking to be nice, but my day is the last thing I want to talk about. I dig into the fridge and grab a sugar-free Red Bull and crack it open. I still have Madeline's deadline hanging over me like a guillotine, so it's going to be a late night.

"A mix of good and bad. I'm pretty sure Mia left the campus willingly, probably by boat on the lake at the back of the property."

"That's good."

"Yeah, but I have nothing on who she left with or where she went."

"That's bad."

"Exactly."

Kenny finishes his artistic seasoning process and mercifully begins eating while I have a few noodles remaining. He starts talking with a mouth full of food. One of his worst habits.

"In training, they talked about how tough missing persons cases are because you usually don't have a crime scene. And serial predators tend to hide evidence by abducting the victims in one location and burying the bodies in another location. If the person's dead, it's usually a long way from where they were taken. There's no pattern of killing."

"I hope she's not dead. But yes, there's no crime scene at all, especially since all the evidence shows she just walked right out the door."

"What about the police? Were they helpful?"

"No."

Kenny frowns as though I've insulted him personally. He's not even a cop yet, and he's already protecting them.

I put a hand up in the air to calm him.

"I'm being too harsh. The detective performed a full investigation and gave me all the information he could and probably more than he should. It's funny, he was actually kind of cute in a goofy way."

I spy a blush rising to Kenny's cheeks. He plays with his noodles.

"Oh, really?"

"Yeah, but most of what he told me I had already figured out on my own. Plus, before I even got there, I got pulled over."

"By the same cop?"

"No, a different guy."

As I finish my last noodle, I pause and stare out our dirt-streaked windows. The wind squeals through the gaps in the sealant.

"What is it?" Kenny asks.

"Nothing. The cop that pulled me over said something strange."

"Really? What did he say?"

"He said something like 'a lot of girls go missing from that place.'"

Kenny stops eating and taps a chopstick against his front tooth. "A lot of girls go missing from that place? Hazel, that could be a lead. If other girls have gone missing in the past, we could have a serial abductor on our hands."

"Yes, I'm aware of that. That's why it stuck with me. And what is this *we* business?" I say, tilting my head to one side.

Kenny stares back down at his noodles. "I mean, *you* might have a serial abductor on your hands."

I give a loud burp. It's nice to be able to burp in front of someone.

"Yeah, maybe. Or it's just a regular children's home with a lot of girls from tough backgrounds who run away. Even the other cop who I spoke with, Bobby, said that half of them come back."

"Yeah, but it's probably still worth looking into, don't you think?"

Kenny springs from the table and grabs his laptop. I admire his enthusiasm. It reminds me of when I started out as a private investigator. I used to love sinking my teeth into a case: performing the research, running the interviews. But over time, you feel like you're pushing a boulder that will inevitably tumble back down. There will always be another insurance cheat or another missing person. Madeline's challenge to me, and the money that comes with it, seems like just another goal out of reach.

What happened to me?

A flash of lightning illuminates the room, followed by the clap of thunder outside. I force myself out of my food coma and slide my chair around to Kenny's laptop. It can't hurt to indulge the guy. One less lead I have to track down.

"Where did you say the children's home was?" asks Kenny.

"Lake George."

Kenny types *Missing person Lake George* into Google News. His leg shakes with anticipation.

"Don't shake your leg," I bark at him. It's bad luck in Korean culture, and we need all the luck we can get.

"Sorry," he says and stops shaking. "You know my family

and I go out to Lake George, right?"

Kenny comes from a wealthy family, and every year they go to Lake George, which he never tires of telling me. The only reason he lives in this crappy little place with me is because his parents cut him off when he told them he was going to be a cop. They were hoping he would take over the family business. Part of me thinks he likes it, though. Probably his version of slumming it.

He keeps pattering on about his favorite summers there, but I've stopped listening. A series of news articles pop up, documenting people who have gone missing. There's a blurb about Mia, but the press gives little attention to missing orphan girls. The other articles cover missing wives and men who left their families, but no missing girls from Saint Agnes.

"Try *missing girls, Lake George*."

Kenny types and hits a button. Another string of articles fills the screen, but these are of missing girls not just from Lake George but from all over upstate New York. The vast majority are little Black girls like Mia, but none are from Saint Agnes.

"Try *missing girl, Saint Agnes Children's Home*."

Kenny obliges and the screen updates, and it is as though I've entered a secret code revealing an unknown world. The first article is about Mia. But the ones that follow are different girls. One from November 2022, one from October 2021, one from March 2021. On and on: the results go back twenty years. And then they stop. I do a quick count. It must be fifty girls over the last twenty years. My heartbeat accelerates.

"That's a lot of missing girls from one children's home," says Kenny.

"Yes, Special K, it is." I roll my eyes at his statement of the obvious.

"I wonder why it stops in 2003?"

I pivot the computer toward me and take over the keyboard.

"Google News only goes back to 2003. Let's try the Google newspaper archive. This keeps articles going back to the 1880s."

I type in the same search term in the Google newspaper archive, expecting to see more missing girls prior to 2003. But there aren't any. It all stops in 2003. At first, I wonder if I did something wrong in the search.

Then it hits me.

Mackenzie.

I grab my notebook from my bag and page through my notes to make sure I'm right. Kenny watches with a scrunched forehead. My fingers flip through the yellow-lined pages of my notebook. In my terrible handwriting, I see what I'm looking for: a scribbled note that says "Thomas Mackenzie at Saint Agnes twenty-five years."

Chapter 14

After wolfing down a second plate of Kenny's noodles and a couple of cream puffs from Beard Papa's, I retire to my room for some research. As strange as it sounds, I do my best work sitting in bed with my computer on my lap. I think it reminds me of home, when I used to sit on my twin mattress studying into the wee hours, occasionally stealing glimpses of my Justin Timberlake poster to fortify myself. My sister, Christina, would already be done with her homework and chatting away with whoever her boyfriend was at the moment. She was, somehow, both better than me at school and more popular. It wasn't the greatest life, but it was home.

The rain falls and thunder rumbles outside as I read through every article or mention of girls who've gone missing from Saint Agnes over the years. I open my case management software and inventory every girl's name, picture, and age and any family information I can dig up from Tracers and the other databases I have access to. Most of the girls don't have any known connections. And there don't appear to be any common threads connecting them. Normally with serial criminals you can identify some type of pattern. All Black girls, or all skinny girls, or something. But looking at these girls, there's nothing.

There's white girls, Black girls, Hispanic girls, straight-haired girls, curly-haired girls, blondes, brunettes, redheads. The only thing that binds them is Saint Agnes.

I clench my jaw and rub my forehead.

Missing adults leave a trail. There are auto records, phone records, credit records, known associates. I've run missing persons investigations where I found the person the day I was hired.

Children are different.

They're too young to have any electronic records. Orphans are even worse. Still, in reading the articles and checking the databases, I find an occasional family friend or relative. Maybe they'll know something beneath the surface appearance that binds these girls. I add them to the file. At the top of the file is a photo of Mia smiling right at me. Seeing her picture reminds me of her in that video of "Time after Time," singing about watching through windows and wondering if she's okay.

Except I'm not wondering if she's okay. I'm certain she isn't. Too much time has passed. Too much evidence has washed away. My case management system has a solvability matrix, which scores the probability of solving the case based on the data you've entered. Currently, the score blinking back at me shows ten percent. Normally, I'm in the eighties or nineties.

I look at the clock. It's two in the morning, and the Red Bull is wearing off. From the absence of *Call of Duty* gun blasts from the living room, I can tell Kenny's already called it a night. I need to go to bed, but I have a ten percent chance and eight days left before Madeline Hemsley's reward expires. The sleep will have to wait.

Faced with so many missing girls, I can't help thinking of my mom. She was convinced that child abductors lurked around every corner. That she watched every procedural cop show, from *CSI* to *Law & Order*, only made it worse. She never let us play with our friends in the neighborhood unless she or another adult was present. My sister didn't mind. I think she liked the attention. But for me, a natural-born explorer, it was stifling. Fortunately, I had my grandmother who lived with us. She was like me at heart—adventurous, curious—but because of a combination of age and culture, she never got a chance to chase her dreams. When my mom was out running errands and my dad was at the shop, she would take me aside and tell me I was strong and smart and that I would be somebody someday. Every New Year, as part of Korean tradition, we would bow to our elders as a sign of respect and well-wishes for the New Year, and they would give us a gift of cash in a small silk bag. She would always give me a little more than my sister and raise a shaky finger to her lips so that I would keep it a secret. She's gone now, and I miss her every day, especially when my mom's fears grip me. I look at the faces of these girls who are gone and probably not coming back, and I can't help but wonder if my mom was right.

Once my list of missing girls and known contacts is complete, I open a background file and list all the children's group homes in the country that are similar in size and scope to Saint Agnes, and their contact information. Based on what I've learned so far about these places, runaways are not uncommon. At one large, underfunded, understaffed home in Florida for emergency shelter, two hundred and fifty kids ran away in one year. Two hundred and fifty. That's a train station, not a shelter. But Saint Agnes is no emergency shelter, and it definitely isn't short on resources.

But before I go back to *Dr.* Mackenzie, I need to be sure. I fire off some emails to the other children's homes, asking them how often they have a runaway, but schedule the emails to go out in the morning, so that I don't look like a psychopath emailing about runaway girls at three in the morning.

After my tenth email, the weight of my eyelids overwhelms me. I shut down my computer and throw it on the floor next to my bed. Tonight is a sleep-in-your-clothes night for sure. I pull my weighted blanket over me and reach over to turn off my bedside lamp when I spot the picture of Mia that her roommate gave me. I can barely see, I'm so tired, but curiosity pulls harder. I turn the picture over and look again at the stamp of the laughing bearded man. There's a reason Penny gave this to me, even if she was too scared to say it.

I take out my phone and open Google Lens, which enables you to take a picture and then search on that image. I take a photo of the laughing man with grapes on each side of him.

Google returns similar images, one of which says *Bacchus* in the search results.

I look up Bacchus.

The result sends a shiver up my spine.

Bacchus. / ('bœkəs) / noun. (in ancient Greece and Rome) a god of wine and giver of ecstasy, identified with Dionysus.

Chapter 15

Eight days left

I wake up with my retainer spilling out of my mouth and an expansive puddle of drool on my pillow. I feel like someone put me in a tumble-dry cycle all night. You know you're getting older when you injure yourself in your sleep. I look at the clock. It's 10:00 a.m.

Shit.

I overslept.

Last night, I stayed up another hour learning more than I ever wanted to know about Dionysus, but it gave me zero insight into what it could possibly have to do with Mia other than the obvious fact that Mackenzie has a picture of him in his office. I grab my phone to see if I missed any important calls. Of course Madeline called. I'm so screwed. But I'm going to need some Red Bull, and probably a two-day-old mochi doughnut, before I talk to that woman.

While I'm trying to rouse myself back to consciousness, I scroll through my emails. Some of the other children's homes have written back to answer my question about how many runaways they've had over the past ten years.

The first one I open shows a long introductory greeting. It's clear that they think I'm a prospect looking to place a child.

After the obligatory pablum, she gets right to the point: five. They've had five runaways in the last ten years.

I open another response.

Three runaways.

I open another.

Seven runaways.

After I'm done, I've found no children's home with over ten runaways in the last ten years. There are only two possibilities: either Mackenzie is incompetent, or he's protecting something or someone, and nothing about that man seemed incompetent. Either way, something at that place isn't right, and the quicker I identify who or what that is, the quicker I can find Mia and get paid.

My phone rings.

It's Madeline again.

I take a sip of water from my nightstand and talk to myself for a second to warm up my morning voice, which currently sounds like Miley Cyrus.

"Madeline, hello. I was just about to call you."

I hear a scoff on the other end.

"Oh, I'm sorry. Did I wake you?" Venom coats her voice.

"No, no. I just have a bit of a cold. I was up until four a.m. working on your case."

"As you should be. I'm calling because I believe we agreed you would report back to me within forty-eight hours, yet here I am alone in your office, and you're nowhere to be found. I've seen my fair share of incompetence in my experience with private investigators, but you're taking the cake."

It's a Madeline Hemsley special: a breathtaking blend of arrogance and condescension.

"Yes, we did, and that's why I said I was about to call you.

I'm not available at the moment, but I can send you a written report or give it to you over the phone if you'd like."

"No, I would prefer it in person, please. I'll wait."

I can picture her smug smile. I bite my lower lip and raise my eyes to the ceiling.

"Great. I should be back at the office in ten minutes."

I jump out of bed and pinch my cheeks to get some color back in them. The good news is that since I slept in my clothes last night, there's no need to change. I throw my laptop bag over my shoulder and sprint into the kitchen to grab a Red Bull and a doughnut. The Red Bull's there, but Kenny took the last doughnut. He better sleep with one eye open tonight.

I take a swig of energy drink, throw on my driving mocs, and run out the door. I sprint past the Yu and Me bookstore— I've always loved that pun—and up Mulberry Street past the vendors selling suitcases, bags, and pretty much any other knock-off merchandise you'd like. By the time I get to Canal Street, I'm already winded. God, that's sad. I swear to myself that I'm going to start working out, but in the meantime, I downshift into a power walk the rest of the way.

When I finally arrive, Madeline is sitting on the bench in the waiting hallway. The same bench that Gene Strauss sat on before he threatened me. The thought of him cinches my stomach. I'm not sure this meeting is going to go much better. She breathes a long, dramatic sigh, as though she's been stuck in my office for days.

"Apologies for the delay, Madeline," I say as I walk past her and open the door to my office.

Madeline purses her overfilled lips. No *Don't worry about it* or *Apology accepted*, just irritated silence. We sit down at my desk, and I pull up the case file on my computer and pivot the

113

screen so she can see it. As the screen fills with information about Mia, I notice Madeline's face transforms from anger to curiosity...and hope. She's a hard woman to impress, but I think I just might have with my preparation.

"I'm pleased to report I've made a lot of progress in the past forty-eight hours. I can go into as much detail as you'd like, but long story short, I can say with a high degree of confidence that Mia left the children's home willingly. And she likely left with someone by boat."

Madeline sighs again. "Yes, Hazel, I know that already. Both the police and your predecessors came to the same conclusion."

That's why you don't hire different private detectives, you bitch, I think to myself. "Yes, I understand, but that's not all I've found. I also discovered that Mia's disappearance might be part of a larger problem at Saint Agnes."

This elicits shock on Madeline's face, or as much shock as you can get through the filler.

"Really?"

"Yes, from our preliminary research, we"—I use *we* like I've got a full team behind me—"were able to determine that at least fifty girls have gone missing from Saint Agnes over the past twenty years, and the real count is likely much higher."

Madeline sits back in her chair, and her neck tightens. Her fingers tap against her handbag, and her eyes drift past me.

"So, you think that whoever did this has done it before?"

"Yes."

"Do you have any leads?"

"No. It's too early. But I would like to reinterview Thomas Mackenzie to find out more about what he knows."

Madeline laughs out loud at this one. Not a joyous laugh. It's a laugh coated in pain.

"Hazel, I've known Thomas Mackenzie for years. The man is an institution in Lake George. He's done more for those little girls in a year than most of us will do in a lifetime. Frankly, I'm disappointed in you."

Blood rises to my face, and I grab my thigh to remind myself not to let Madeline get to me.

"Yes, I know that he's well regarded, but I'm telling you something isn't right. Girls have been disappearing for years on his watch, and he doesn't seem interested in helping."

Madeline stands up from her chair. She's heard enough.

"Hazel, please. You're trying to tell me that Thomas Mackenzie's master plan was to go to work as a headmaster at a girls' home, bide his time, and then start abducting girls? C'mon now. You're going to need to do better than that if you want to get paid. I'd go back to the drawing board if I were you."

She wields her money like a knife, carving into my desperation. She knows I need this and revels in the power. I have to fight everything in me not to tell her to go to hell, but this money would change everything for me. I can finally be the private investigator I've dreamed of being. Taking only the most stimulating cases. Turning down the scumbags like Gene Strauss. Making a name for myself. Showing my parents.

I clasp my hands together and nod.

"I understand, Madeline. I'll keep at it."

She taps her knuckles on my desk and turns toward the door.

"You better. You only have eight days left."

For the first five minutes after Madeline leaves, I pace the office like a tiger before mealtime. If there is one thing in this world I hate, it is being disrespected. When you're a short Korean girl, your life is one long litany of disrespect. You watch people do funny Asian accents in movies or tell you that you can't drive or ask you where you're from. But it's not just the disrespect, it's the inability to do something about it. If you disrespect me and I punch you in the face, that's one thing. But if you disrespect me and I have to swallow it, that's a soul crusher.

Eventually, I get over it by telling myself that this is the last time. That once I hit the Madeline jackpot, I'll be free to tell any rogue clients to eff themselves. And despite what Madeline says, I know Mackenzie knows more than he's letting on, and Goolsbee and Paver are hiding something too. The way Paver talked about his boat. The way Goolsbee bit his tongue when I asked him about what happened to Mia. The thought of it makes my skin crawl.

I grab my phone and call Saint Agnes, continuing to pace around the office while the phone buzzes. The chirpy receptionist from the other day answers.

"Thank you for calling—"

"Dr. Mackenzie, please."

"May I ask who's calling?"

"Hazel Cho."

The receptionist responds a little too quickly. Her words are sharp and clipped.

"I'm sorry, he's not available."

"Do you have any idea when he will be available?"

"No, he's quite busy."

I take a deep breath and disguise my irritation. Is it possible to choke someone through a phone? "Okay, can you put me through to his voicemail?"

"I'm sorry, he doesn't have a voicemail."

I throw my hands in the air. Of course. Why would he?

Mackenzie's stonewalling me. That's not suspicious at all.

"Okay, can I speak to Mr. Goolsbee, then?"

"I'm sorry, he's unavailable as well."

"How 'bout Ms. Barreto, then?"

To my surprise she says, "Yes, one moment."

The phone rings again.

"Hello, this is Sonia."

Sonia's soft accent puts me at ease. There's a kindness and steadiness in her voice that makes you feel like everything's going to be all right. I've always envied people like that. Life never seems to faze them, only interest them.

"Sonia, hello. This is Hazel Cho."

Her voice lights up.

"Hazel, my love, how are you? I'm sorry I didn't get to say goodbye to you after our friendly chat the other day. How's the investigation going?"

"We're making progress, but I have some more questions for Dr. Mackenzie and I can't seem to get through to him. And Mr. Goolsbee doesn't seem to be available either."

Sonia lowers her voice.

"Yes, I'm sorry about that. After you left, Dr. Mackenzie was very upset. He said he's done talking to private investigators, and we've been instructed not to speak to you as well. But I told our receptionist to forward your call to me anyway if you rang. This conversation is our little secret."

"I see. I appreciate you speaking to me, Sonia. I promise I'll keep this conversation confidential. Is there anything you can do to get through to him? I'm just trying to help find Mia, and I would think that he would want that as well."

"Yes, I tried to tell him that, but Thomas is stubborn and doesn't always listen to me. You have to understand that we've had a number of private investigators on this case with little result, and I think at this point Thomas just wants to leave it to the police. And Mr. Goolsbee will do whatever Thomas says."

A horn honks in the background, and Sonia curses in Spanish.

"Are you driving?" I ask.

"Yes, I was just about to tell you. I'm headed into the city today for a fundraiser we're hosting, so if you're free this afternoon, we could have lunch and talk more then."

"Today? Yes, that would be great. What part of the city?"

"Tribeca."

"Okay, how about we meet at Bubby's in Tribeca at one p.m.?"

"One p.m. it is."

I hang up the phone and look out the window. Mia is out there somewhere, and if Mackenzie and Goolsbee won't give me the keys to find her, maybe Sonia will.

Chapter 16

I sit down at an outdoor sidewalk table at Bubby's restaurant and am once again reminded of the life I want but am nowhere near living. The sun shines overhead, and an unseasonably warm breeze floats along the sidewalk. Couples composed of strong-jawed men and tanned women sip mimosas and laughingly feed their babies small nibbles of pancakes. It's a Friday. Doesn't anybody work anymore?

The smell of baked goods wafts across my nostrils, and my stomach rumbles. Bubby's is one of my favorite spots. My sister's celebrity man-crush, John F. Kennedy Jr., used to go here with his girlfriend Carolyn Bessette before they died in that horrible plane crash. I was only six, but Christina would show me pictures of him and even cried when he died. In some dark corner of my mind, I'm hoping their glamour will rub off on me. It hasn't happened so far, but in the meantime, I can drown my sorrows in Bubby's delightful blueberry pie.

My eye catches Sonia walking down Hudson Street toward me. But this is a different Sonia. She has traded in her admin wear for an outfit that announces herself to the city. She wears a bright-red patterned linen maxi shirtdress with the collar popped in the air, and colorful hoop earrings. The mélange of color bursts against her tan skin, and she walks like a force of nature. I watch women's eyes at the neighboring tables move up and down her tall frame, evaluating her, asking themselves the same question that I'm asking myself: How do I be like that?

It's funny. When I'm doing investigative work, I'm confident and comfortable. Despite the ambiguity and lack of information associated with a case, I always know the path forward—that if I have the time, I can question the right people, check the right leads, and discover the truth. There's a process. But once I'm out of that world, I'm flailing, never knowing what to wear, what to say, how to act. And even when I make the right choices, I feel like an impostor just waiting to be exposed.

One look at Sonia, and I know she won't relate. This is a woman who knows who she is and knows what she wants. Saint Agnes would come crashing to the ground without her, and even in the brief time I was there, I could see how those girls love her. But I can't let my envy distract me from what I need from this meeting: access to the people in that institution.

As Sonia approaches, I extend my hand.

"Hazel, mi amor," says Sonia, ignoring my hand and embracing me. Her floral perfume reminds me of my mother's garden. I'm surprised by how good it feels to be wrapped in Sonia's arms, to feel her soft chest against my head. I haven't had a lot of luck on the dating scene lately, and my parents were never big huggers. We're all still just kids in need of affection, I guess.

We both sit down and order. I refrain from ordering the blueberry pie. I feel like Sonia will judge me. Maybe I can sneak it to go after she's gone.

"Thanks for taking the time to meet with me today," I say.

"Are you kidding? This is a treat for me. A girls' lunch in the city is exactly what I needed."

My mouth curls into a smile. A girls' lunch. I would like to have many more girls' lunches with Sonia. I don't normally cut out for socializing during the workweek. It's something that's been ingrained in me since I was a kid. That was one of the biggest battles with my parents growing up. I always wanted to go out with friends, but my parents always thought school should be my one and only priority. I remember once I wanted to go to the big basketball game on a Tuesday night, and I thought my mom and dad were going to pass out. Tuesday nights were for studying, not for fun. That mentality sticks with me. Having a girls' lunch on a Friday during work hours, I feel like I'm cutting class. I shoot Sonia a mischievous grin at the thought.

"Yeah, I meant to ask you what brought you into the city. You said you had a fundraiser?"

Sonia rolls her eyes and adjusts the bangles on her wrists.

"Yes, we're hosting our annual black-tie gala to raise funds for Saint Agnes tomorrow. It's quite a spectacle. Thomas is very well connected, so many of New York's wealthiest families are there. There's a dinner followed by a party. We have an event coordinator who takes care of most of it, but guess who gets stuck with making sure it all comes off?"

"You?"

"Exactly."

"Sounds like quite an event."

"It is. It's a lot of work, but it is so good for the home and the girls. We raise a great deal of money, and we bus the girls in so they get to dress up and go to part of the event, so it's sort of glamorous for them. But enough about me. Let's talk about you, Hazel. How's the investigation going? Any luck tracking down Mia?"

The smile fades from her face, and her jaw hardens as she inquires. I'm reminded that I wouldn't like to be in detention with Sonia Barreto. The waiter delivers our food, and I take a bite of my pancake flight. The warm buttery pancake, combined with a drizzle of caramel, melts in my mouth. Is it possible to black out from taste? I swallow the pancake down quicker than I would have preferred so that I can answer Sonia's question.

"No luck yet. But that's why I wanted to talk to you. We now know that Mia left the grounds willingly and that she likely traveled with someone by boat on the lake."

"Who?"

"We don't know that yet. But in my research, I discovered that an unusually high number of girls have gone missing from Saint Agnes. Are you aware of that?"

I watch Sonia's answer carefully.

She shifts in her seat and clears her throat and plays with her salad. I watch the fork dance left and right, sliding from one lettuce clump to another.

"Yes, I know that several girls have run away over the years. It's not something we're proud of, but you must understand it is in the nature of what we do. When you take in orphan girls who have come from difficult circumstances, some will run away, and many of them come back. So many of these girls have been in tough placements before and find it hard to fit in anywhere. We've taken several security precautions to reduce the likelihood of it happening, but it still happens. We're not a prison, after all."

Her tone is firm but not defensive.

"I understand that. But are you aware that you have way more runaways than any other orphanage—I'm sorry, children's home—of a similar size and type?"

Sonia sits up straight in her seat and raises an eyebrow that could cut glass.

"Yes, I'm aware. It's an issue we take very seriously and are constantly trying to resolve. We're in regular contact with the police and local community organizations, but it's a real challenge to get their attention. The fact is, most people don't care about what happens to poor, brown-skinned little girls. That's part of why we have this gala, to raise awareness of the issue. No one cares for those girls like we do. You've been there. You've seen."

I take in Sonia's demeanor. The fork trembles in her grip, and her eyes dart left and right as though searching for something. I reach out a hand and put it on hers. It's coarse. She has the hands of a hard life, harder than she lets on.

"I know you do, Sonia, but I think there's something bigger going on here. And I think Thomas might be able to fill in the blanks."

Sonia's face flushes, and she sits back in her seat, crossing her arms. I feel like I'm watching the seven stages of grief in real time.

"I've known Thomas for twenty-five years, Hazel. He's a good man. Besides, I told you, he refuses to meet with you. There's no way I'm going to convince him. Once he's made up his mind, it's made up. But you have to trust me. His heart is pure."

"Will he be at the gala?"

"Yes, of course."

She takes a bite of her salad and looks beyond me, and I see the idea spring to her mind. She nearly jumps out of her seat and grabs both my hands.

"Hazel, you must come to the gala."

I flash her a broad smile.

"I thought you'd never ask."

She takes another bite of her salad as she considers the logistics. She places her pointer finger on the cleft of her chin.

"There's no way I could get you into the dinner. That's five thousand dollars a head, but I could get you a ticket to the after-party. You can't tell anyone I gave you a ticket, though, or our director of development will kill me. Thomas will be there. I think once you have time to get to know him, you'll see that you're barking up the wrong tree."

"That would be perfect. Thanks, Sonia."

"You're very welcome. But you have to promise me you'll be careful. Thomas has powerful friends, and I don't want you to get on the wrong side of them."

There's a quiver in her voice.

"Don't worry. I'll be careful. This isn't my first rodeo."

"Good. Then it's settled."

She claps her hands together and taps her feet on the ground, doing a little dance in her chair.

"I'm excited. Normally, at these events, I'm stuck with a bunch of stuffy old men, but now I'll have a friend with me. I think this calls for champagne and a piece of pie, don't you?"

I think I've found my new best friend.

Chapter 17

I return to the office from lunch with Sonia, buoyed by two glasses of champagne and the idea of cornering Mackenzie. I'm looking forward to catching him away from his home turf. I give Yanush, the hot dog vendor, a wave as I turn toward the office entrance. I rub my stomach to signal that I've just eaten and won't be indulging in his treats today.

It still hasn't sunk in that I'm going to a gala tomorrow. It would be nice to have a date along with me, but my Bumble dating lineup is not up to snuff, and I'm pretty sure Kenny would trip and knock over a priceless work of art. I guess I'll just be the mystery woman, Cinderella-style. Speaking of, I need to get a dress. That will have to wait for tomorrow, though. Right now, I need to dial for dollars. That's what I call the litany of phone calls I throw myself into once I get my bearings during a case.

Before I start my calls, I take a moment to straighten up my office. Something about Sonia has inspired me. I saw her office, immaculate to the last inch, and then I saw the woman that came along with it when we had lunch. Now I see my office, covered in dust and paperwork, and I look in the mirror and see the woman that comes along with that. Maybe if I clean up the office, I can move on to cleaning up myself.

Once I've dusted the entire office and filed my paperwork, I throw away the duster, which now resembles something from *The Grudge*, and sit down at my desk. I crack the window open to let in the crisp fall air. The fresh air and lemony scent of Lysol wipes brace me, and I pull up Mia's case file.

Normally, my first step would be to call all the people who knew Mia to get a better understanding of who she was, her movements, her habits, her hopes. But since Mackenzie has me blackballed from Saint Agnes for now, that's not really an option. What I do have is a pattern, though. Mia isn't the first girl who's gone missing. If I can reach out to the people that knew those girls, maybe I can find a common thread. Let the dialing begin.

I put in my earbuds and look at the girl who went missing most recently before Mia: Malika Washington. She has an aunt living in Boston. I dial the number listed for her. I get the shrill "This number is no longer in service" message. Could they make that beep any more unpleasant? I dialed a wrong number. I didn't kill anyone.

"Tough start," I say to myself. I find talking to myself in between calls keeps the juices flowing.

I go to the next girl who went missing before Mia: Brooke Anthony. She has one known contact: her cousin Lindsay Anthony, age twenty-two, living in Staten Island. I dial Lindsay's number, and Lindsay answers on the third ring.

"Hello, Ms. Anthony, this is Hazel Cho. I'm a private investigator looking into missing girls at Saint Agnes."

"Okay."

Her voice is low and nasally and on guard.

"I believe your cousin Brooke Anthony went missing two years ago?"

"Oh, yeah. Um, I didn't really know Brooke. We hung out a couple times when we were kids, but that's it."

"Did Brooke ever contact you or tell you she planned to run away?"

"No, like I said, we hadn't talked since we were kids. The last I heard about her was when the children's home called, looking for her. Look, I'm late for a meeting, so I gotta go, but good luck on your investigation."

She hangs up. A sense of dread fills my stomach. There's a reason these girls were sent to a children's home. They don't have parents, and anybody else in their life is either too far removed or too selfish to care.

I spend the next few hours dialing every known acquaintance of the girls who have gone missing. All I get is a series of old phone numbers that are out of service or reassigned, or people who hadn't talked to the missing girl in years and only found out about them when someone from Saint Agnes called. Say what you will about Madeline Hemsley, at least she cares.

I'm reaching the end of my list but keep plowing forward, not because I think it's likely to lead anywhere but more so that I can update the case file and check that angle off my list and take a different tack. One of the misunderstood things about detective work is that you find a lead right away and chase it down and solve the case. Most of the time, you don't find a lead. The lead emerges only after you've eliminated the alternatives. It's a daunting process, but it keeps you from running around in circles. Maybe if Madeline sees the work I'm putting in, she'll give me a little extra time.

On my third to last call, I reach an actual human being.

"Hello?"

I'm so surprised at hearing a voice that I look back at my

case file to make sure I know who I'm talking to. It's Sarah Blankenship. My file says she's the cousin of a towheaded girl named Olivia Blankenship who went missing a decade ago.

"Hello?" she repeats.

"Uh, hello, is this Sarah Blankenship?"

"Yes, it is."

Her voice is buoyant but cautious. She's wondering if she's dealing with another telemarketer.

"Hi, Sarah, my name is Hazel Cho, and I'm a private investigator looking into girls who have gone missing from Saint Agnes Children's Home."

"Oh, thank God, finally," she says.

I did not see that coming. I give a polite chuckle.

"Why do you say that?"

"I'm sorry. I just wasn't impressed by the investigation after Olivia went missing."

She speaks slowly and carefully, like she's giving a presentation at work.

"Well, that's why I'm calling. Were you close with Olivia before she disappeared?"

Sarah breathes into the phone as if she's grappling for the right words.

"Honestly, no, we weren't that close. I was eight or nine years older than her. Before her mom died, she would bring Olivia over to our house for Christmas once every few years, and I would play with her Barbies with her. She was obsessed with my old Easy-Bake Oven. But our families eventually lost touch. I think my mom and her mom had a falling out."

"Is that why your parents didn't take her in?"

"No, when Olivia's mom died, my mom was battling cancer, so I don't think my parents felt like they could take on Olivia as well. She never seemed to resent it, though. She would write me letters—Saint Agnes discouraged computer use—and I would write her back. She always wrote in pink bubble letters. Always pink. But I'm ashamed to say, I didn't think about her that much. I was too absorbed in my own college drama."

"I understand. Are you aware that several other girls have gone missing from Saint Agnes over the past twenty years?"

"Really? I haven't heard anything about that in the news. The only reason I know about Olivia is because the headmaster called me the day she went missing."

"Thomas Mackenzie?"

"Yeah, that's right. Is he still there? He must be a hundred years old."

"And what did you tell him?"

"I told him I hadn't spoken to Olivia in months, and she hadn't said anything about running away. In fact, she had written me a letter a couple weeks earlier, before she went missing, about how she was so excited because she thought she had been discovered."

"Discovered?"

"Yeah, she was really into singing and theater, and she said that after one of their little performances, the choir teacher said she could be a star."

I think of Mia's enchanting voice singing that song.

"Did she ever do any theater outside of those performances?"

"Not that I know of, but she said something once about a theater that she was going to perform at someday. To be honest, I sort of dismissed it as the dreams of a little girl."

"Do you know the name of the theater?"

"Hmm, it's been a long time. It had a funny name. It started

129

with a *D*."

I rack my brain for theaters in New York City that start with a *D* but can't come up with any.

Sarah continues to try out words. Her voice is steady, professional, methodical.

"Donnelly, Diossi, Diocese..."

"Dionysus?"

"Yeah, that's it. Dionysus. Have you been there?"

I stand up from my desk and run my hands through my hair. My palms sweat. This case gets stranger by the minute.

"No, I've never heard of it. But it may help us find Mia. Mackenzie is obsessed with Dionysus."

Sarah snorts on the other end of the line. The girl's got confidence. I'll give her that.

"Thomas Mackenzie? The headmaster? There's no way he's involved with this. He's the only one who seemed to care when Olivia went missing. I know he's a bit of a grouch, but he's a good egg. He would follow up with me all the time and give me updates. That security guy is the one you should look at if he's still there. I went to one of Olivia's shows once, and he was standing in back, taking an inordinate interest in the young ladies, if you know what I mean."

That's not what I wanted to hear, but if I got upset every time I heard something I didn't want to hear, I would have left this business a long time ago.

"I know what you mean. Thank you so much for your time, Sarah. Do you still have those letters?"

"Now that you mention it, I don't. I think the police took them for the investigation and never returned them."

"Okay. I'll reach out to them and see if I can get those for you."

"That would be wonderful. They're pretty much all I have left of Olivia. We were never that close, but part of me feels like I should have done more."

"I understand. I'll be in touch."

I hang up the phone and stare out my window at the alley below. The more I learn about this case, the more it sprawls. It started with a missing girl and a suspicious headmaster. Now it's turned into multiple missing girls, a mysterious theater, and a litany of questionable people. When you're a private investigator, you get a sixth sense for moral rot like something gone bad in your refrigerator.

I can smell it. I just don't yet know the source.

Chapter 18

even days left

S The following night, I'm at home preparing for the gala with a feeling of pure dread. Oddly, the dread stems more from the fact that I have to go to a formal event than the thought of all these missing girls. After this case, I need to go to a therapist who can explain to me why I'm more fearful of elite social events than child abductors.

Earlier in the day, Kenny and I went dress shopping, much to his chagrin. I didn't think Madeline would approve of me expensing a gown to her account, so the two of us hit the Chinatown consignment store circuit. It wasn't pretty. But after weeding through one matronly garment after another, I finally found a red polyester dress that will suffice.

When I squeeze my way into the dress and look in the mirror, I'm surprised by what I see. The dress looks a little prom-ish, but it's emphasizing what needs to be emphasized and disguising what needs to be disguised. I flash back to my younger days, when I turned heads, and blow a kiss into the mirror. "I've still got it," I say to myself. I pull my hair into a tight bun, mostly because I have neither the time nor the skill to style it. I throw on some eyeliner and foundation, and I'm ready to go. I look dangerous and sexy.

The smell of pajeon, a type of Korean pancake, pulls me into the kitchen. That's one thing I love about having Kenny as a roommate. He's an excellent cook and loves food almost as much as I do. And when he cooks Korean food, it transports me back to when my mom used to cook for us. Except he doesn't lecture me about doing homework or finding a husband.

I throw on my worn heels and shuffle out into the main room. Kenny stands at the stove in his standard sweatpants and T-shirt and shuffles the pajeon around the skillet. I hear the sizzle and smell the light fragrance of cooked vegetables. My stomach grumbles. I wish I could just chill on the couch, stuff my face, and watch some Korean soap operas with him, but duty calls.

Kenny turns, and his jaw hits the floor.

"Hazel. You look...you look...gorgeous," he says as his eyes survey me, unsure of where to stop. He still has that crush on me.

I mock a curtsy to make it less awkward.

"Thanks. I couldn't have done it without your keen eye for women's fashion."

He blushes, grabs a couple of plates and places them on our pseudo–dining table, and then slides the pajeon onto them. He also grabs a couple of plastic take-out cutlery sets. We don't have a dishwasher, and our sink is frequently clogged, so this cuts down on the cleanup. The savory scent goes straight to my head, and I'm not sure whether to eat or faint.

"Dinner's served," he says.

I clap my hands at Kenny's presentation.

"This looks incredible. I've always meant to ask, Where did you learn to cook like this?"

"From my mom. She was never much of a talker, so this was

sort of our way of bonding. It's pretty much the same to this day. I'll go over there, say hello, and then we just get to work making dinner. It's different, but it works for us, I guess."

I run into my bedroom and throw on my powder blue ten-year-old bathrobe. I can't afford to ruin this outfit. I ease into one of our folding chairs ever so gently, trying to avoid stretching the dress.

"Yeah, I have a bit of a love-hate relationship with Korean food," I say.

"Really? Why's that?"

"The smell, mainly."

"What do you mean? I love the smell."

My mind goes back to high school.

"Yeah, I used to love it too. But when I was a freshman in high school, I was dating this white guy. And we were standing by my locker, and this Vietnamese kid named Bao had a locker a couple of lockers down from me. So, Bao opens his locker, and he must have had his lunch in there or something, because this powerful aroma of Vietnamese food hits me in the face. And being the bratty teenager that I was, I turned to my boyfriend and said, 'Woof, that stinks.' And my boyfriend, who was the sweetest guy but not the most worldly, says earnestly, 'Yeah, kind of like your clothes smell sometimes.'"

Kenny slaps his forehead with his palm. "Oh man, what did you say?"

"Well, at first I didn't really know what he meant, so I just said, 'What are you talking about?'"

"And what did he say?"

"He was pretty sheepish and said, 'Oh, I'm sorry. You know how sometimes your clothes and hair smell a little different.' As you can imagine, I was absolutely mortified. I wanted to crawl inside my locker. I mean, basically my boyfriend is standing there telling me I stink."

"What an asshole."

"No, it wasn't his fault. He didn't know any better. But you know how sometimes it's the little things that stick with you? Well, that one stuck with me. I told my sister about it, and for the rest of high school, the two of us would hang our clothes out in the garage so that they didn't smell. We would double-shampoo and condition our hair and then run out of the house. We were completely paranoid about it. Looking back, I feel awful about the whole thing. I think it hurt my mom a lot more than she let on."

"I hope the smell from my pajeon doesn't ruin your night tonight."

He's joking, but the truth of it lingers. The old high school insecurities come back, and I fight the urge to smell my dress and open the windows. People think that we're defined by the big moments in our lives: births, deaths, successes, and failures. But I think the little moments matter more because those are the moments that shape your self-perception and who you want to become. I change the subject to get my mind off it.

"What's the occasion for this feast, anyway?"

"It's a little celebration dinner. I just finished the last page of my officer's training study guide. Now I just got to pass the test and you're looking at Kenny Shum, supercop."

"Oh, Kenny, congrats. That's awesome. I knew you would do it. And I know you'll pass that test. We need more cops like you. I wish you were handling the Mia investigation. Then I could see the case file and get some real help."

Kenny joins me at the table, and we both take bites of the

pajeon. I close my eyes and delight at the airy texture. The food is phenomenal, but I'm coming down off my initial high. It's difficult to maintain the dangerous and sexy feeling when you're staring at a lime-green Formica cabinet set.

"Thanks, Hazel. We need more PIs like you too. What's the update on the investigation?"

I groan.

"I'm making progress, but it just feels like one obstacle after another."

"It sounds that way. What are you expecting to find at this gala, anyway?"

The gala.

The taste of the pajeon almost made me forget about going out tonight. I look at my watch. It's eight thirty already. I don't have time to eat any more, plus I'm not sure the seams on this dress can handle the extra strain. I drop my plastic fork and stand up from the table.

"Sorry to cut this short, but I've got to get going if I'm going to catch the people I need to interview. I'll have to tell you all about the gala later. And we need to celebrate you passing the exam properly. Can I take a rain check?"

Kenny's eyes drop to the floor, and he swallows hard. "Oh, okay. We can do it another time. I'll just pack up your meal and throw it in the fridge so you can have it when you get back."

I put a hand on his shoulder and then grab my purse and keys.

"Thanks, Kenny."

I throw open the door and head out to a gala that I have no business attending.

* * *

The Harvard Club cuts a stunning figure in the evening light. Uplighting surrounds the neo-Georgian building, giving the feeling that it stands apart and above everything else. Much like most of the people at this party, I would imagine. As I get out of my Uber sedan with one hubcap missing, I can't help feeling a little ridiculous. Other guests are stepping out of stylish SUVs or valeting luxury cars, carrying the self-assuredness of wealth. And here I am standing alone in my consignment dress, like a kid who got lost on the way to the school dance.

I take a deep breath and fall into line with the other guests on the sidewalk in front of the entrance. Fortunately, I'm arriving after the dinner portion of the party, so the line is short. Red velvet ropes and a plush dark-blue runner separate the sidewalk from the entrance to the club. I show the security guard my phone with the ticket and barcode Sonia sent me. He scans the code and gives me a skeptical look but then lets me in. I wonder if he thinks I'm some guy's escort or something. It stirs memories of when my sister would bring me to one of the cool-kid parties and they'd look at me as if I'd gotten lost. Maybe red was not the best choice for blending in.

I step into the lobby and feel like I've been transported to another world from my Chinatown apartment. A giant chandelier shaped like blossoming flowers hangs from the ceiling. Wood that looks like they harvested it from the *Mayflower* wraps the walls. Men in tuxedos and women in gowns considerably more appealing than mine glide across the shining floors. I should have asked Bobby to be my date. He'd look good in a tuxedo.

I look up at the paintings of old white men high on the walls. It's as though they're looking down on me, saying *You don't belong here.* They remind me of Thomas Mackenzie.

I turn the corner into a grand, high-ceilinged ballroom of more mahogany-paneled walls, flowers, and sparkling crystal. Circular tables with white tablecloths dot the ballroom floor and face a temporary stage, presumably for tonight's musical act and obligatory appeal to donors. My eyes run past the bevy of white-haired men and artificially enhanced women. And there he is, Thomas Mackenzie, holding court with a burly man and two couples who are lapping up every word he says. I recognize one of them as the sheriff of Warren County. That's interesting. I take a few surreptitious photos. I'll have to dig into that more later.

The dinner is over, and people have made their way from the large circular tables over to the small bars that line the room. I grab a glass of champagne from one of the waiters and sidle up next to an oversize fern. As I watch Mackenzie, I'm struck by how different this man is from the man I met at Saint Agnes. This Thomas Mackenzie is all charm and mirth. He uses his great height to his advantage, placing his large hands on people's shoulders or slapping their backs. Leaning in, bent at the waist to listen to their stories. He seems more like a US senator than the headmaster of a children's home. I can see why people are so charmed by him, and it makes me wonder if my focus on him has been misplaced.

I take a sip of champagne to calm my nerves. It's desert dry and delightful. My eyes scan the room, and I spot Sonia at the bar, looking like a modern-day Evita. Her lipstick is deep red, and she styled her hair with a curl. She wears a glittering black dress that accentuates her voluptuous figure. There's no worse feeling than seeing another woman with something you can't have. And Sonia Barreto has it in spades. She's drinking a martini and chatting with a group of men, presumably prospective donors. They're lapping up everything she's saying with lascivious looks. I'm struck by how she and Thomas together must be quite the unstoppable force. She throws me a wave and a broad smile. She makes a zipped-lips motion at me and laughs. I would say hello, but I don't want to spoil her fun. Besides, I'm not here for a social call. I'm here to find out what the hell's going on at Saint Agnes.

Sonia leads the men off into a side lounge that, from my angle, looks like a library. I see ancient rugs, overstuffed leather chairs, and books lining the wall. There must be a big donation ask coming. She shuts the door behind them, and I return my gaze to Mackenzie.

We make eye contact, and his eyes squint into slits. A sigh escapes from his mouth. He turns to his guests, raises a finger in the air to ask for a moment, and charges in my direction. He stops inches from me. As he leans in, he blocks the light from the chandelier, and a shadow passes over me like a solar eclipse.

"Hello, Dr. Mackenzie," I say with a wry smile.

He counters my smile with a scowl. "Ms. Cho. What are you doing here?"

"I'm supporting Saint Agnes. Is that a problem?"

He straightens up and crosses his arms. "I'm sure you are. No, that is not a problem. Are you here to cause trouble?"

"Of course not. But while I'm here, I was hoping to ask you a few more questions."

His face reddens, and he clutches his crystal tumbler so hard I can see his knuckles turn white. "I've said everything I have to say to you. I wish you all the best in locating Mia, but this is neither the time nor the place. If I see you harassing any of our guests, I'll have you thrown out of here. Understood?"

"Oh, you mean like the sheriff over there?"

He ignores my questions, spins away, and heads toward his guests.

"Dr. Mackenzie," I say.

He stops in place and cranes his neck to the side but refuses to look at me.

"Are you aware that an unusually high number of girls have gone missing from Saint Agnes?"

He turns and raises a long finger in the air, his face scrunching into a scowl. For a second I think he might break. But then he puts his hand down, buttons his tuxedo jacket, and returns to his guests. He smiles and backslaps like nothing happened.

He's a tough one, that Mackenzie. It's going to take more than unsubstantiated accusations to get him talking. I need to find someone else who can break through the Saint Agnes wall of silence.

I shift my gaze from Mackenzie to the other patrons. As I take in the scene, my eyes catch sight of Goolsbee. He's standing alone at the portable bar next to the stage. He's dressed in a tuxedo that's two sizes too small on his generous frame, and he wears his discomfort on his sleeve. The other people at the bar ordering drinks ignore him, and he seems frozen with social anxiety. I actually feel sorry for him. His face is beet red, and he's stroking his gray broom mustache, staring backstage, but I can't see what or who the subject is.

This is my chance to find out what he knows.

I've begun walking across the parquet dance floor when I'm intercepted by another girl in a red dress. She's young, about twelve or thirteen. She must be one of the orphan girls. We're almost matching.

As she approaches, I give her a smile and point to her dress and then mine, while still keeping one eye on Goolsbee. She gives a giggle and jogs toward me. She sports long blonde hair and freckles and a big gap between her two front teeth. I hate to delay my confrontation with Goolsbee, but who can say no to that smile?

"We're matching," she says as she walks up to me.

"We sure are," I say in my warmest voice. Goolsbee turns to the bartender and orders another drink. He's not going anywhere.

"I'm Nora," she says and sticks out a tiny pale hand.

"I'm Hazel," I say, returning the shake. Her fingers feel so small in mine. I can't help wondering if this was what Mia's hand felt like.

"Did you go to Saint Agnes too?"

"No, I'm just a guest of So— Ms. Barreto."

I take another sip of my champagne.

"Oh, she's the best. So, are you here to adopt someone?"

I nearly choke on my champagne and start coughing, but I stifle it so as not to hurt the girl's feelings. She's so earnest in her questioning that it makes me question myself. Am I here to adopt a girl? I quickly come to my senses and remember that I'm having trouble taking care of myself, let alone a little girl.

"Um, no. I'm just here to support the home."

Her shoulders slump, and she kicks at the polished wood floor.

"Why? Do you want to be adopted?"

"Yeah, I mean, I think so. Saint Agnes is nice and all, and I have lots of friends, but I'd like to have my own family and my own house and a big dog like a Saint Bernard or something.

And—"

She pauses.

I press. "And what?"

Nora continues, "I don't know. Sometimes I don't know why I try. There's so many other pretty girls, see?"

She points to the other side of the room, and I see what she means. Entering through the doors are all the girls of Saint Agnes. That's who Goolsbee was staring at. To my horror, they're all wearing red dresses just like mine. I look like one of the orphan girls, except more weathered.

This is humiliating.

I backpedal, and one of my heels catches on the floor, and I fall backward. I've braced myself to hit the deck and make a complete ass of myself when a pair of powerful hands catches me and in one seamless move pulls me back upright. I look around, and no one has even noticed.

"Are you all right?" I hear a honeyed baritone voice say.

I spin my head around, and my heart stops in my chest. The man looking back at me is quite simply the most handsome man I've ever seen. You know those people who when they walk in the room, everybody stops what they're doing and just stares? He is that person. He has baby blue eyes, a small triangular nose, and a firm jaw covered in movie-star stubble. His sandy-brown hair is side parted, and his smile seems too bright to be real. Add that to the fact that he's holding me in his arms like we just finished a dance, and I'm wishing there was a pause button so I could freeze this moment.

I'm so shocked by his appearance that I start to say "Wow" and then catch myself and just end up saying "Wha."

He crinkles his brow, and the corner of his mouth rises upward. His eyes are kind and genuine, unlike the cold arrogant eyes of other good-looking men I've known.

"Did you just say 'Wha'?"

"Yeah, I was a little surprised. I thought I was going to hit the floor. I'm all right, thank you."

He places me back on my feet and extends his hand.

"It was my pleasure. I'm Andrew DuPont."

I shake his hand and hold it for an extra beat.

"Nice to meet you, Andrew DuPont. I'm Hazel Cho."

"It looks like your glass is empty. Would you like a drink?"

I look back at Nora. I'd like to talk to her more about Saint Agnes, but even she knows what's going on. She mouths "O-M-G" to me, and I give her a covert thumbs-up. She gets it. Goolsbee is going to have to wait.

"Yes, I'd love a drink."

We walk out of the banquet hall and into a side room with a beautiful carved walnut bar and lit-up bottles of sophisticated liquor. Other couples have spilled into the room, but there's a pair of open seats at the rail. Andrew pulls out one of the green leather upholstered stools for me, and I sit. I can feel the other patrons' eyes fixed on me, wondering who this woman is with Adonis. He wears a tailored black tuxedo, and I can make out the outline of his chest and biceps. There's an effortlessness about him that's intoxicating. It's like watching a master artisan performing their craft, except Andrew's craft is simply being.

He orders me a glass of champagne and a martini for himself. As the bartender shakes his drink, Andrew turns to look at me. I swear it's like being injected with heroin, looking at this guy. Your senses dull, your brain slows, and all you feel is an inchoate sense of euphoria.

"So, Hazel, what brings you here this evening?"

I was afraid he was going to ask that. My mind vacillates between lying about being a guest or telling him the truth. I go with the truth. Who knows, maybe he'll know something about Saint Agnes or Mia.

"I'm actually here for work."

I take a sip of my champagne and feel the flush on my face. I'm going to need more of this if I'm going to keep talking to this guy without having a panic attack.

"Really? What kind of work?"

"Well, I'm a private investigator."

I'm expecting Andrew to recoil like most men do when I tell them about my profession, but he does the exact opposite. His eyes light up like I told him I was a movie star. He puts a warm hand on my shoulder and leans forward in his seat.

"That's incredible. I've never met a private investigator. So, you're a prettier version of Sherlock Holmes."

"Exactly," I say, while desperately trying to disguise the fact that my mind is exploding that this man just called me pretty—well, *prettier*, but close enough.

The bartender hands Andrew his martini. He thanks the man and raises his glass to me.

"Well, cheers to you, Ms. Holmes. I'm so glad we bumped into each other."

"Literally bumped into each other," I say, raising my glass to his. We clink glasses and share a satisfied sip.

"I have to say, you win the prize for the most interesting profession tonight. I feel like everyone I talk to is in finance, marketing, fashion, or law. If I have one more conversation about the stock market, I'm going to shoot myself."

"That's nice of you to say, but really, it's not that interesting. Most of my work is following around cheating husbands or wives."

"Don't sell yourself short. Adultery is very interesting when it's not happening to you."

"Fair point."

"So, what exactly are you investigating?" he says. "I hope it's not me, or this is going to get a lot more awkward."

"No, fortunately, I'm not investigating you. I'm investigating a girl who went missing at Saint Agnes."

His brow furrows, and he taps his glass's stem with his finger.

"I'm sorry to hear that. Have you had any luck so far?"

"I'm making progress, but it's tough with kids because they don't leave as much of a trail as adults do."

Andrew nods, absorbing the information. His cobalt eyes sparkle with interest. It's incredible. I've known this man for about two minutes, yet I feel like I'm talking to an old friend and we're the only two people on earth. There's a full-blown party going on around us, but he focuses entirely on me. And he listens. Normally, on a date, I feel like I'm at a lecture as the guy tells me about how cool he is or how much money he makes. My favorite is when a guy spends the entire night talking about himself and then tells you how much he likes your personality.

"How about you?" I say. "What brings you here tonight?"

"My great-grandfather supported the establishment of Saint Agnes back in the early nineteen hundreds, and my dad's a big donor."

He's rich too? I might have to tie this guy up and lock him in the back of the Tesla so he doesn't slip away. I really should track down Goolsbee, but Andrew's eyes are like a tractor beam. I rationalize staying by telling myself that maybe I can learn something from him about Mia's disappearance.

"So, you know Thomas Mackenzie?"

His nose crinkles, and a smile creeps across his face. I notice he has the most adorable spattering of freckles running along the bridge of his nose onto his cheeks.

"Oh, yes. He's an old family friend. I've known him since I was a kid."

Strike one, I think. I guess nobody's perfect.

"What do you think of him?"

"I think he's a saint. He's given his life to that place, and I can't tell you how many girls have gone into the home in tatters and come out as incredible women. Have you looked at that alumni list out there? Doctors, judges, elected officials, business leaders. It's like a who's who of New York."

Great. The man of my dreams likes one of my suspects in Mia's abduction.

"What about the choir teacher, Gregory Goolsbee? Do you know him?"

Andrew takes a sip of his martini and shakes his head.

"Neil Paver? The security guard?"

"No, that doesn't ring a bell. This might shock you, but I'm not really dialed in to the security or girls' choir scene these days."

"Yeah, me neither."

Out of the corner of my eye, I see a striking older tuxedoed gentleman with salt-and-pepper hair waving at Andrew, then beckoning him. His face is kind, and he gives me a warm smile.

"I think someone's looking for you," I say.

Andrew glances and smiles and shakes his head.

"That's my dad. Duty calls."

Apparently, handsomeness runs in the family. He steals a

last sip from his martini glass and places it on the bar as he rises. I'm tempted to tackle him and never let go. It's like a dream I'm trying to hold on to, afraid I'll wake up and never get it back.

He takes my hand and kisses it with his perfect lips. Goose bumps break loose on my arms. I hope he doesn't notice.

"Hazel, it has been an absolute pleasure."

"Likewise," I say with a schoolgirl's giggle. I'm thirty years old and still boy crazy.

"I would love to take you out to dinner some night this week, if you're available."

"I would love that too."

"Perfect. I'll call you."

We exchange numbers, and Andrew glides out of the room.

Chapter 19

I stumble home to my dingy apartment that evening with my head still buzzing from meeting Andrew. When I open my door, my heart jumps in my chest. Kenny is sitting on our secondhand couch in silence. No TV, no video games, just him on the couch with his arms crossed, drinking wine from a black box that looks like the juice boxes I took to school as a kid.

I flinch and drop my handbag to the ground.

"Jesus, Kenny. You scared the shit out of me. What are you doing up?" I ask.

"How was the gala?" he says, putting *gala* in air quotes.

"Oh, give me a break." I let out an exaggerated breath and remove my heels. I plop down on the couch next to him. "Are you jealous?" I say, punching his arm.

He makes brief eye contact, and then his eyes flit from side to side.

"No, I'm not jealous. I was just worried about you."

"Worried? Why were you worried about me? What's going to happen to me at a charity gala?"

He recrosses his arms and looks out the window. "I don't know. From everything you've told me, it seems like somebody's abducting girls *from* Saint Agnes, so you going to a fundraiser *for* Saint Agnes seems dangerous."

I put a hand on Kenny's knee to calm him.

"I'm a grown woman. I can handle myself. This is my job. You know that."

After a few seconds, Kenny nods and hands me a box of wine as a peace offering. I've already had a couple of glasses of champagne, but I figure, Why not? It's the weekend. I grab the box and start drinking. The wine tastes cheap and fruity.

"So, how did it go tonight?" he asks.

I lean back on the couch and feel the warmth of the wine rise to my face and the afterglow of meeting Andrew embrace my body.

"It...was...amazing."

"Really? Did you find some fresh evidence?"

"Oh. No. It was a disaster from that standpoint. Everybody I spoke to about Mackenzie seemed to think he was one step short of Mother Teresa. And Goolsbee, the choir teacher who I've had my eye on, left early, so I didn't even get to talk to him. Paver, the security guard, wasn't even there."

Kenny scratches his head.

"So, what was so great about it?"

I can't keep myself from sighing as I say it: "Andrew."

"Who's Andrew?"

His round face droops. I don't want to hurt his feelings.

"Oh, no one. Just a guy I met at the event."

Kenny takes a long pull from his wine. He's trying to be nonchalant, but it's not working.

"So, what's his story?"

"I don't know much about him yet. He's just this cute guy I met at the party who looks amazing in a tuxedo."

I hate that I've said *amazing* twice in five minutes.

149

Kenny stands up from the couch and crushes his wine box in his hand. He tosses it in the trash, shaking his head.

"Wait, you're not talking about Andrew DuPont, are you?"

"Yeah, why?"

"His family's one of the richest in New York. When my family went to Lake George every summer, his family owned half the town. He was one of the cool kids, so I didn't hang out with him, but he was always super nice."

"Hmm," I say, trying to play it cool. "Yeah, I get the feeling that pretty much everyone at the gala was from one of the richest families in New York."

He shoots me the side-eye. "Hazel, doesn't all this make you a little nervous?"

"What?"

"The fact that all these powerful families have been support-ing Saint Agnes for years and girls have gone missing from Saint Agnes for years."

The champagne and wine have fully taken over my brain, and the last thing I want to do is get into an argument with Kenny. I lie down on the couch and close my eyes.

"Yeah, it's disconcerting, but I don't have a lot of choice right now. I need the money, and if you haven't noticed, there aren't a lot of clients banging down our door. What do you want me to do, quit?"

Kenny sees that I'm fading away and grabs the old multicol-ored blanket my grandma knitted for me. He drapes it on top of me.

"No, I'm just saying that these are powerful people, Haze."

I pull the blanket over me and roll onto my side.

"Yeah, yeah, yeah."

"Promise me you'll be careful. The person who's taking

these girls might be right in front of you, and you wouldn't even notice."

"I'll be careful," I mumble.

"Don't say I didn't warn you."

He turns out the light, and I drift away into drunken oblivion.

Chapter 20

Six days left

The next morning I awake to a grating buzzing sound and a splitting headache. I take a moment to get my bearings. I'm in the living room. I must have slept on the couch all night. Our nineteenth-century radiator must be misfiring again, because the room feels like it's eighty degrees and sweat soaks my underarms. The buzzing continues to drill a hole through my skull. It's my apartment's entry buzzer. I've got an unexpected visitor.

I heave myself off the couch, and nausea crawls through my stomach. I push the intercom button.

"Who is it?"

"It's Madeline Hemsley."

I step back from the intercom like it might infect me with the plague. Madeline Hemsley? What is she doing here? I glance at myself in the mirror next to our door. It isn't a pretty sight. My mascara has bled into a Rorschach blot around my eyes. My lipstick looks like it's trying to make a break for it, and my hair clings to my head. I look like a sad clown.

More buzzing.

I swallow hard to keep last night's champagne from coming back up and hit the intercom button again.

"Good morning, Madeline. What are you doing here?"

"I stopped by your office, and you weren't there. I came to get a status update."

The intercom exaggerates the shrillness of her voice.

"You know it's Sunday, right?"

"Yes, I'm well aware it's Sunday, but since you have only six days left to find Mia before I find another private investigator, I assumed you'd be working. Now let me up."

I roll my eyes at no one in particular and hit the entry button. I unlock my door and leave it ajar so Madeline can come in.

At warp speed, I grab the empty wine boxes, throw them in the trash, fold the blanket onto the couch, toss my hair up into a ponytail, and use a dish towel to wipe the worst of the makeup off my face. I hear Madeline's footsteps climbing the stairwell like the grim reaper. Before she enters, I take one more glance in the mirror. I've improved my appearance from sad clown to hungover girl. I'll take it.

Madeline opens the door and steps into my apartment. I have to give it to her: she commands a room. She wears an all-black yoga outfit with a high-collared jacket on her taut frame. It makes her look like she's about to captain a spaceship. Her hair is blown out, and her face is caked in foundation and bronzer, which makes me wonder exactly how much yoga she will actually do today.

She gazes around the apartment with undisguised disdain, then pulls her luxury purse closer to her as though my apartment might dirty it by osmosis.

"Welcome to my humble abode," I say to Madeline, attempting to lighten the mood.

Madeline sniffs and crinkles her nose. Without asking, she walks to the window and, after several tries, heaves it open. I have to admit the cool, fresh air feels good.

"Yes, quite humble."

Fresh air or not, when Madeline says things like that, I'd like nothing more than to kick her to the curb. But if I don't get that money, I won't have an apartment to kick her—or anybody else—out of. I guide her over to our kitchen card table and pull out a folding chair for her. As I do, I check the hallway to our bedrooms. Kenny's door is closed. I pray he doesn't wake up. I don't even want to think about Madeline's reaction to me having a roommate.

She pulls a disinfectant wipe from her purse and wipes the seat. Part of me doesn't blame her. It's covered in crumbs. We both sit.

"How can I help you today, Madeline?" I say through gritted teeth.

"As I said through your charming little intercom, I'd like a report as to your progress."

I lean my elbows on the table and meet her eyes.

"You know, you could have called, or we could have scheduled a meeting. I don't think coming to my house unannounced is appropriate."

"Well, I don't think your level of effort in this case is appropriate, but here we are."

She could start an argument in an empty room. My temples throb.

"How did you get my address, anyway?"

"I have my sources."

Her haunting green eyes pierce me, daring me to challenge her. I decide to let it go. Whether or not I find Mia, I'll be done with this woman in a few days, so I just need to bite my tongue and get through this. When it's over, I can tell her what I really think of her.

Madeline continues to press. "I heard you were at the gala last night. Did you have a good time? From your breath, it seems like you did."

I give an insincere chuckle at her slight.

"The gala was entertaining, but not particularly fruitful. One of the staff members I was hoping to speak with left early, so I didn't have a chance to interview him, and the rest of the guests echoed your opinion that Mackenzie is a stand-up guy."

"Wonderful. It took you three days to confirm what I already know."

Madeline's tone reinforces what I've always felt is the biggest problem with the vendor-client relationship. It throws the power dynamic completely off balance. It allows one person to say things they would never say because they know the other person is powerless to do anything about it. That's why I need this money. It will grant me that elusive power to say no.

"I'm making progress, Madeline. We now know that this isn't an isolated incident. Whoever has been doing this is coordinated and serial. We know that it's an inside job. There's no way that someone could gain access to so many girls without having help from someone on the inside. We know Mia left willingly and was likely taken by boat. We know we need more information from the people who work there. But since Mackenzie has banned me from the Saint Agnes campus, it's going to be tricky, particularly because most of the key players stay on campus. I'm not the police. I can't compel people to speak to me."

Madeline crosses her legs and arms and leans back in her chair.

"So, what you're saying is you have nothing."

In my mind, I say *Yes, I have nothing*, but I know that if I tell Madeline that information, I'm not even going to make it a few more days. I get up and grab a Red Bull from the fridge to buy myself a moment to think. I intentionally don't offer Madeline anything. It would only give her another opportunity to insult me in my home. I take a sip of the Red Bull and decide to play my best card.

"No, I have something."

"What?"

"The Dionysus Theater."

Madeline's eyes widen. She uncrosses her legs and leans forward, placing her hands on the table. I notice one of her polished nails is slightly off. She's been biting it.

"What is the Dionysus Theater?"

"I don't know yet. But I know that in both Mia's case and the case of at least one other girl, the name of that theater has come up, and the girls seem to have wanted to perform there. Have you heard of it?"

"No, never. And I know every theater in New York."

I'm sure you do, Madeline, I think.

"Me neither, but I'm confident that if I can find out what the Dionysus Theater is, then I can find out what happened to Mia."

For a moment Madeline's mask of pretentiousness breaks, and I see the glint of hope in her eyes. A tear forms, but she rises from her chair and turns away.

"Good. I want you to find out everything you can about this Dionysus Theater today and report back to me tomorrow at eight a.m. at your office."

Madeline gives me the order as though she'd thought of it

and I wasn't going to do exactly that anyway. I guess that makes her feel like she's doing something when, in fact, she's just an obstacle.

I nod my agreement.

She heads toward the door of my apartment and opens it.

"And no more of this drinking and going to parties with my money, Hazel. That's not what I hired you for. You do it again and you're fired."

I squint my eyes but say nothing. I tell myself this is Madeline's way of saying *Good job*.

She shuts the door behind her.

I turn the lock and crumple into a ball on the couch.

Chapter 21

For the next fifteen minutes, I try to go back to sleep, but it's not happening after Madeline's surprise visit. I tell myself not to dwell on her impertinence, but something about that woman crawls under my skin. My head aches at the thought of her.

Six days.

I curse Madeline in my mind. It's hard enough to find a missing girl, period, let alone with some arbitrary deadline hanging over your head. I think of Mia and how she deserves so much more than this pill of a godmother. Then I think of what my mom used to tell me in Korean, growing up: "Ha-neul"—that's my Korean name—"it's better to get beaten by the whip first." Looking back, it was a strange phrase to say to a child, but it meant that if you're going to have to endure something painful, it's better to just get it over with. Fortunately, my mom never beat me with an actual whip, just steady helpings of guilt and displays of disappointment.

I grab Kenny's leftover pajeon and pop open my laptop on the card table. Hopefully the pancakes can absorb some of the alcohol rotting in my stomach. With a mouthful of pajeon, I type *Dionysus Theater* into the browser bar. The first thirty search results cover the Theater of Dionysus, which is an ancient theater in the Acropolis in Athens. I skim the history of the theater, which seems like any other theater. Until I see two words that shake me: *ritual sacrifice*. The theater hosted sacrifices every year as part of the spring festival of the god Dionysus. Not a festival I'd like to attend.

I know full well that this is not the theater I'm looking for, but the more I learn about Dionysus and the traditions that surround him—ritual sacrifice, hedonism, madness, frenzy, ecstasy—the more I'm certain that someone lured Mia into something sinister. In my business, I've found that symbols matter. What people choose for their car, their passwords, their screen names, their brand provide a window into who they truly are.

I keep scrolling through the search results, realizing that whoever selected this name for their theater was brilliant. The search results are so dominated by the theater in Athens that whatever this underground Dionysus Theater is can exist in virtual anonymity. On the fortieth search result, I find something different. There's a group called the Dionysus Theatre Company in Connecticut. For a moment, my heart skips at the thought that this might be something. But I'm quickly disappointed as I look at the Facebook page of the group, which is littered with pictures of middle-aged folks performing *A Doll's House* or *Hamlet*. It's just a nice little theater troupe in Vernon, Connecticut. I highly doubt that they're abducting little girls.

I keep searching and keep hitting dead ends. I'm losing hope when I find a Reddit thread entitled "Dionysus Theater? Been? Heard of it? Know anyone there?" The post is from a month ago and has only one reply: an address.

522 West Thirty-Eighth Street.

That's Manhattan. It's a long shot, but it could be what I'm looking for. I jump out of my chair and accidentally knock it over, banging it against the floor. I cringe—Kenny is still sleeping—but I can't stifle the excitement of finally finding a lever to pull. The post is fresh enough that there may be something there still.

Kenny rustles out of his bedroom in Yoda boxers and a T-shirt that says *Free Hugs*. His sleep hair is matted into mohawk shape, and he rubs his eyes as they try to absorb the daylight. They look like they're taped shut.

"Hazel, what are you doing out here? I'm trying to sleep."

I pick the chair up off the floor and shrug my shoulders.

"Sorry about that, sleepyhead. I just got a break in the case."

"That's nice," he says, stifling a yawn.

I shuffle into my room and grab some joggers and a hoodie. I throw them on in the living room over my pajama shorts and tank top. I hear the coffee maker gurgling and run back out into the kitchen.

"No time for coffee, Special K. Get dressed. You're coming with me."

Kenny, who's gawking at the coffee maker like it's the fountain of youth, leans his head back and stares at the ceiling. He runs his hands through his hair. He's used to my impulsiveness by now, but it doesn't mean he likes it. I can't help but laugh at his pain.

"Ugh. Really? I'm so hungover. I was planning on just chilling and gaming all day."

"Yes, really. It's almost one in the afternoon, and you've always said you wanted to be my partner and help with the casework. Well, now's your chance."

He looks down from the ceiling to the floor, searching his

foggy mind for an excuse, but he's got nothing.

"Fine, let me get some pants on."

I smile as he stumbles back into the bedroom to change.

Today's going to be a good day.

Chapter 22

Kenny and I burst out of our apartment building, brimming with enthusiasm. An enthusiasm that the weather quickly dampens. Dark clouds slide through the sky, and a cold mist hangs in the air. The city itself feels weighed down by the dreary autumn. The streets of Chinatown, normally bustling with activity, mope, forlorn and empty. The old Chinese folks that play go or chess in the park have stayed home. Buildings that gleamed and glistened in the sun now hover and lurk.

We bolt through the drizzle into the subway station. The dampness from outside seeps into the concrete, creating a raw chill in the station as we wait for the train. Kenny's jumping up and down, shivering. He's here, but his body hasn't woken up yet.

A man follows us into the station. A long scar runs across his jaw and down his neck, which is dotted with acne marks. His sharply receding hairline comes to a widow's peak. It reminds me of Dracula in the old black-and-white version. Another favorite of my dad's. He's looking down at his phone and texting. I feel like I've seen him before but can't place where.

Kenny doesn't acknowledge him.

"So, what are you dragging me to now, Haze?" he says in

more of a whine than a question.

"Something called the Dionysus Theater."

"Okaaay. What's that?"

I was afraid he'd ask.

"I don't know, exactly. I think it's some type of underground theater of some sort. But I think Mia might have been interested in it, and I know for sure another girl that went missing from Saint Agnes was."

"So, is this like a movie theater or a theater with plays and stuff?"

"Honestly, I have no clue. I don't even know if where we're going is the theater. I just found the address on a Reddit thread."

Kenny stuffs his hands into the pockets of his bright-orange fleece and rocks back and forth. In that color orange, it looks like he's going hunting.

"Sounds terrible. I think I would have preferred you taking me to the gala last night."

He looks at me, and his lips pinch and move to the side. He's trying to tell me something without telling me something. I brush it off to lighten the mood.

"I bet you would. But I don't think your tuxedo game is up to it. Besides, I think that place has a quota for Asians. Only one at a time."

We both laugh. The train pulls up with a screech, and we enter and slide into the multicolor plastic seats. It's our lucky day. We got a new subway car.

Kenny looks away for a moment to make it less awkward and then down at his phone. He starts playing *Mario Kart*, so I look elsewhere. I notice the man with the scar boarding the next car down. He stands at one of the metal poles, and I can see him through the train car window; or rather, he can see me. The conductor barks something indecipherable overhead, and the train pulls out from the station.

"Just so you know, I can't stay long. I have Collector's Club in an hour," says Kenny over a series of beeps and boops chirping from his phone.

Collector's Club is Kenny's vintage knife collecting group. They collect different knives from the Civil War or the Second World War and then show them off to each other. When Kenny first told me about it and showed me his knife collection, I was pretty creeped out. The idea of a bunch of lonely men with knives didn't seem like an elite club to be in, but now that I've learned more about it, it seems harmless. I think it's just an excuse for guys to get together, drink beers, and talk, sort of like a book club for women.

I pat Kenny on the shoulder.

"Yeah, I don't think this is going to take too long. This could be a wild-goose chase. I'm not even sure we're going to find anything. You can take off whenever you need to."

He nods and stares back at his phone, disappointed. What was he hoping for? That I'd say "No, Kenny, you can't go to Collector's Club. I need you. Stay with me"? I think he watched too many romantic comedies growing up.

Five minutes later, we pull into our stop at Thirty-Fourth Street and Hudson Yards. The man with the scar stays behind on the subway, but the feeling that I've seen him before hangs with me. We walk out of the station and a few blocks north to the address. It's not what I expected. This part of Manhattan has been transformed over the past decade. Parks have sprouted up along the river. Offices and condos have been constructed. But this street seems like the lone holdout. A faint aroma of sewage hangs in the air, and an open construction site stands on one side of the road. The rain falls on the dirt, turning it into mud and sludge. On the other side, a row of abandoned horse-drawn carriages lines the curb. I'm assuming they're the ones used for tourists in Central Park. They must store them here because there's no other place to put them. Off the street, a series of broken-down buildings frown like death row inmates, waiting to be taken from this earth.

Kenny and I scuttle down Thirty-Eighth Street through the drizzle until we reach a nondescript two-story, smoke-colored building. At first glance, the structure appears to be abandoned. Bars cover the windows. The paint flakes off the facade. No signs hang from the exterior, and the landscaping consists of mud and little else. But as I step closer, I notice evidence that people gathered here not that long ago. A few empty glasses linger by the front entrance. The front door is locked, but footprints mark the ground where people would have been standing. I pull out my phone and record the scene.

"This is what you woke me up for?" says Kenny. He pulls his jacket hood over his head and then kicks at the mud with hands on hips. When he's irritated, he braces his back with both hands like a pregnant woman. His intent is to convey annoyance, but to me it's straight comedy.

I ignore his snark and grab a drinking glass with a gloved hand. I smell it.

"It's booze, and it has to be recent or the smell would have faded by now."

Kenny raises an eyebrow. Despite his annoyance, he's becoming intrigued. While I continue to inspect the front of the building, he strolls around the back. My eyes scour the ground, looking for anything that could tie this dump to the Dionysus Theater. But the drizzle has washed away whatever was here. I'm rapidly losing hope when I hear a noise from behind the building.

"Haze! Come back here. You're going to want to see this," bellows Kenny.

I race through the mud to the rear, expecting something dramatic—a dead body, a secret entrance—but it's just Kenny standing there.

"What is it?" I say, my brow furrowing in confusion.

His round cheeks rise on his face, and he points to the right corner of the building. It's faded, but the painted emblem of the bearded man from the card Mia's roommate gave me gazes back at me from the brick. I give Kenny a big hug and a kiss on the cheek.

"You're a rock star!"

His face turns as red as it was after a few drinks last night. That was probably a mistake.

I pull my lockpick kit from my bag to change the subject.

Kenny's flush recedes, and his jaw drops.

"What are you doing?"

I crouch down to the ground, grab a bump key from my pack, and work the lock on the back door. It's a standard Schlage, so it shouldn't be too difficult.

"I'm checking out the inside of the building. Will you look out for me?"

Kenny grabs my arm.

"Haze, you can't do that. It's breaking and entering."

I stop wiggling the bump key for a moment and straighten up to look him in the eye. He looks away, his eyes never connecting.

"You can't be serious. This is why I don't invite you along with me to my work."

"What's that supposed to mean?"

"You know what it means. Sometimes, as a private investigator, you have to do things that are a bit...sketchy."

Kenny rubs his palms together, and he spins around, checking if anyone is watching.

"Yeah, but this is illegal. If we get caught, my police career will be over before it's started."

"Then go," I snap. "Go to your Collector's Club. There's no one here. I'll be fine."

Kenny sighs and looks like he is about to say something but thinks better of it.

"Okay. It's your funeral. I'm going to go, but call me if you need anything."

"Don't worry, I won't."

Kenny sulks away, and I return my focus to the lock. I know I can be mean to him sometimes, but his passive-aggressive bullshit gets under my skin. I'll apologize to him when I get home. Right now, I need to find out what's behind door number two.

I wiggle the bump key back and forth until I feel the tumblers in the door lock settle into position. I ease the key ninety degrees, and the lock gives. The hinges squeak as the door creeps open.

The inside of the building is not at all what I expected. At first glance it resembles a Prohibition-era jazz club. To the left sits an empty dark wood bar. To the right, a small stage barely large enough to fit a quartet. The carpet is worn and stained but holds a rich burgundy pattern that hints at past glory. Beyond that, the place sits empty. Still, I can't help feeling that something is off.

Really off.

Although the place appears old and abandoned from the outside, there's something alive in here. I can smell a faint combination of cigar smoke and perfume. The bar and stage shine and are free of dust. I can almost hear the music that played here recently. The bloodred stage curtains are drawn as though a performance is about to take place. People have been here, and their energy echoes through the building.

I spot a small stairwell to the right of the bar and climb the stairs. The stairwell is narrow, and the stairs whine with each step. God, I hope nobody else is in here because if they are, they've heard me. As I ascend, the smell of perfume grows stronger, fruity and thick, almost as if someone painted it onto the walls themselves. A rat scurries across the top step, and my heart leaps into my throat. New York hosts a lot of rats, but I'll never get used to them. I pause and breathe in and out to calm my pulse, then resume climbing.

The top floor appears hollow: just a long hallway with five empty offices with gray unfinished floors lining the left and right sides, probably for the old jazz-club management. But as I pass the second office, my eye catches something. Two slight scrapes mark the floor, and next to them is a small stain about the size of a penny. I tiptoe closer, hoping it's not what I think it is.

The stain has turned brown with time, but that's definitely blood. And by the looks of it, I'm guessing it can't be more than a month old. I try to imagine what could have taken place here. Some type of fight club? An underground medical procedure? My mind goes to the darkest places. What kind of jazz club has bloodstained floors? I bend over and take a photo.

A noise from downstairs breaks my concentration.

Someone's entering the front of the building.

I hide beside the doorway, blood pounding in my temples.

I catch a man's voice through the floor beneath me. The sound vibrates from the floor up my spine. I think back to the man with the scar on the subway. Could he have followed me? Is this a setup?

I poke my head outside the room. The one with the blood. It could be my blood staining the floor if I don't get out of here.

The hallway appears empty. I hear more muffled talking. There are two men. I can tell from how the sound of their voices travels that they're moving around the first floor.

They're coming.

They'll be at the stairwell soon.

I tiptoe closer to the stairs to see if I can hear what they're saying. The top step of the stairs moans.

The voices stop.

They heard me.

It's silent. Only my pulse rings in my ears.

I stand motionless, preparing myself for a fight, but then I realize I left my purse, along with my Taser, at home. It's just me now. I consider texting Kenny, but he'll be too far away to help. I dart my eyes back to the window in the office. Is it too high to jump?

Mercifully, the voices resume talking. They must have assumed it was the rain. Their conversation grows louder, and I lean into the stairwell to listen, my mind preparing for the worst.

"I think you're going to love this space, Tom."

"I don't know, Rick, it seems like I'm going to spend more on the reno than on the land."

"Really? I don't think it will be bad. A little elbow grease, and you should be all set."

Unbelievable. It's a real estate broker giving a tour of the space.

I release a long breath and wipe the sweat from my forehead. I creep down the steps. With any luck, I'll be able to slide out the door without these bozos noticing. If they see me, I'll pretend to be another broker interested in the space. I slip my head around the corner.

The broker and his potential client stand with their backs to me, inspecting the stage.

"Look at this woodwork, Tom. When was the last time you saw something like this? Imagine having a little jazz band here. It would really make the restaurant pop."

I seize the opportunity when their backs are turned and slide along the rear wall toward the back exit. As I pass the bar, I notice a small card sitting on the corner. I must have missed it when I came in. I don't have time to inspect it now, but I see a familiar face staring back at me, so I grab it and sidestep out the door.

Once outside, I take a deep breath and sprint around the building, feet slipping and sliding in the mud. I race down the sidewalk past the carriages to get as much distance as possible from whoever was inside. I glare behind me to see if anyone's following me. No scarred men, no real estate agents.

Once I've reached a safe distance, I duck under the awning of a closed Greek restaurant to escape the drizzle and look down at the card. It's a thick white card stock with a glossy finish. On the front is the familiar smiling, bearded Dionysus, surrounded by bunches of grapes on each side of him. The back of the card shows a simple URL and a phrase that raises the hairs on my arms.

Thyrsus.io

"Wine and children speak the truth."

Chapter 23

For the next forty-five minutes, I walk south toward my apartment. I want to get as far away from that place as I can. I would take the subway, but something about the idea of going underground right now freaks me out. It's a long walk home from here, but the rain has subsided, and I need the fresh air. The farther away I get, the more the anxiety metastasizes in my stomach. My hands shake, and my breaths are short. The charcoal overcast of the afternoon makes it feel like night, and all I hear are my footsteps shuffling over the grimy sidewalks.

Cars splash through puddles in the street as I walk. New York never seems so lonely as when you're afraid. Every face, every sound, every shadow spooks you to the core. I read the card in my hand again. The quote on the card, "Wine and children speak the truth," and the fact that girls are going missing seem like more than a coincidence. Was it left there intentionally for me or someone to find? And the blood on the floor? That's even more perplexing. In some ways, it would have been easier if it was a pool of blood, the kind you'd see from a gunshot wound to the head. But this was just a small stain. It's a metaphor for this case: something mundane with ominous implications beneath the surface.

I keep trucking and thinking about the evidence. Fear clings to me like a shadow, and I check behind me every so often to make sure I'm not being followed. It's clear to me now that this isn't the work of one man. This whole affair reeks of something more organized and coordinated. Sometimes the safest place to hide is in broad daylight. It reminds me of a few encounters I had with the mafia, but with a more sophisticated edge. The mafia doesn't reference Dionysus.

The thought of Dionysus brings me back to the card. As I turn down Canal Street and head toward home, I look at the URL on the bottom. I pull out my phone while I stride, being careful not to step on the few remaining street vendors who've braved the weather. I type in *thyrsus.io*, and it leads to a blank page with a message: "This is a secure site. Enter your password to continue."

Of course it needs a password to continue. Nothing about this case is easy. Can I get one damn break? I pause my journey and raise my head up to the sky, hoping the clouds will give me insight into what the password could be. As I stop and look up, I notice that two men across the street and thirty feet behind me stop abruptly as well. I pretend that I'm confused about where I am and looking at street signs, and shoot a side-glance in their direction. The first man is tall, with a flattop, dark skin, and striking blue-gray eyes, like a zombie. I've never seen him before. My eyes settle on his partner. I have seen him before. It's the balding guy with the chin scar from the train.

My heart drops to my stomach.

The familiar nausea from before rises again in my gut.

I look back down at my phone as though nothing's wrong, but my hand trembles so hard I can barely see the screen.

I walk faster.

Out of the corner of my eye, I see that they've continued walking and are now crossing the street. I look ahead hoping Yanush is there, but he doesn't work weekends. The Gene Strauss encounter reverberates in my mind. I should probably run, but I hesitate, since the last guy I ran from gave me a Tesla. My house is several blocks away, but my office is only two streets down, so I quicken my pace and head toward Cortlandt Alley. I hear the sound of steps behind me breaking into a run. I feel them gaining on me, but the alley is only a few feet away.

I turn right into the alley and am launching myself into a sprint when I feel a hand grab the collar of my coat and yank me back against the brick wall. I open my mouth to scream, but the man with the scar covers it with his hand, while the other man gives him cover. I smell stale cigarette smoke on his left hand and feel him raise a knife blade to my neck with his right. The blade burns against my neck and freezes me in place. I glance at his partner, who grins with fire in his eyes. I search the alley for cameras, but the brick is bare. Cheap-ass landlords.

I remember the Stabby Kitties self-defense weapon on my keychain. If I can get to it, I could jab him and get some space between us. But the knife is too close to my neck. One wrong move and I'm dead.

The man with the scar pushes his face closer to mine. I look into his beady brown eyes. There's no fear, no excitement, no uncertainty. I can feel it in the blade's steadiness as he presses it against my artery. This is his job. He terrorizes people for a living. Panic overtakes me.

"I come here with a message," he says. His voice is high pitched but gravelly, just above a whisper.

I nod to show I understand. I clench my neck as the blade

presses closer. I pray the message won't be delivered with the knife.

"Stop investigating the Dionysus Theater. You understand?"

I nod again, tears streaming down my face.

"You only get one warning. You understand?"

I blink, afraid to move.

"If I have to visit again, I'll be the last person you ever see. You understand?"

I blink one last time, hoping for a reprieve.

He releases me, and he and his partner turn and walk away into pedestrian traffic on Canal as though nothing happened. It took them no more than thirty seconds to terrorize me. And like that, they're gone.

I drop to the ground.

Chapter 24

I sit in the alley on the wet pavement. Pedestrians stroll by and either don't notice or don't care. Tears stream down my face, my body shakes, and I realize that everything I've been keeping inside is now trying to escape. In my day-to-day life, I put on a brave face, but I have no idea what I'm doing. When that knife blade touched the skin on my neck, I saw everything I am and everything I'm not in one moment. I'm thirty years old, broke, and living in a run-down apartment, and my only hope right now is a narcissistic rich lady whose case might get me killed. I think about the look in Zombie Eyes' face, and something in me breaks.

The life that I wanted has turned into the life I want to escape.

It's ridiculous, of course, but I can't help blaming myself. I should have taken an Uber home. I should have had my Taser ready. I should have ducked into a store. I should have fought back. I replay the confrontation on a loop in my mind, and the rage builds inside me.

I hear my mom's voice in my head, telling me to quit. To turn my back on this life, these toxic, dangerous people. This isn't worth dying for. Madeline definitely isn't worth dying for. I could live in the suburbs with Dr. Lee and leave all this behind.

And then I think of Mia. Alone, scared, hoping that someone will save her. I think of how I feel right now in this alley. How I've felt before. This is why I became a PI, so that victims wouldn't have to feel alone anymore. If I don't find her, no one will. She'll be lost in the system, just like I was once. If I quit now, what was it all for? Perry used to tell me "You can hope for the good times, but it's the bad times that make you." This is one of those times.

My phone rings as if to say *Stop feeling sorry for yourself.* I look at the screen. I'm expecting to see my mom's face, but there's no picture, just a name: Andrew DuPont.

Now?

Really?

Any other time, I would be ecstatic to get this call. Right now, my stomach is one big knot. But I don't want to let this chance slip away. I sniffle and clear my throat so I don't sound like a girl who's this close to throwing herself off a building.

"Hello?"

"Hello, is this the one and only Hazel Cho?"

Andrew's voice is like a warm breeze on a chilly day.

"Yes, it is. Is this the one and only Andrew DuPont?"

The tears in my eyes dry, and I wipe away the ones on my face.

"It sure is. Hey, is everything all right? You sound a little... off."

I pull the phone away from my head and bend over at the knees to catch my breath. I don't want Andrew to hear me like this.

"I'm fine. Just a little out of breath. I've been walking."

"Oh, cool. Just wanted to make sure you're okay. I was calling to see what you're doing right now."

177

I look around for a lie that sounds a lot better than what I'm actually doing, but all I see is a damp brick wall. Another metaphor for my life.

"Actually, I'm currently standing in the alley outside my office."

"Your office? On a Sunday? No, no, no. We can't have that. I'm cooking up a nice little dinner tonight, and I have more food than I could ever eat, so I think you should ditch the office and come join me."

I can hear water running and pots and pans clanking in the background. An involuntary smile appears on my face.

Andrew's given me oxygen.

I swallow the tremor inside me. My first reaction is to tell him no, go back to my apartment, and try to forget what happened to me. His timing couldn't be worse. But then I think to myself, *What could be a better distraction than Andrew?* I force a smile on my face and brighten my voice.

"That sounds like a wonderful idea. Do you need me to bring anything?"

"Nope. Just a nonjudgmental attitude. I'm a questionable chef."

I envy wealthy people like Andrew. Life comes so effortlessly to them, they spend about ninety percent of their time enjoying it while the rest of us grind away.

"I can do that. I need to run home real quick and change, and then I'll be over. What's your address?"

"Eleven East Sixty-Eighth Street. Just tell the doorman that you're visiting me when you get here, and he'll let you up."

He lives in the Upper East Side. It's a long trip from Chinatown, but I need this after the day I've had. This and a Valium. Better than wallowing in my bedroom while Kenny taps on my door, asking me what's wrong.

"Great. I'll see you soon."

I hang up the phone and look around me as though I've awakened from a trance. Andrew has that effect. When you're talking to him, his lightness carries you away from whatever neuroses are gripping you at the moment. But now I'm firmly back to reality, remembering how close I was to death. I watch as New Yorkers dodge the puddles on the sidewalk, oblivious to my presence. It almost feels like I dreamed the assault from Jaw Scar and his sidekick. I have to figure out what I'm going to do about this case, but not right now.

Right now, I need to change into a decent outfit.

* * *

An hour and a half later, I'm pulling up to Andrew's place in a cab paid for with Madeline's money. The clouds have broken, and the rain has washed away the air pollution. The stars pop against the bright black sky. It reminds me of a joke my dad used to make about rich people: "They're so rich it doesn't even rain on them." I step out of the cab and take a long inhale of the crisp fall air. The knot in my stomach from my visit from Jaw Scar and Zombie Eyes stays with me, but I do my best to ignore it. I think back to how my therapist told me that's the worst thing you can do with trauma, but I don't have time for trauma right now.

The street, lined with old trees and multimillion-dollar brownstones, is silent. Blissfully silent. I see Central Park just a block away. Must be nice.

I walk into the lobby of the cream brick building and am greeted by a kind doorman with rosy cheeks, in a hunter green uniform and hat, who seems to have been expecting me. The lobby is small and cloaked in a warm light that nestles on blond wood. He points me to the elevator. I ask him the floor, but he just waves me off, and when I get to the elevator, I see he has selected the floor for me. Thank God, because I wouldn't want to sprain my finger by pushing a button. The elevator opens to the ninth floor, but instead of a hallway, it leads right into Andrew's apartment.

For a moment, I think I'm in the wrong place. I mean, I've seen apartments where the elevator opens directly into the foyer in the movies, but never in person. But then I hear Andrew's voice from the kitchen.

"Is that Hazel Cho I hear?"

"It is," I shout back as I step onto the gleaming black-and-white-tiled floor.

As I'm taking my shoes off, Andrew comes around the corner and gives me a big hug and a kiss on the cheek. Whatever cologne he's wearing goes straight to my head.

I'm in trouble.

He grabs my hand with his buttery-soft palm and drags me into the kitchen. It's the most gorgeous kitchen I've ever seen. A beautiful island made of dark wood and marble stands at the center, white cabinets with gold handles surrounding it. Paned windows line the walls, providing a gorgeous view of the city. The sink is filled with a mishmash of pots and pans, as though Andrew has been slaving away for hours. A dining table crafted from a single piece of wood sits a few feet from the island, with two plates of steak-and-vegetable stir-fry.

Andrew points to the table.

"Your timing is perfect. Dinner is served."

We sit down at the table, with Andrew at the head and me on

one side. He pops open a bottle of wine that looks like it might be older than I am. It hasn't really sunk in that I'm here right now. I wasn't meant to go from being attacked to utopia this quickly.

I force a smile and say, "This is beautiful. Thanks for cooking," but Andrew sees through me.

He places a hand on my shoulder.

"Is everything okay?"

"Yeah, it was just a really hard day."

I shove down the tears. I cannot let him see me cry on our first date.

"Do you want to talk about it?"

I shake my head.

"I understand. I've had days like that."

I highly doubt it, I think to myself.

Andrew pops his pointer finger in the air and leaps up from his chair.

"I have an idea. Come with me."

He walks me into the living room, which is somehow more gorgeous than the kitchen, and points me to a velvet camel couch that begs for you to melt into it. I take in the walls, wallpapered with rich steel blue silk, and the stunning artwork hanging on them.

"You look like you could use a cozy couch. Well, this is the coziest couch in the city."

"What about dinner?"

"We can eat dinner out here. Just promise me you won't spill or I won't invite you back again."

I laugh and flop onto the couch, and Andrew throws a striped Pendleton blanket over me. He's right. This is the coziest couch in the city. My body groans at the feeling of the plush

THE ORPHANAGE BY THE LAKE

velvet cushions. I didn't realize how much tension I was carrying, and now it's dissipating. Fatigue overcomes me.

A few minutes later, he's back with the wine and the stir-fry in two bowls, so we can eat on the couch without spilling all over ourselves. I take a whiff, and the smell of steak and soy makes my stomach leap to life. We clink our wineglasses. I can feel the day's fear melting away and my strength returning.

"You have to let me know what you think of the stir-fry. I've been really working on my cooking, taking cooking classes, the whole deal," says Andrew.

I take a closer look at my bowl. The vegetables are scorched, and the meat looks a little undercooked. He may need to take more classes. I take a cautious bite. Andrew watches me as I chew.

"Mmm," I say as I force the oversauced meat portion down my throat. It tastes like I just took a shot of soy sauce.

"You like it?" he asks, forehead crinkling with hope.

I nod and gulp, then snatch my wineglass off the table to drown the taste. It's terrible, but he's so excited I don't have the heart to tell him.

Andrew's eyes squint, and the corners of his mouth rise. He takes a self-satisfied bite and chews for a few seconds, and then the smile fades.

"Oh, this is terrible," he says.

I drop the act. "Yeah, it's pretty bad."

Andrew and I share a laugh over his culinary disaster. He takes another bite and shakes his head.

"Dang. I was feeling so optimistic this time. Ah well. Back to cooking class."

I smile and rub his back. "Don't worry about it. I'll eat anything. Besides, the wine is incredible." I take another bite and wash it down with cabernet. "This is a beautiful apartment, by the way."

Andrew sets down his bowl and takes a sip of wine. "Thanks. It's been in my family for decades. My parents used to use it as a city getaway before my mom died. After that, my dad didn't really want to use it, but I don't think he had the heart to sell it. It had nothing but wonderful memories for me, so I took it."

I place my hand on his hand. There's a vulnerability to him I hadn't seen before.

"Oh, I'm so sorry. I didn't know your mom died."

Andrew takes a bite of stir-fry and swallows it down, but he's clearly swallowing more than just the food.

"It's okay. It was a long time ago. It's been me and my dad ever since."

"How did your mom die, if you don't mind me asking?"

He puts down his fork and looks out the window.

"She committed suicide."

"Oh, Andrew, I'm so sorry."

He puts his hand on my shoulder and squeezes. His glacier-blue eyes meet mine, and I see the pain and anger behind them.

"I appreciate that. Yeah, it was really difficult at the time, especially because she didn't show it. She was an amazing mom, always happy, always playing stupid games with me. Then she was gone. But it's been over twenty years now, so I've come to grips with it. And I'm thankful for the time we got to spend together. And it's really brought my dad and me closer together."

"Do you and your dad work together?" I ask, trying to figure out what exactly Andrew does without directly asking. I don't want him to think I'm a gold digger.

"No, I'm not really a workhorse. I'm more of a show horse."

He laughs.

"What does that mean?"

"It means I don't really have a job. I'm still figuring out exactly what my calling is. I thought it might be cooking, but given tonight's performance, that's not looking good."

And there it is. I'm on a date with a trust-fund baby. I thought it was too good to be true. I should probably head home now, but one look at Andrew's face and I'm back in.

He pivots on the couch and sits cross-legged so he can look at me.

"Enough about me. What about you? What's your story?"

I put my bowl down on the coffee table and cross my legs and turn toward him.

"I don't have much of a story. Grew up in Palisades Park in a pretty strict Korean household. I'm a youngest child. One sister. Went to college at Union College, upstate, then law school at NYU. Never married."

Andrew smiles and says, "Thank God for that."

I blush and pull my hair over my ear.

"How's your big case going? Have you found the missing Saint Agnes girl yet? It's just awful that happened."

"I can't really go into the details, but I'm making progress. Painfully slow progress."

"I'm sorry to hear that. What does Mackenzie say about all this?"

"I know you love him, but honestly, he hasn't been very helpful."

Andrew's eyebrows pinch together, and he scratches the stubble on his chin.

"That's terrible."

He hums and stares at one of the priceless art pieces on his wall. It's an impressionist painting of children playing by a lake. I can see the wheels turning.

"I'm going to call them tomorrow. My father's on the board, for crying out loud. We should be able to give Mackenzie a kick in the ass."

I pat him on the knee.

"Easy there. I appreciate the gesture, but I can handle Mackenzie. I don't need you and your dad getting everybody's guard up."

Andrew leans back on the couch and takes a sip of wine.

"You're right. I apologize. You clearly don't need my help, given what you've accomplished. All I did today was watch football and recover from last night's hangover. How did you become a private detective, anyway?"

I pause. I'm not sure I want to tell him the story this early in our relationship.

"That's a story for another time, but let's just say when I was in law school, something bad happened, and my attorney was worthless, and my parents weren't much better. The only person who would help me was a private investigator. From that moment on, I knew that's what I wanted to do. Or at least I thought that's what I wanted to do. Now I'm not so sure."

"What do you mean?"

"Nothing. It's just a tough and dangerous business, and I'm not sure I can hack it anymore."

Andrew puts a hand on my leg.

"Hazel, I've known you for a few hours, and I'm a hundred percent confident you can hack it at whatever you set your mind to. The second I met you and you told me about being a private investigator and everything, I was like 'This girl is different,' and I wanted to know more. I just think it's so cool what you've done. Building your own business. Solving mysteries. Taking down bad guys. You're unlike any woman I've ever met."

"That's sweet," I say and give him a kiss on the cheek, which lingers into a kiss on the lips. His lips are perfect, and it's so clear that he knows what he's doing. Unlike most guys, whose desperation for sex emanates from them like body spray, Andrew kisses like this is all he would ever need.

When we're done with dinner, he puts on *The Proposal*, which is nothing more than an excuse for us to continue making out. The only thing I can think about is being with him tonight, but it's not the right time, and he knows it too. We kiss and hold each other on the couch, and eventually fade away into a perfect bliss. My last thought as I drift away is *I've never felt so safe.*

Chapter 25

ive days left

F I wake up on Andrew's couch to a blinding sunrise. Both of us passed out without shutting the blinds, so the morning rays are beaming through the windows unimpeded. I wipe the sleep out of my eyes and look over at Andrew. Aaaargh. He's so ridiculously handsome that even when he snoozes, he's pretty. He looks like an ad for a mattress company where the guy is sleeping but still has perfect hair. His strong, rounded jawline cuts at perfect angles, and his smattering of tiny freckles is the imperfection that makes perfection. It's almost enough to make me forget about the fact that he does nothing all day. I catch my reflection in the window and am reminded that I have my own issues. My mascara has smudged around my eyes, and my hair shows a tragic oily shine. I need to dash out of here before he wakes up, or he's going to wonder who this ghoul is that he allowed into his home. Plus, I need to get to work. I only have five days left before Madeline cuts me loose, and I'm nowhere near solving this case.

I quietly gather my things and leave him a note, thanking him for the wonderful evening. As I'm leaving, he stirs for a moment and says the three words you hope to hear after spending the night together: "Dinner this week?"

I nod my confirmation with a smile and tiptoe out of the room. I step out of his building, and it feels like I've traveled in time. Was I really just with that male model in his immaculate penthouse? Is it too late to go back and say goodbye to my previous life?

My phone rings and delivers a harsh dose of reality. I look at the screen, but I don't need to. I know who it is.

It's Madeline.

"Hello, Madeline," I say through gritted teeth, as though I was expecting her call at six thirty on a Monday morning.

"Hazel, you're awake."

She never misses an opportunity to get a dig in.

"Yes, I am. How can I help you?"

"I'm just confirming our eight a.m. progress report meeting this morning."

Shit. In my preoccupation with Andrew, I totally forgot about our meeting.

"Yes, of course. I will see you at my office at eight."

"Wonderful."

Madeline hangs up. No goodbye.

I run home to my apartment, shower, change, and turn onto Cortlandt Alley by seven thirty. There's no way in hell I'm going to let Madeline beat me. But as I turn, I see the spot where Jaw Scar attacked me, and it all comes back. The fear of being killed. The shame that I didn't do anything but cry like a little girl. Bile rises in my stomach.

I sprint up the two flights of stairs in my building and throw open the hallway bathroom door. I get to the stall just in time. I vomit and can smell the wine from last night. Oddly, it feels good, like I'm purging the anxiety that has been hanging over me since yesterday. After a few minutes and multiple retches, I'm ready to go. I throw in a piece of gum and splash some water on my face.

As I open the bathroom door and step into the hallway, I hear Madeline's low, imperious voice.

"Did you get your days and nights mixed up again, Hazel?"

I swear this woman is the bane of my existence. Whenever I'm at my lowest, she's there. It's like she has an emotional tracking device on me, and whenever I'm at rock bottom, she gets an alert and shows up. Like a genie, but instead of rubbing the lamp, you just feel like shit, and she appears.

I throw her a condescending smirk.

"No, it must have been something I ate."

Madeline's eyebrows rise, and her forehead would have creased except the Botox prevents it.

I open the door to my office across the hall and let Madeline in. We both sit in silence while I pull up my case file on the computer. I'm still not sure whether I should tell Madeline about my unexpected visit from Jaw Scar and Zombie Eyes yesterday. On one hand, I want her to know what I'm going through to solve this case; on the other, I'm pretty sure she won't care, and I'm certain she won't be helpful.

"So, have you found anything more about this Dionysus Theater?" Madeline says. She raises one eyebrow. She expects me to have nothing.

"Actually, I did."

She sits up in her chair and pulls her curled blonde hair behind her ear.

"Really?"

"Yes, I found what looks like a former location of the theater in the Garment District."

"A former location? What good does that do us?"

For every solution, Madeline has a problem.

"It does a lot of good because I found the website for the theater."

"And?"

"And I'm hoping that will lead us to where the theater is now."

Madeline scoffs and her hands flail. "Hoping? Why are you hoping? How hard is it to read a website?"

I wonder if Madeline thinks everyone is this stupid or just me.

"It's not hard to read a website, unless it is a secure site with a password, like in this case. Unless you have some computer hacking skills that I'm unaware of?"

I pull up the URL from the card and spin my computer screen so Madeline can see. Her face reddens, and she taps her thin fingers against the desk. "Well? What's the password?" she asks. Her gestures become more violent the more agitated she becomes.

"I don't know that yet, Madeline." I say her name like an expletive.

A vein bulges in her head, and she stands up and paces the room. Her heels knock against the floor. After a few seconds of huffing, she turns to me and points.

"I swear, Hazel, you're as worthless as the others."

That does it. I've been taking shit from this woman for too long.

"What the fuck is your problem?" I say as I rise from my desk.

"I beg your pardon?"

"You heard me. What the fuck is your problem, Madeline?

From the moment I've met you, you've been riding me. Yet, as far as I can tell, I'm the only investigator you've hired that has produced any results. And what do I get for my efforts? Bullshit from you and threats from strange men."

Madeline scoffs. "Threats? What threats?"

"Oh, you mean you didn't know? I thought you knew everything. I guess not. Yeah, yesterday, right outside this office, two men accosted me, held a knife to my throat, and told me to stay away from this case. Any idea why that might have happened?"

She raises her hand to her mouth and takes a step back, and for a second, I glimpse another crack in the facade. But it's not anger or surprise I see through the crack, it's sadness. I want to feel sorry for her, but I'm so angry that I can't stop my mouth.

"I mean, why do you even care about Mia? She's just your goddaughter. You didn't even have the decency to take her in when her parents died, but now you're apparently so interested in what happened to her. Maybe if you had cared for her at, I don't know, any other point in her life, she wouldn't be missing right now."

I slam my hand on the table.

Madeline's fingers clench into fists, and for a moment, I think she's going to strike me. Then her face contorts, and tears burst from her eyes. And these aren't the controlled tears of sadness; they're the unvarnished tears of heartbreak. I'm so shocked at this unexpected display of humanity that I freeze at first, but then have enough good sense to grab a few tissues from my tissue box. I walk around my desk to hand them to her, and Madeline surprises me again. She raises her arms to hug me.

I hug her back. Her bony frame shakes as the sobs roll from her lips. She cries so much on my shoulder that I can feel my blouse dampening. After a minute, Madeline releases me and sits back down. Her perfectly curated makeup is ruined. Black lines run down her face. For the first time, she looks human.

I return to my chair and hand her more tissues. She wipes her cheeks and nose and then looks me in the eye. The Madeline that puts on airs is gone, and I can envision what she might have been like before she created this false image of who she is.

"I'm so sorry that happened to you, Hazel. Why do you think those men attacked you?"

"I was about to ask you the same question. All I know is that they didn't want me asking any more questions about the Dionysus Theater. Are you sure you don't know anything about it?"

"I swear. Until you told me about it, I had never heard of the Dionysus Theater in my life." She pauses and dabs at her eyeliner with a tissue. "But there is something you should know." She twists the sapphire ring on her right hand.

"Okay," I say, afraid of what I'm about to hear.

"Mia isn't my goddaughter. She's my daughter."

The news hits me like a brick. I lean back in my chair so hard that I hit my head on the wall behind me.

"What?"

"When I was in college, I played tennis. There was a boy there—another tennis player."

Her face brightens at the memory.

"He was beautiful. Tall, strong, a fabulous tennis player. All the girls on the team, including me, were obsessed with him. One day just before the end of my senior year, he asked me if I wanted to sneak out and go to the beach with him. One thing led to another.

"The school year ended. I came back home from school for the summer, and a few weeks later I started feeling nauseous in the morning."

I should write this down, but I'm too shocked at what I'm hearing. This is definitely not the Madeline I know.

"Did you tell your parents?"

Madeline chews on her bottom lip.

"I didn't really have a choice. My morning sickness was pretty bad, so my mom put two and two together."

"How did she react?"

"She was mortified. She harangued me about how I could be so stupid. She told me I was going to ruin our family name."

I think about my mother and how she would react. It wouldn't be pretty. I guess avoiding unplanned pregnancy is one thing I got right.

"Then what happened?"

"I stayed in lockdown at my parents' house for the next eight months. They were strict Catholics, so terminating the pregnancy was not an option. My mother insisted that I have the child, and my father was constantly working, so he went along with whatever she said. At first, my parents intended to keep the baby and tell people it was theirs. My mother was twenty-two when she had me, so it was possible. That's when I had to drop the bomb on them."

I place my hands on my cheeks.

"You mean that the guy at college was Black?"

"Yes."

My entire image of Madeline has shattered into a million pieces in five minutes. This woman's got a lot more depth to her than I ever thought possible.

"I'm guessing your parents weren't the most enlightened folks?"

"That's a charitable way of putting it. My mom is just a flat-out racist. The idea of having a Black child in the family was totally unthinkable to her."

"So, what did you do?"

"I thought about just having the baby and running away with her, but I wasn't that strong. My parents said they'd cut me off if I did. I was fresh out of college and had been sheltered my whole life, so I didn't know how to make it on my own.

"My mother said she would take care of it, and like an idiot, I let her. She and Thomas were old friends. He told my mother he could help."

"Thomas?"

"Mackenzie."

"Thomas Mackenzie told your mother he could take in Mia and pretend that she was an orphan?"

Madeline lowers her head, and her voice cracks.

"Yes. Every time I would visit Mia was agony. We would go into town and get ice cream, and I'd see that sweet smile, and she reminded me of the girl I used to be. It killed me not to tell her, not to take her out of that horrid place. But I'd lied so long that I was afraid that if she knew the truth, she would never forgive me. When she disappeared, it felt like God was punishing me, saying *You abandoned her, now she's going to abandon you.* This is my chance to change things. To make it right."

"Wait, I don't understand. I researched you and Mia. There were no birth records. Did you do a confidential birth certificate?"

"Yes, she'll have access to it when she's eighteen, but until then we can keep it private."

"But what about Saint Agnes? Usually, when custody of a child changes hands, there's paperwork requirements. You know, child services and all that."

She clears her throat and brushes her platinum hair from her face.

"You'd be surprised. It's actually easier than you'd think. When Mia was a baby, my mother saw in the paper that a couple with the last name Ross had died in a car accident off I-87, so she changed Mia's last name to Ross. That way, there would be no obvious association, and if someone inquired about the parents, there would be an explanation. Then Thomas enrolled her at Saint Agnes under the name Ross and told the staff and eventually Mia that she was an orphan. It was almost like enrolling your child in a boarding school, but just doing it so young that she never knows her parents. We never legally declared her as an orphan or changed custody, so there was no paperwork or interaction with child services. We just shoved her out of our lives. It's sad, really, but if no one is complaining, nobody really cares about what happens to a child."

"I'll need you to send me that birth certificate."

"Of course."

"Why didn't you tell me this?"

Madeline raises her head, and the stubborn stare returns.

"It's an embarrassment to the family. I can't do that to my father and mother. No one can know."

"What about Mia's father? Did you tell him?"

"No, he doesn't even know. My mother didn't want him around."

A pang of sympathy runs through me. I've misjudged

Madeline. I used to see her haughtiness as a reflection of her shallowness—a sign of a woman who cares for nothing but herself and her status in her clique of socialites. But it's a defense mechanism, protecting a softer side of her that's always coming second to the needs of her family. No one's ever stood up for her. Maybe it's time for that to change.

I jump up from my chair and start packing up my day bag.

Madeline stands, her eyes dancing left and right.

"Where are you going?"

I throw my bag over my shoulder. "I'm going home. I've got some loose ends I need to tie up, and then tomorrow I'm going to drive up to Lake George and knock on Mackenzie's door until he lets me in. I know you think he's a saint, but he definitely knows more than he's letting on."

I put my hand on her back and lead her out of the office with me.

"We're going to finish this thing."

Chapter 26

our days left

FThe next morning, I hop into the Tesla and head north to Lake George. As I drive, my mind sifts through everything I've learned about this case. I spent the rest of my Monday researching and working the phones to see if I could find out how Mia navigated that lake. The more prepared I am for Mackenzie, the better. I used Google Maps to mark every property on the lake within a five-mile radius of Saint Agnes. Then I used a reverse address lookup tool to find the residents of those properties and their phone numbers. Once I had a full list, I worked the phones to see if any of the residents have cameras pointed at the lake, and if so, whether those cameras caught any boats passing by the night of Mia's disappearance. It went about as well as everything else in this case. Most people didn't answer my call. That is what is so infuriating about Madeline's deadline. If I had more time, I could spend weeks knocking on the doors of the houses I missed earlier, reviewing their camera footage, and maybe find a glimpse of the boat that took Mia. But instead, I'm working the phones, hoping for a miracle.

Of the people that did answer my calls, many don't have cameras on their property. Of the ones that do have cameras, most of them don't point at the lake because burglars don't come by boat. If they had a boat, they wouldn't need to burgle. I found one guy—with an amazing name, Benjamin Smylie III— who does have a camera pointed at the lake, but he's "sailing off the coast of Italy right now," so unable to check the footage. He assured me he'll check his camera footage online when he gets in from his sail, but I'm dubious. Like I said, the core of detective work is crossing things off the list. I'm officially crossing boat camera footage off my list. Maybe Benjamin Smylie III will surprise me, but I'm not counting on it. My answers lie within Saint Agnes and the Dionysus Theater.

As I drive, the frustration rises. Thomas Mackenzie is going to talk to me whether or not he likes it. I merge onto I-87 and slam on the accelerator. Dark clouds crash overhead, and a steady rain falls. Even the weather wants to keep me from Saint Agnes. The outskirts of New York are a dreary place in the rain. An old industrial wasteland frozen in time.

It's a Tuesday morning, so the traffic is thick. I do my best to wind through the mess of commuters, but there's a limit to what I can do. I fire up my Best of EDM mix on Spotify to clear my mind, but my thoughts keep snapping back to the case. Madeline hired me to find answers, but all I discover are questions. What is the Dionysus Theater? What is Mackenzie hiding? What else is Madeline hiding? Who else is involved? My brain revs like an engine in neutral, stuck in place like the traffic in front of me.

Mercifully, after thirty minutes of dwelling, my phone rings, and I see that it's Detective Riether: a welcome distraction. Per his instructions, I haven't called him since I was last in Lake George. I wanted to stay on his good side in case I really need a favor. Before I pick up, I give a brief prayer for good news.

"Bobby Riether, please tell me you have something good for me."

A nervous chuckle pops through the phone.

"No *Hi, how are you?*"

"Sorry. Hi. How are you?"

"Too late. But I do indeed have something good for you. It would be better to discuss it in person, though. What's your schedule this week?"

His raspy voice sounds tight.

"I guess it's my lucky day because I'm headed out there right now."

"Really? What for?"

His voice cracks a little, and I feel a smile rise on my face.

"I'll tell you about it when I see you."

"All right, looking forward to it. What time do you think you'll get here?"

"Should be about one."

"Okay, I'll meet you out front of the station. Better we talk outside."

There's something cute about Bobby Riether. When I talk to him, I'm reminded of the time in my life when I thought being a PI would be fun. I thought maybe I'd meet a cute cop and we could solve mysteries together. I know. It's cheesy, but sometimes the dreams of the young are cheesy.

By the time I pull up to the police station, it's afternoon, but it looks like dusk outside. The rain hasn't started yet, but it's coming. The wind carries a fierce chill that cuts through me. Bobby paces in front, smoking his white filtered cigarette, seemingly oblivious to the cold. He walks with one hand placed on his lower back, and his little paunch leans out over his beltline. When he sees me, he gives me a cool-guy wave with his cigarette hand.

Real James Dean energy.

"You brought more wonderful weather with you," says Bobby, pointing at the doom-filled sky above us.

I shake his hand and notice how rough it is, unlike Andrew's. A man's hand.

"Yeah, it seems to follow me wherever I go. Should we go inside?"

"In a minute. Let's take a walk. I wanted to talk to you first."

"We're not going to that café again, are we? I don't think I can take any more of that waitress's stares. I felt like I was on a date being chaperoned by my mother."

Bobby releases a small laugh, but his mouth barely moves.

"No café today. We can just walk around the block here."

I cross my arms. This sounds serious. We walk, and I take in my surroundings. The neighborhood around the police station is a modest array of lake cottages and picket fences. Much more modest than the opulent mansions on the lake. Fall is rapidly turning into winter, and the colored leaves of the trees hang on for dear life. The streets are empty on account of the impending storm, so Bobby and I stroll down the middle of the road. The neighborhood sits silent except for the soft crunch of our feet against the leaves.

"Okay, what's up?" I say.

"I'm not sure you should keep pursuing this case."

He stares at me with his deep-brown eyes, and I notice the red around the edges and the bags underneath.

"Why?"

He takes another drag from his cigarette and kicks at the ground with each step, searching for the right words. He runs his tongue over the chip in his front tooth.

"I wish I could give you a simple answer, but there's no one thing. But everything about this case tells me you might be in danger."

His eyes drift up to the sky as we walk. A whiff of fireplace smoke slides by my nose. I put a hand on his shoulder, trying to get him to look at me. It's bony. He's thinner than he looks.

"What do you mean?"

"The best way I can say it is that nobody seems to want this case solved. Anytime I ask for additional resources to investigate, the sheriff says no. Any person I try to interview either declines or stonewalls me. I look back at the cases on other missing girls, the ones that even exist, and it's the same thing: obligatory investigation with no follow-up. Yesterday, I was complaining to a couple of my colleagues about it, and they told me I should focus on my other cases."

"So, what are you saying? You think the sheriff's department is involved in this?"

He takes another drag from his cigarette and blows smoke out of his mouth like he's extinguishing a candle. We pass a small yellow cottage with a golden retriever at the window who looks as confused as I am.

"I don't know what I'm saying. What makes it so hard is that everything they're telling me is true. We have limited resources, so it's not crazy to say that we shouldn't spend them on finding a girl who all the evidence says ran away. And Saint Agnes is an institution in this community that has done a lot of good, so nobody wants to see it torn down with police investigations. But I can't shake the feeling that everyone is best friends with the headmaster and seems to want to sweep this under the rug. I don't know. All I know is I can't sleep."

The headmaster.

Mackenzie hovers over this investigation like a wraith. I see now how alone Bobby is. He's a good cop trying to find Mia, but he's on an island. He doesn't know who to trust, and the scary part is, neither do I. We take a right at the next street. The fireplace smoke I smelled earlier drifts from a chimney on a sand-colored Tudor house up the road.

"Yeah, I know what you mean. Ever since I started this investigation, I feel like I've been fighting with two hands behind my back. Even Madeline Hemsley—who hired me, for crying out loud—won't give me the full story."

Bobby stops in his tracks. Leaves tumble across the road in front of us.

"What do you mean, Madeline won't give you the full story?"

I debate with myself about how much to trust Bobby. Until now he's been nothing but helpful, but I learned a long time ago that in this business you can't trust anyone. Unfortunately, I have little time to solve this riddle, so I need all the help I can get. Sometimes your only choice is to trust and hope.

"Okay. What I'm telling you is between us, all right? You can't put this in the case file. You can't tell your colleagues."

Bobby raises his right hand, and for the first time I see his hawk nose crinkle and his mouth break into a genuine smile.

"I swear," he says.

I smile back, and for a moment, I forget about Andrew.

"Madeline isn't Mia's godmother. She's Mia's mother."

Bobby immediately starts coughing out smoke.

"What? How?"

He pivots left and right, looking around like he thinks the explanation is going to jump out of a bush.

"She got pregnant when she was young, and it was an embarrassment to the Hemsley family. Apparently, Mackenzie said he would take Mia in at Saint Agnes and keep it secret."

Bobby runs his hand back and forth through his buzz cut, processing what he's just heard. After a few seconds, he grabs both my shoulders and gives them a friendly shake.

"Hazel, you're a genius. This explains so much."

He resumes walking, leaving me behind. I hustle to keep up with him, wondering what exactly about this makes me a genius.

"How does it explain so much?" I ask.

His pace quickens, and his hands dance as he talks. I keep a healthy distance so as not to get stabbed in the face with a lit cigarette.

"When I started the investigation, I did the standard preliminary research into the Hemsley family, since most child abductions are committed by a family member or someone who knew the victim. At first, I didn't think there was much there. The Hemsley family's been in the Lake George area for generations. There's no criminal record, no records of abuse, no family legal or custody disputes of any kind."

"Yeah, rumor has it they made their money in bootlegging to the resorts during Prohibition. But why is that relevant?"

We make another right turn and head back toward the station. An elderly gentleman in a raincoat walks toward us with an amiable-looking bulldog. Bobby gives him a wave but lowers his voice so as not to be heard.

"The Hemsleys have been big donors to the Saint Agnes Children's Home for years. Of course, rich people donate to charities all the time, so I didn't think much of it. But if Mackenzie's holding that secret, he has them over a barrel. He could be extorting money from them."

"I guess that's possible, but I don't see how that helps us

find Mia."

Bobby shoots me a Cheshire cat grin.

"That's why I called you. The other thing I found when I was poking around was that the Hemsley family has a trust set up in Mia's name. I thought that was a little odd when I first found out—setting up a trust for a godchild—but I've seen rich people do weirder things. But, Mia being Madeline's daughter, this makes so much more sense."

"Agreed, but I'm still not following how this helps."

Bobby shakes a finger at me.

"You have zero patience. The other thing I found out is that if Mia dies, then Madeline gets her share of the trust."

Now it's my turn to stop in my tracks. My mind swirls with the possibilities. If Madeline stands to benefit by killing Mia, then she's the primary suspect. But then—

Bobby interrupts my thoughts.

"So, what I'm thinking is that makes Madeline a suspect. But if Madeline killed Mia for the money, why would she hire you and the other investigators she's hired?"

I grab a damp twig off the ground. Having something in my hands helps me think. The two of us keep walking, gears turning. A crazy thought crosses my mind, but if I don't say it, I'll burst.

"Could it be because she killed Mia but hid it too well?"

Bobby screws up his face.

"What do you mean?"

"I mean, picture this: She kills Mia and hides the body. But she hides it too well, so that neither you nor any of the private detectives she's hired have found it. So, now there's no proof that Mia's dead, and she's being written off as just another runaway. As long as she's a runaway, Madeline doesn't get paid."

Bobby stubs out his cigarette on the road and then puts it in his pocket. Better than littering, I guess. He shakes his head as he thinks. He looks at the station up ahead.

"I don't know. That seems like a pretty ballsy move. It's not like Madeline was in the poorhouse before Mia died. And that's her daughter, for God's sake."

"Yeah, a daughter she gave to Thomas Mackenzie the first chance she got. Maybe they're working together?"

Bobby nods and says nothing. We've arrived back at the parking lot in front of the police station. He weaves through the cars and taps his hand on an SUV parked out front, signaling to me that he's headed into the station and back to work. I grab him by the arm. I don't want to let this treasure trove of information slip away. I shoot him the sweetest look I can muster.

"Do you think there's any chance you could make a copy of what you found on Madeline and the Hemsley family?"

He rolls his eyes and bites his lower lip.

"I knew you were going to ask me that."

"Please. I promise this will be my final ask."

It definitely won't be my final ask.

Bobby laughs as if he's thinking what I'm thinking and gestures toward the entrance.

"Why don't you come inside and warm up, and I'll make you a quick copy."

"You're a good man, Bobby Riether."

We walk into the station, and Bobby points me to one of the waiting room chairs. The lackadaisical assistant glances up from her phone and flashes me a dead smile. I wonder how in the world she got a customer service job.

"I'll be back in a minute," says Bobby.

While I sit in the lobby, waiting, I grapple with what I've just heard. Could Madeline Hemsley be a killer? I still can't wrap my mind around it. My neurons fire with the possibilities. Could she have done it alone? No. She would have had to have help on the inside. I don't picture Madeline murdering and then disposing of a dead body herself. She can barely sit on a dirty chair in my kitchen. Was the plan for Mackenzie to help her and the two of them split the money? It's possible, but I can't help thinking that it just doesn't feel right. Madeline is not my favorite person, but her concern for her daughter seemed genuine, and I just don't see her being a killer. And Mackenzie is a seventysomething-year-old man. It's hard to imagine him tromping around, disposing of little girls' bodies. And none of this would explain the other missing girls. There must be something more. The clock in the lobby ticks away, and I'm reminded of Madeline's deadline bearing down on me.

As I continue to ponder the case, my eyes drift around the waiting room. Pictures of cops in the sheriff's department dot the walls. There's the sheriff, who has a big round face, a mustache, and bright-red cheeks, like Santa Claus would look if he shaved the beard. There's Bobby, who looks surprisingly handsome in full uniform. Leave it to me to meet two good-looking men in the same week when I've been roaming through a dating desert for years. When it rains, it pours. My eyes continue along to the pictures of the other cops whom I've never met. But as I scroll, I see a familiar face.

A malevolent face.

Jaw Scar. The man who accosted me in the alley. I'll never forget that jagged scar running from his chin down his neck. I'll never forget that blade pressed against my skin.

He's a cop.

He's working with Bobby.

And right beside him on the wall is a picture of Zombie Eyes.

The realization sucks the air from my chest. I can't breathe. I clutch the chair's armrests. I look around to see if anyone has noticed me panicking, but the sheriff's office continues with business as usual.

I gotta get out of here.

I rise from my seat, and the assistant squints at me.

"I left something in my car. Back in a second," I say to her.

She gives me an appraising look, as though she doesn't believe me, but after a moment returns her attention to her phone.

I exit the station and take a deep breath of the cold air, trying to steady myself, but terror grips me. I break into a sprint to my car. I don't look back. I just keep going. I hop in the driver's seat and slam on the accelerator. The tires screech against the wet tarmac as I fly out of the lot.

I don't know where I'm going, but I can't stay here.

Chapter 27

I point my car toward the lake. There's something about the cool blue water wrapped by rolling hills that seems safe. I drive along East Shore Drive and look out the glass as the storm gathers over the water. My hands clutch the wheel like a vise. I roll down my window for some fresh air, and the crisp northern breeze passes through my nostrils. My heartbeat slows, and my mind clears.

None of it makes sense.

Why are those cops stalking and threatening me? How are they involved in Mia's disappearance, and what do they have to gain? Are they in league with someone in some type of blackmail scheme? Is Bobby a part of it, playing the good cop to their bad cop? And what about Madeline? She stands to gain from Mia's death, but why hire me and all the other private detectives? Just to confirm Mia's death so she can get the money? It seems like an enormous risk to take when you consider that if Mia is dead, someone will probably find her body eventually.

I see a bolt of lightning, and seconds later, thunder rips through the sky. The wind builds, and the lake crests. The walk with Bobby chilled me to the bone, and I feel like this case is doing the same to my spirit. I want nothing more than to go home to Manhattan and open a bottle of wine with Andrew and cozy up on the couch together.

Then I hear Mia's melodious voice in my head, and I'm reminded why I came here.

I think of Mackenzie saying how her disappearance didn't bother him, it disappointed him. Well, it bothers me. From the first day I met him, I've suspected that he held the keys to this puzzle. But every step of the way, I've been thrown a breadcrumb in some other direction. The choir teacher. The security guard. The Dionysus Theater. Madeline. The cops. Each one more confusing than the last. But all of them have one thing in common. They all connect to Mackenzie. He hired Goolsbee and Paver. He has a painting of Dionysus on his wall. He took in Mia when Madeline's mother wanted to give her away, and he seemed to be best buddies with the sheriff at the gala. Is it possible that they're all involved in Mia's disappearance and Mackenzie's just sitting back, the puppet master? Not to mention the fact that Mia's not the only missing girl. There are others. Many others. And Mackenzie has been headmaster the whole time this has been going on.

Normally, I would take more time to investigate the man. Tail him in his daily routine. Talk with known acquaintances. Search his online records. The basic private investigator's tool kit. But there's no time. It's Tuesday, so after today, I only have three more days to find out what happened to Mia. I have to confront him.

I flip a U-turn, and my tires scream as I veer back toward the campus. I roll past town, and all the restaurants are bringing in tables and chairs, and everyone is hustling inside to prepare for the storm. It reminds me of the Old West when there's going to be a gunfight and everyone knows it.

After a few minutes I turn onto Scholar's Way, the road where Neil told me the headmaster and some of the other teachers at Saint Agnes live. Fortunately, it's outside the gates, so I don't have to cut past security. The wind shreds the fall leaves off the trees, whipping them across the street. It's not raining, but a thick fog crawls along the ground. Halloween decor dots the yards: ghosts in trees, jack-o'-lanterns on stoops, headstones on lawns. The historic houses that line the block, which must look so beautiful and quaint on a sunny day, look more like haunted houses now. Each one has a single light on inside, bright enough to lure you in but dark enough to trap you.

I pull up to Mackenzie's house. The blue paint and yellow trim have turned a sickly shade with time. A white porch surrounds the front of the home, and a porch swing creaks back and forth in the wind. Above it hovers a steeple roof and an attic with a dim light in the window. My heart thumps in my chest, and I can feel the sweat pooling through my sweater.

I check the clock on the dashboard. It's 4:00 p.m., but it looks like eight outside. There's a light on in the living room. Mackenzie should be back from his office now. The girls finish their day at three. Reasons why I shouldn't be here, why I should slam this car in reverse, tumble through my mind.

I close my eyes and take a deep breath, searching for a place of calm. Normally, I don't mind confrontation. It goes with the job. But there's something about this man. I don't know whether it's his sheer height or the fact that he's been bossing young women around for decades, but I feel small in his presence. Not just physically small but timid and insecure. I revert to the girl I was in junior high, not the woman I am now. The thought of the horrors of junior high reminds me that maybe life isn't so bad. If I can handle Jocelyn Wheeler and her mean-girl posse, then I should be able to handle Thomas Mackenzie.

I grab my bag and double-check that my Taser is inside and charged and ready to go. The incidents with Gene Strauss and Jaw Scar still stick with me, crawling up my spine at unexpected moments. Violence makes an imprint.

I exit the car, and as if God is firing one last warning shot, lightning cracks and the rain starts. I can hear it coming from behind me like an oncoming herd. Then it's here, pattering against my head and jacket. I jog up Mackenzie's front steps and pause under the porch overhang. There's a full-on downpour now. I swivel and look into the house. Mackenzie is sitting in an overstuffed leather chair, reading a book. A gold glass holder sits beside him, cradling a crystal glass of what looks like scotch with an oversize ice cube. If you didn't know any better, you'd think he was just a nice grandpa relaxing after a hard day.

I ring the doorbell and remind myself that looks can be deceiving.

Mackenzie rises from his seat, looking startled, and heads toward the door. He opens it with a cheery grin that drops into a frown upon seeing me.

"Ms. Cho, what a pleasant surprise," he says, his lips pursing in disappointment. He has to lean forward to speak to me.

I try to kill him with kindness.

"Sorry to bother you, Dr. Mackenzie, but I have a few more questions I need to ask you. I know from my previous phone calls you don't want to speak to me anymore, but I was in the neighborhood and thought you might give me fifteen minutes in person."

I flash him my most innocent, pleading smile.

He places a hand in the pocket of his army green cardigan, takes a deep breath, and sighs.

"In the neighborhood, were you? From Manhattan?"

"That's right."

He looks over my head out at the rain, and I can see the wheels turning in his mind. Would God send him to hell if he sends this tiny woman back out into the rain? He decides he would.

"All right, Ms. Cho, let's get you out of this storm."

He opens the door for me and ushers me into his home, which has a distinctly masculine aroma of leather, smoke, and scotch. Wood burns and crackles in the fireplace. The living room is beautiful and filled with light. But the rest of the house lurks in darkness. My dad's voice echoes in my mind: *It's what we can't see that scares us.*

Mackenzie crosses the mustard-and-crimson rug anchoring the room, resumes his seat, and gestures for me to sit down. The rich harmonies of Chopin drift through the room. I'm parched from all the panic sweating I've been doing today, so I notice when he doesn't offer me anything to drink. He wants me out of here. That's something you get used to as a private investigator. Most of the people you talk to want you to leave as soon as possible.

I sit down on an ancient red velvet chair that feels like it might collapse under my weight. To my right sits an elegant marble chessboard with hand-carved jade pieces. The place recalls another era. An antique timepiece on the mantel ticks behind me as if to remind me I'm on the clock.

Mackenzie crosses one long leg over the other and splays

out his giant hand to me.

"You said you had some questions for me?"

I grab my notebook and pen out of my purse and press them firmly against my lap so he can't see my hands are shaking.

"Do you remember how Mia ended up at Saint Agnes?"

His jaw sets, and he puts one hand over the other in his lap.

"I'm sure I don't."

I know he's lying, but the certainty with which he embroiders his lies is a marvel.

"What do you mean?"

"I mean I've had thousands of girls in my charge over the years, and I'm an old man and can't be expected to remember how every one of them came to Saint Agnes."

"Hmm, that's interesting, because Madeline does."

Mackenzie uncrosses one leg and crosses the other.

"Is that so?"

"It is so. According to her, Mia is her daughter, and when the family couldn't stand the 'scandal' of having a Black daughter out of wedlock, you offered to take her in at Saint Agnes."

Mackenzie smiles, and his yellow, crooked teeth jut out like fangs. He takes a slow sip of his scotch, then purses his lips.

"It appears you have wrong-footed me, Ms. Cho."

I feel my voice rising in my throat. I can't hide my exasperation at his coyness.

"I'm not trying to wrong-foot you, Dr. Mackenzie. I'm just trying to find out what happened to Mia."

He takes another sip of scotch and clinks the glass with his fingernails. Clink. Clink. Clink. He clears his throat in a violent ahem.

"Well, I guess since Madeline has told you, I can drop the charade. Yes, Lake George is a close community, so I had known the Hemsleys for years when Madeline became pregnant. Madeline's mother was...not fond of Black folks. When she found out that the father was Black, she reached out to me to ask what I could do. Obviously, I was appalled that the family would turn their back on a child just because of their skin color. I tried to convince her of the error of her ways, but some people are just too far gone. When she refused to let Madeline keep the child, I was furious. But I also knew that no one would care for little Mia like we would at Saint Agnes, so I offered to take her in. She accepted and asked that I keep it under the strictest confidence."

"Was there any monetary compensation offered for this favor you were doing the Hemsleys?"

Mackenzie's eyes pinch, and he sits upright in his chair.

"What do you mean by that?"

"I mean after Saint Agnes took Mia in, the family made substantial donations to your endowment. When I was touring the campus, I noticed they were in your platinum circle of donors."

Mackenzie scoffs and takes another sip of scotch. His lips sour, but I can't tell if it's from the scotch or the conversation. The clock continues. Tick-tock. Tick-tock.

"Please spare me the accusations. While it's true that the Hemsleys were grateful and have been very generous over the years, there was no quid pro quo. Ms. Cho, you forget that this is what we do at Saint Agnes. This is our mission."

I've had it with his holier-than-thou bullshit. I lean forward to shrink the space between us. I need to make him uncomfortable. This is Interrogation 101.

"Is part of your mission losing little girls?"

"I beg your pardon?"

"Because according to my calculations, over fifty girls have gone missing since you took over as headmaster, and you don't seem to care."

Mackenzie stands up from his chair, leaning the full power of his treelike frame over me. I swear he could blot out the sun. He points a bony finger in my face. He is not intimidated; he intimidates.

"What exactly are you accusing me of?"

"You tell me. You lied about Mia. You lied about Madeline. Girls have gone missing. The police won't investigate. How do you explain that?"

"The police? What do they have to do with this?"

"Oh please, don't play dumb. I saw you backslapping with the sheriff at the gala. And a few days later, a couple of his men assaulted me in an alley."

Mackenzie's mouth drops open, and his forehead creases.

"What? Who assaulted you?"

"Two officers."

A vein rises in his forehead, and the scotch glass shakes in his hand.

"From the sheriff's department?"

"Yeah, that's right."

"You must be mistaken."

I rise from my chair and pull down the collar of my coat to show him the mark from the blade. I feel my voice rising to a shriek.

"I'm not mistaken. This is where he held a fucking knife to my neck. Now why don't you stop protecting people and help me?"

A flush bursts through his face, and his pale-blue eyes water with hurt and rage. He stomps out of the room into the hallway and beckons me.

"Follow me," he says. I take a few cautious steps and watch as he opens the door to what looks like a basement stairwell.

I hear thunder rumble overhead and notice the light fading outside. The house seems to get lonelier.

"Why?"

"You said you wanted to know who I'm protecting. They're down here."

Chapter 28

Y ou know that moment when you're watching a horror movie and you see the woman descending into a dark basement and you're like, "You're such an idiot. Don't go down there"?

Well, this is one of those moments.

And I am that idiot.

I know I shouldn't follow Mackenzie down the creaky wooden steps into the bowels of this ancient house. But the investigator in me can't resist the pull of finally discovering Mia's fate. Plus, I reassure myself, he's just an old man. I've got a Taser in my bag and a few self-defense moves up my sleeve. I wonder if it's a thought that other women have had before. Unease coils within me as I take the first step down.

Mackenzie opens the door wider, and as if my dread couldn't get any worse, the hinges let out a long, mournful creak, telling me *Don't even think about it.* Fortunately, he goes down the steps first, which makes me feel a little better. His shadowed form limps downward, the meager light barely illuminating the stairs. I pause, imagining one of his cronies lurking nearby to lock me in this tomb. But it appears we're alone, for better or worse.

As I descend, mildewed air presses down, that unique combination of mold, dust, and age that inhabits basements in old houses like this. A lone light bulb hanging from a string hovers over the center of the room. Dripping water echoes off the concrete walls, probably from the deluge outside. But to me it sounds like the steady ticking of a clock, reminding me that time is running out to find Mia.

Drip.

Drip.

Drip.

When he reaches the bottom of the steps, Mackenzie shuffles into the center of the room. I emerge from the last step and immediately notice the walls.

They're covered in photographs of girls.

Hundreds—no, thousands—of girls pinned up in neat rows.

Bright, beaming smiles masking uncertain fates.

My blood turns to ice. Every instinct screams at me to bolt back up those stairs. But morbid curiosity roots me in place. I can't look away from this disturbing shrine.

Mackenzie gestures proudly to the photo collage. "Every girl who has attended Saint Agnes during my tenure," he announces, having to hunch under the oppressively low ceiling. "Quite a collection, wouldn't you say?"

I take another look at the pictures. They're class photos, moving chronologically from left to right. You can tell by the resolution and dated hairstyles roughly when the photographer took them. I look at the smiling faces of all these girls and wonder how many of them shared Mia's fate. The thought slithers inside me. I return my attention to Mackenzie. His icy eyes carry a mixture of pride and pain.

"Why are you showing me this?" I ask.

He purses his lips, and his shoulders slump.

"Because I want you to know that this is more than a job to me, Ms. Cho. This is my life. This is every girl that has been entrusted to me at Saint Agnes. Every one of these young women is important to me. I lost my wife to cancer twenty years ago, and ever since she died, I've given everything I've had to building up this institution and the women in it in her honor. And I can't have you tearing down everything we've built."

He takes a few steps closer to me, and I can see the agony etched into his features. I backpedal until my calves hit the first step out of the basement.

"I'm not trying to tear down what you've built. I'm trying to find out what happened to Mia and all the other girls that have gone missing."

Mackenzie takes another stride toward me and grabs my shoulders with his long bony hands, his stale, scotch-laced breath hot on my face. A phone rings upstairs, but he makes no move to answer it.

I reach for the Taser in my bag, but I stop when I hear what he says next.

"You don't think I want to find out what happened to Mia? You don't think I want to find out what happened to the other girls? Who do you think put up those gates? Who do you think put in the state-of-the-art security system that they assured me would keep this from happening again? Why do you think I was lobbying the sheriff at the gala? But no matter what I do, they keep disappearing."

As he speaks, he shakes my shoulders as though he could physically shake me loose of my convictions. Mackenzie sees the terror in my eyes, looks at his hands clutching my shoulders, and realizes what he's doing.

He takes a step back and raises his hands, catching himself.

"Forgive me, Ms. Cho. I...I...don't know what came over me."

I take a step back up the stairs to get some more air space between the two of us and to give myself a shot at escape.

"If you want to find Mia and these girls so badly, then why are you covering it up? Why the lies?"

Mackenzie senses my fear and takes another step back. His face twists in anguish while he searches for what to say.

"Because this place is me. These girls. This is my legacy. And I refuse to be remembered as the headmaster who allowed girls to disappear."

Tears well in his eyes, and I glimpse the fragility in the man.

"Dr. Mackenzie, if you help me find Mia, I will make sure that you're remembered as the headmaster who not only educated hundreds of underprivileged girls but also saved the ones who ran away."

I take a step back down the stairs and put my left hand on his shoulder but grip the Taser as a precaution. Mackenzie wipes the tears from his eyes. I search his face. I'm still not sure he doesn't have something to do with this, but I'm damn sure he's not the mastermind. There's too much confusion, too much pain.

"But how, Ms. Cho? Think how many people have investigated this and come back with nothing."

"Yeah, but they weren't me."

I flash him a grin to lighten the mood. The corners of his mouth quirk up. I was wondering if he even could smile. The grin drops as quickly as it rose.

"Be serious, my dear. What makes you think you can find Mia?"

I step away from him and survey the pictures of girls on the wall. I spot Olivia Blankenship. I'd recognize her platinum blonde hair anywhere. I remember what Sarah Blankenship told me, and I turn to him.

"Dr. Mackenzie, what can you tell me about the Dionysus Theater?"

His forehead creases.

"The Dionysus Theater? The one in Greece?"

"No, the one in the United States."

"I've never heard of it. Why do you ask?"

Mackenzie shrugs his shoulders. I can't tell if it's sincere. I decide to bluff, my eyes boring into him.

"Oh, c'mon, I know you know what it is."

He steps back and fires me a stern headmaster glare.

"Ms. Cho, I can't fathom what you're talking about."

"You're telling me you have a painting of Dionysus in the center of your office and you don't know what the Dionysus Theater is?"

Mackenzie chuckles to himself, and for a second I think he's going to confess.

"I know who Dionysus is. I just don't know what the Dionysus Theater is. Not that it matters, but that's not even my painting. Mr. Goolsbee gave it to me as a twentieth anniversary present of the two of us working together. I'd say you should talk to him about it, but he called out sick today."

The news sends my mind spinning, sorting through the possibilities.

Goolsbee.

The girls started vanishing when he came here, not when Mackenzie did.

Chapter 29

I bust out of Mackenzie's house and sprint through the downpour to my car. The rain rolls down in sheets, and I can see my breath as I run. After our conversation, I'm inclined to think Mackenzie's innocent, but I don't feel the need to tempt fate. Not after seeing that basement.

I hook a right at the end of Scholar's Way and head toward the campus. I have to find Gregory Goolsbee. That painting can't be a coincidence. My mind flashes back to my interview with him in the choir room. He was going to tell me something. He wanted to tell me something.

I pull up to the wrought iron gates of Saint Agnes, which appear even more menacing in the storm. Neil Paver stands in the guard shack, talking on the phone, a look of concern plastered to his face. When he sees me he forces a dead-eyed plastic smile. I roll down my window a sliver so that I can hear him but keep the rain out. He puts the phone down.

"Ms. Hazel, I didn't expect to see you here."

"Hi, Neil. Yeah, I was in the neighborhood, and I thought I'd stop by to say hello."

"That's awfully kind of you. What can I do for you?"

I notice that he's not opening the gates.

"I was actually hoping to speak to Mr. Goolsbee. Is he

available?"

Neil grimaces and looks to the ground. He scratches his head and shoots me a sheepish look.

"I'm sorry to be the one to tell you this, ma—Ms. Hazel, but Mr. Goolsbee is no longer with us."

I roll down my window all the way, thinking I must have misheard.

"Did you say he's no longer with us? Like he left town?"

He gives a crooked smile.

"No, ma'am. He's dead."

My mouth drops open. Goolsbee dead? It can't be a coincidence.

"When?"

His tongue slides across his cracked cherry-red lips.

"They just found him. Apparently he was feeling under the weather today, so one of the faculty members went to check on him and found him dead. I was just calling Dr. Mackenzie, but he won't answer his phone. Everybody at Saint Agnes is real broke up about it."

"Do you know how Goolsbee died?"

"I'm pretty sure it's a suicide."

"How do you know?"

"He slit his wrists, ma'am."

I search Neil's face. His cheeks and lips sit in a frown, but his eyes remain frozen. A feeling of dread crawls through me. I scan my rearview mirror, preparing to slam it in reverse.

"Did he leave a note?"

"No, ma'am."

Only a quarter of suicides leave a note, so that's not surprising, but it's yet another loose end in a case that's fraying by the day.

Neil takes a step outside the guard shack and places his hand on the roof of my car. Rain patters against his head, but he doesn't acknowledge it.

"The cops are on their way. My golf cart's in the shop, but if you let me hop in there with you and give me a ride, I can take you inside and we can wait together until they get here."

Something in the way he says it stands the hairs on my neck on end. His yellow skin molds into a smile, but the eyes stay locked on me. I have no desire to see the cops, and it almost seems like Neil knows it.

I shift the Tesla's gears into reverse but don't move.

"Thanks, Neil, but I can't stay. I just thought I might catch Mr. Goolsbee, but I need to head back to the city. Please pass along my condolences to everyone."

He leans in closer and runs his hand through his overly gelled hair.

"Ah, that's right. I keep forgetting you live in the city. What part again?"

"Manhattan," I say, not wanting to give him any specifics.

"That's too much city for me. Here, let me open the gate for you so you can turn around."

"No need. I'll just back out." I glimpse irritation cross his face, but then it vanishes under the plastic smile.

"Okay. Suit yourself. Good to see you again, Ms. Hazel. I wish it were under better circumstances."

"Yeah, me too. Take care."

I slam on the gas and reverse into the road. A horn blares as a car careens around me. I was so focused on Neil, I almost got myself T-boned. I pause for a moment to get my bearings, then speed down the road. I need to get as much separation between myself and Neil Paver as humanly possible.

I head back to the city. For the first five minutes, I barely notice where I'm going. I just stare into oblivion, trying to absorb everything I've seen and heard in the last few hours. Neil's words ring in my ears: *Goolsbee's dead...took his own life.* But why? Was he the one behind the missing girls, and the guilt or fear of being caught finally caught up with him? Did he know too much and take his life before someone could take it from him? Or did someone kill him and make it look like a suicide?

What Mackenzie said about Goolsbee rattled me. His death shakes me even harder. I need to know what Bobby and the police find in Goolsbee's apartment. The problem is, the cops are involved in all of this somehow, and I don't know if Bobby's in on it. My instincts tell me no. From the day I met him, Bobby has been pursuing this case diligently and responsibly, given the resources he's been provided. And I'm guessing the sheriff doesn't want to give him many resources because he doesn't actually want this case solved. I ping-pong the scenarios back and forth in my mind until I realize there's only one way to find out. I don't have a choice. I have only four days left to solve this case, so if Bobby's in on it, in four days it won't matter anyway.

I tap the touch screen to call him as I merge onto Route 9. Rain pelts my windshield, but the Tesla's windshield wiper sensors don't seem to be aware. While Bobby's phone rings, I futz with the wiper settings until they're finally firing at full throttle. Still, the rain is winning the battle. It's going to be a white-knuckle ride home.

"I thought I was going to have to start investigating another runaway," says Bobby as he answers the phone.

I smile to myself. The man plays the perfect cop. Everything about him is earnest and true and makes you feel safe. I just hope it's not an act.

"Yeah, I'm sorry I ran out like that."

"Are you okay?"

"I'm fine. Is this phone number your personal number or a work line?"

"It's my personal. Why? Are you about to tell me something juicy?"

I can feel his excitement through the phone. He's a crime junkie, just like me.

"Yeah, but you're not going to want to hear it."

"Oh, boy."

Better to just get it over with.

"I think there are cops in the sheriff's office that are involved with this."

I'm expecting Bobby to fly off the handle and protect his brothers and the institution, but he does the opposite. He just sighs.

"Bobby, did you hear me?"

His raspy voice carries a few extra cracks as he speaks.

"Yeah, I heard you. Truthfully, I've been suspecting the same thing. I just didn't want to believe it. What makes you say that?"

I swallow hard. The memory of the alley and the knife to my throat curdles in my stomach. I can barely get it out.

"A few nights ago, I was walking home, and two men threatened me with a knife and told me to drop the case."

"Oh my God. Hazel, I'm so sorry. Are you okay?"

I note his reaction. His first instinct is to see if I'm okay. If he's faking, it's Oscar time.

"Yeah, I'm fine."

"But I don't understand. What does that have to do with the sheriff's department?"

I feel my chest tighten as the memory crystallizes in my mind.

"One of the two men had a long scar on his neck. The other had gray-blue eyes like a zombie. The same scar and the same blue eyes I saw in the pictures of two officers in your lobby."

Bobby's voice drops an octave. His frustration vibrates through the phone.

"That would be DeGrom and Hanley. I'll kill 'em. What did they say to you?"

"They told me to stop investigating the Dionysus Theater."

"What's that?"

"It's a long story I'll tell you about later, but in the meantime, you can't say anything to them about this. I just needed you to know."

"Okay. I won't say anything for now. Thanks for telling me, because this tracks with what I've been seeing. DeGrom and Hanley are the detectives I told you about who were encouraging me to move on to other cases."

"Makes sense."

"Yeah, but they couldn't have done these abductions alone. Believe me. They're dumber than a box of rocks. They would need someone on the inside of Saint Agnes. Plus, girls have been going missing for decades. They haven't been on the force that long."

"I agree. They're definitely not pulling the strings, but they're involved somehow. My guess is that they're the hired muscle."

"Who do you think is pulling the strings?"

I squint to search for the lane lines in front of me.

"I don't know, but they just found Gregory Goolsbee dead."

"The choir teacher?"

"Yeah. Apparently some of your colleagues are on the way. Interesting that you didn't get the call. I need you to find out what, if anything, Goolsbee left behind."

"Got it."

"And can you discreetly keep an eye on DeGrom and Hanley to see if they lead us anywhere, and make sure they don't kill me?"

Bobby gives a sad chuckle. "No problem. They're out right now, probably headed to Saint Agnes, but I'll bird-dog them once they get back."

"Thanks, Bobby. Let's talk tomorrow."

"Sounds good. Be safe."

I hang up the call and look out the window. Blurry, rain-soaked spruces line the highway like soldiers. The downpour is growing now, so it's difficult to see the car in front of me. I take my foot off the accelerator, throw on my hazards, and check my rearview to make sure the people following me get the message.

And that's when I notice it.

The SUV from the police station parking lot. The forest green Suburban Bobby tapped when he went inside.

Two cars back.

It's got to be DeGrom and Hanley.

They're following me.

My phone rings, and without thinking about it, I hit the green button, hoping it's Bobby.

"Hello."

But it's not Bobby, just ominous, heavy breathing on the other end.

In and out.

In and out.

Fear paralyzes me, and for a moment I'm thrown back to law school. To where my life changed forever.

But this isn't law school.

This is now.

And I'm different now.

I flip off the hazards, slam on the accelerator, and swerve into the opposing lane of the two-lane highway, ripping past the car in front of me. I look over at the man in the car I'm passing, who looks at me like I'm a psychopath for doing that move in this weather. I don't blame him.

I peer in my rearview, and the green Suburban is passing as well, but more slowly. A Suburban can't keep up with a Tesla. I continue to push the speed, water spraying in every direction, but the rain is so thick I can't see far enough ahead.

The good news is, neither can they.

I've driven this road enough to know that in about three hundred yards, there's a hairpin turn that comes out of nowhere. One minuscule sign gives you warning, but if you're not looking or there happens to be a torrential downpour, you can miss it.

I only hope that they miss it. God only knows who else is coming with them.

Two hundred yards.

I accelerate even more to put distance between us and to force them to speed up. The tires of my car hydroplane on the slick surface. Sweat beads in my palms as I grip the wheel tighter and tighter. I can almost hear my heartbeat.

One hundred yards.

I look behind me. They're gaining. They must be going at

least a hundred. I turn the car lights off. They might catch my brake lights, but in this rain, they might miss them. And by then it will be too late.

Fifty yards.

I hit the brakes and slam the wheel to the right. I can feel the tires sliding on the slick surface and thrusting me off the road toward the ditch.

I'm not going to make it.

At the last second, the tire tread catches the road, and the car lunges forward through the turn and onto the straightaway.

I stare into the rearview.

It's working.

They're coming on too fast.

As they roar around the turn, I see them try to spin the vehicle back on the road, but it's too late. I hear the vicious squeal of tires and watch as the Suburban slides off the asphalt and into a ditch. The sound of metal against rock thunders through the valley as the Suburban fades into the rain in my rearview.

I keep driving like nothing happened, wiping the fog of panicked breath from the windshield.

Chapter 30

When I get back to Manhattan, I'm completely spent. It's as though my mind and body have run through their supply of fear, anxiety, and adrenaline and now just plod forward. After twenty minutes searching for a parking spot, I find one on Mulberry Street a couple blocks down from my apartment.

I get out of the car into the damp night air. The rain has stopped, leaving the streets quiet except for the occasional swoosh of a passing car. I know that those two cops couldn't possibly still be following me after tumbling into that ravine. Even so, I feel like any moment someone is going to jump out from behind a corner and attack me. Fear is like a cancer—it starts with an actual moment but then multiplies and gains hold of you until it's bending your experience of everything around you.

I throw my bag over my shoulder and jog down the slick street toward my apartment, my boots splashing in the puddles. The earthy smell of rain and worms rising off the streets somehow settles me. I get to my building door and look around cautiously. The street is empty except for a man walking his dog under the yellow glow of the streetlights.

I'm home.

I'm safe.

For now.

Or so I think, until I throw open the apartment door and see what's on Kenny's computer screen.

Kenny is sitting in our '80s-style BarcaLounger with a laptop perched on his thighs. But instead of his typical police study guide or video game on the screen, all I see is a picture of Mia. Her crinkled brown hair and dimpled smile are unmistakable.

Kenny flinches, minimizes the window on his computer, and turns to me, his cheeks reddening. His thin black eyebrows rise in surprise.

I throw my bag down on the hardwood floor with a thud, like a mom who's come home from work to find her son ignoring his homework. I know it's probably something harmless, but I don't need this right now. My apartment is supposed to be a refuge from all the shady characters I deal with daily. I don't need one sleeping five feet away from me.

"Kenny, why do you have a picture of Mia on your laptop?" I demand, my voice sharp.

Kenny pivots the BarcaLounger to face me but keeps his eyes glued to the floor.

"No reason," he mumbles.

"What do you mean, 'no reason'? You're freaking me out a little." My hands stiffen at my sides.

"Sorry, Hazel. I was just doing some research. I thought I might help you with the case."

His explanation both calms me and infuriates me further. I'm glad that Kenny isn't some creep looking at pictures of little girls, but I'm annoyed that he's meddling in my investigation without asking.

"Kenny, when are you going to get it? I don't need your help.

I've got this. You're not even a real cop yet. Spend five years on the force, then call me."

Kenny's eyes roll back down to stare holes in the floor. I see his hands clench tighter into white-knuckled fists. For a second, I wonder if he's going to come at me. But then I remind myself: This is Kenny, after all. Harmless, kind Kenny.

"You know, Hazel, you're always underestimating me. Someday I'll show you."

He sits back down and resumes working on his computer.

I'm hungry—no, scratch that—I'm hangry after the day I've had, so I don't even dignify Kenny's comment with a response. I spot a red-and-white Bleecker Street Pizza box sitting on the counter and make a beeline for it. With each step, I pray he hasn't eaten all of it. Mercifully, two big slices remain inside. The smell of warm cheese, tangy tomatoes, and oregano soothes my foul mood. I take a couple of big, satisfying bites and let him stew in his guilt while I chew.

After I polish off the first slice, I turn back to Kenny, who looks like a scolded puppy still slouched in the lounger. I tear off one more giant chunk, packing my cheek full, and mumble through the wad of dough, "I'm sorry, Kenny. That wasn't fair to you. I'm the one who asked you to help in this investigation. I've just had one hell of a day."

"What happened?" Kenny asks, leaning forward, desperate to get back on my good side.

"Oh, nothing much," I say flippantly. "The headmaster of Saint Agnes lured me into his creepy basement, one of my prime suspects killed himself, and then a couple of crooked Lake George cops tried to run me off the road on my drive home. Just another day in the life, right?"

Kenny's eyes widen to the size of saucers, and he jumps up

from the chair. He shuffles over and awkwardly puts a hand on my arm.

"Geez, I'm so sorry, Hazel. That sounds awful."

This small show of human kindness melts away the last of my anger. My eyes water, and I quickly spin back around and look into the fridge to hide it.

"Thanks, Kenny. I'll be okay." I find a water bottle and then grab the last slice of lukewarm pizza and plop down on the sagging couch, pasting a smile on my face. Time to change the subject before I have a full meltdown.

Kenny returns to his chair, regarding me carefully.

"So, what exactly did you find in your, uh, research?" I ask between bites of congealing cheese.

The corners of Kenny's mouth turn up slightly. "Oh, nothing really."

I prod him again. "Come on, tell me! I promise I won't get mad this time."

Kenny looks left, then right, as if debating whether to divulge his findings. I lock my tired eyes on his until he folds with a sigh.

"Okay, fine. But you have to promise you won't get pissed off again."

"I promise," I reply, drawing a cross over my heart for emphasis.

Kenny takes a deep breath. "I think Andrew's dad, Preston, might be involved in these abductions somehow."

I nearly choke on my pizza. So much for not getting pissed off. I force it down my throat and set the half-eaten slice down.

"You've got to be kidding?" My voice comes out as more of a shriek than I intend.

"Just hear me out," Kenny says, holding up his hands to

calm me. He lays out his research connecting the uptick in donations from the DuPonts to the time frame when girls started disappearing. By the end, I'm practically shaking. Andrew is my one escape from this godforsaken case. I refuse to believe his family has anything to do with this.

"That evidence is circumstantial at best," I counter, standing up to throw the remains of my dinner in the trash. My appetite evaporated the second Kenny mentioned Andrew's father. "I'm sure if we looked at any wealthy donor to any nonprofit, we could find a coincidence like that."

Kenny stands, too, laptop clutched to his chest like a shield. "Yeah, but don't you at least think it's worth investigating? I know he's your boyfriend, but—"

I cut him off. "Don't go there, Kenny. He's not my—this isn't about Andrew. It's about you sticking your nose where it doesn't belong."

Kenny's entire face goes scarlet. "Hey, I'm just trying to help!" he protests. But I'm already brushing past him toward my room, done with this conversation.

I make it two steps before Kenny calls out "Wait! Can I at least give you something before you go?"

I stop short and turn halfway back. "Give me something?"

"Yeah, just...come here. It's in my room." He shuffles into his bedroom.

With a resigned sigh, I follow.

Kenny stands next to his nightstand, where a large black leather case sits. He unclasps it and opens the lid. The hairs stand up on my neck when I see the contents—row after row of hunting knives, each lovingly nestled into its own slot. His collection has multiplied since the last time I saw it. Kenny's rapidly transitioning from collector to compulsive.

I take an involuntary step back. "Kenny, what the hell?"

Oblivious to my horror, Kenny extracts a switchblade and hands it to me gingerly. "It's hazel wood," he explains with a lopsided grin. "You get it? Hazel, wood. I thought it would be good for you to have some protection beyond the Taser. I worry about you with everything that's going on."

My hand trembles as I take the weapon. Everything about this feels wrong. Between the knife collection and his obsession with me, I'm questioning if I really know the person I've been living with at all.

"Um, thanks," I manage weakly, already backing toward the door. "I'm really beat, so I'm just gonna crash."

"Sure, get some rest," Kenny says. "Sleep well, Hazel."

I close the door firmly between us and lean against it, letting out a shaky breath. Is everyone around me insane? Between the headmaster's lair, the cops trying to kill me, and now my unhinged roommate, I feel like I'm surrounded by psychos.

I turn the lock on my bedroom door.

Exhaustion weighs on me, but I take a minute to shove the knife under my mattress for now. I'll figure out what to do about it, and Kenny, tomorrow. Right now, I just need to sleep.

I queue up the recording of Mia singing "Time after Time" on my phone, letting her sweet, innocent voice wash over me. It transports me to simpler times, before my life became a maze of monsters I can't escape. Her lyrics blur together as I finally drift off into a fitful sleep.

Chapter 31

Three days left

I spend my Wednesday doing the boring part of detective work. The work you never see in movies. I talk with Sonia, who informs me that the police — surprise, surprise — didn't find anything of note in Goolsbee's apartment. No suicide note. No evidence of foul play. If I'm going to discover Goolsbee's role in all this, I'm going to find it through the side door. Someone else knows. The question is, Who?

I compile everything I've learned about Goolsbee, Thomas Mackenzie, Madeline Hemsley, the staff at Saint Agnes, the crooked cops, and even Preston DuPont into my software. I have profiles on every one of them, and none of them is flattering. It's gotten to where just having an association with Saint Agnes is a stain on your reputation. Guilt by association. But I've run background checks on every one of them, and I've mapped their whereabouts the night Mia went missing. They're all clean. I even ran a background check on Andrew while I was at it. He doesn't even have a speeding ticket. Not that it matters. Girls have been going missing from Saint Agnes almost as long as Andrew's been alive.

I have dinner with him tonight. Normally, I would be excited, but now I'm filled with dread. I have to ask him about his father, but I'm not sure how to do it without offending him. I'm tempted to just let it drop, but Kenny made a compelling case.

I need to know.

In my years of being a private investigator, I've learned ways to ask questions without the person knowing I'm asking them, but I don't want to do that to Andrew. I like him too much. My mom once told me that a relationship built on a lie is destined to crumble, and that's one thing we both agree on. Plus, I'm afraid Andrew will see through me and then think that I'm just using him to get information.

When I arrive at the Polo Bar in midtown, there's an officious man with a clipboard out front who looks like he's auditioning for a Ralph Lauren runway show. He wears khaki pants and a navy blue wool blazer with an indecipherable crest. I'm wearing a black turtleneck sweaterdress that, combined with my black hair and black eyeliner, makes me look like a mysterious assassin—or so I'd like to think. He looks me up and down with a judgmental eye, but the second I drop Andrew's name, his face brightens and he ushers me into the restaurant. Inside, the dim lighting casts soft shadows on the caramel-colored leather booths. I scan the room, taking in the beautiful people laughing and sipping wine as if they belong here—unlike me. My fingers fidget with the hem of my dress.

Andrew throws me a gentle wave, his captivating smile lighting up the room. He's wearing a pink gingham shirt and gray worsted sport coat. He looks perfectly at ease in this place, like he's in his living room. Like I would feel at a good Korean barbecue. I push aside my hesitation and walk toward him.

"You look absolutely stunning," he says, his ocean-blue

eyes locked onto mine. Stunning? I don't get that a lot. Cute. Spunky. Quirky. Irreverent. Pain in the ass. Those are more typical Hazel words. My cheeks flush at the compliment, but then I remember there's more to this dinner than just a date.

"Thanks. You don't look so bad yourself," I joke, trying to ease the tension that cinches in my gut. He gives me a big hug, and his chest presses against mine, and I'm reminded of the power underneath the dress shirt. It makes me want to do that thing where I just rip the shirt open and buttons fly everywhere. I've never done it, but it always seemed like it would be a cool move.

I sit down, and we exchange small talk and polite laughs, our eyes locked on each other. A part of me wants to lose myself in this world, where money is no object and my Prince Charming flatters me with gifts and luxurious dates, but another part— the private detective inside me—won't let go of the nagging question about his father's donations to Saint Agnes.

I gaze around the room at the customers and realize that we're probably the youngest ones in the place.

"So, were you ever a little kid? Or did you just come to the Polo Bar in a blazer at age five and down a bowl of Frosted Flakes?" I say, cutting through the din of clinking glasses and laughter that fills the room. I need to know more about him, about his family, even if it's just the surface stuff for now.

He raises his eyebrows and adopts a mock hurt face. "Of course I was a little kid. In Lake George, I was a very typical little kid, swimming in the lake and canoeing with my mom. I was really into baseball. I used to have entire imaginary nine-inning games in my backyard with just myself and a Wiffle-ball bat during the summer. I drank a lot of Squirt soda. Do they even make that anymore? My father was always busy with work, so I spent most of my time with my mother." His eyes darken for a moment, and I can see a hint of pain hidden behind his charming smile. He pauses.

I can't help but feel a pang of sympathy for him. Losing a parent would be devastating, but losing one to suicide must be unbearable. I admire how well he seems to have processed the pain.

"It was a tough time, but my father and I had each other, you know?"

"Yeah, thank God for that. When I was touring Saint Agnes, my heart just broke for all those orphan girls. I can't imagine if I lost both my parents. Your mom must have been young. If you don't mind me asking, how did she commit suicide?"

Andrew's eyes crinkle, and small crow's-feet gather around the edges.

"I don't mind you asking. The more I talk about it, the less it hurts. It was a complete surprise. She took a ton of pills, and my father found her in their bed."

I nod along empathetically. I feel for Andrew, but his mother's death only adds to my concern surrounding his father's involvement with Saint Agnes and the missing girls.

The waiter brings us our dinner, and Andrew uses it as an excuse to change the subject.

"Enough about my past," he says, pasting on a smile. "How about you? I assume both your parents are among the living?"

"Yeah, they're both alive and well. Still together. My dad plays golf and cards all day, and my mom loves cooking and nagging her daughters."

"What does she nag you about?"

"Ah, nothing major. Just that I should quit being a private investigator and get married and have kids."

"Why would she want you to quit being a private investigator? That's one of the cool things about you. Anybody can do the stupid stuff I do every day. You're doing really interesting work. It's one of the many things that attracted me to you."

Many things, I say to myself. We'll have to dive into that later.

"It's difficult to explain. In the Korean community, the jobs your kids have reflect on your success as a parent. You want your kids to be doctors or lawyers or in finance. Me being a private investigator reflects badly on the family. They think I haven't accomplished anything. And I'm not certain they're wrong."

As I'm saying it, I'm surprised by how much the words sting.

Andrew reaches across the white tablecloth and puts his hand on mine.

"Well, I don't think you could possibly reflect badly on anyone. There's a great quote I read once that says 'To be yourself in a world that is constantly trying to make you something else is the greatest accomplishment.' So, the way I see it, you've accomplished a lot."

I squeeze his hand in mine.

"Thanks, I really appreciate you saying that."

"You have to tell me. What got you into this business? Last time we talked, you said it was a story for another time. Well, this is another time."

He looks at me so innocently and earnestly that the words come out involuntarily.

"I was raped."

For a second, it feels like the restaurant has gone still, but then I realize it's just me and Andrew. I told my boyfriend at the time about it, and he blamed me. I don't think my heart

241

could take it if Andrew did the same. I watch his face, hoping he'll react the right way.

After the longest five seconds of my life, he does.

He slides out of his side of the booth and sits down in mine and gives me a big hug.

"I'm so sorry that happened to you, Hazel."

I say nothing and just bask in his warmth and kindness. He releases me, and I sip some champagne. I slide over in the booth and put one of my legs up so I can face him. Andrew grabs both my hands in his.

"I totally understand if you don't want to talk about it."

"No, it's fine. You're probably right that the more we talk about these things, the easier it is to deal with. It's not much of a story, anyway. I was in law school, and I was out at a bar on Bleecker. We had just finished our final, so my whole law school class was in full celebration mode, including me. I broke the cardinal rule and took a drink from a guy I had just met. I vaguely remember him taking me back to my place in a cab, and the next thing I knew, I woke in my bed naked, and he was gone."

"He roofied you?"

"Yep."

"What did you do then?"

A waiter drops off a basket full of popovers. Without thinking about it, I grab one and throw a chunk down my throat. It helps hold down the pain rising in my stomach.

"First, I told my sister and my mother. They were sympathetic but reminded me I shouldn't have taken a drink from a stranger. As though rape was just the punishment you get for a social faux pas."

"Oh, that's awful."

"Yeah, I lost my two best friends too. They shrugged it off and said that I shouldn't have been drinking so much. Once word got out, everybody in the school looked at me different too. I felt like the woman in *The Scarlet Letter*. The police and prosecutor's office were even worse. They interviewed my classmates to see if they saw the guy I left with but got nothing. Everybody at the bar was pretty blackout. They said that if I didn't know who the guy was, then there was no case."

"That's it? They just dropped the case? And that was it?"

"Yep. I had basically resigned myself to the fact that this guy who raped me was going to get away with it. Until I met Perry."

"Who's Perry?" There's an endearing hint of jealousy in Andrew's question.

"Perry was a private investigator who contracted with the prosecutor's office. He had done a little work on the case and thought everyone gave up too easy. So, in his own spare time, for no money, he tracked down some security footage of the guy and then went around knocking on doors to see if someone recognized him. He found out the guy's name, which then enabled the police to obtain DNA, and the rest is history. He went to prison."

"Perry sounds like a pretty amazing guy."

"He was. He's dead now, but he was quite the character. He had an Afro that was straight out of the seventies and smoked clove cigarettes and had a cackle that would wake the dead. He was from rural Georgia and used to have all these funny southern phrases. I remember he'd let me tag along on some of his cases, and whenever I threw out a theory that didn't have a lot of evidence behind it, he'd say, 'Hazel, that dog won't hunt.'"

Andrew grins.

"And that's why you became a private investigator."

"Exactly. I saw what someone with smarts and perseverance who wasn't a part of the system could do, and I thought I might help someone in the way Perry helped me."

"Like Mia?"

I take a sip of champagne and swallow hard. I'm not sure I will be able to help her.

"Yeah, like Mia."

"I'm so sorry that happened to you, Hazel, but I'm glad you could make something good come out of it. How is your investigation going, anyway?" he asks.

The question catches me off guard after our brief therapy session, but I decide it's time to be honest with him. The candlelight flickers across my face, casting shadows that, I hope, hide my anxiety. "Now that you ask, there's something I've been meaning to discuss with you," I say, my voice barely a whisper. "I was researching Saint Agnes, while doing my normal investigative due diligence, and I noticed your father started donating sizable sums of money to Saint Agnes about twenty-five years ago."

Andrew's forehead bunches in confusion.

"That sounds about right. But I don't understand why that's a big deal."

I raise an eyebrow at him.

"That's about the time that girls started disappearing from Saint Agnes."

I pause for a moment to let my meaning sink in.

Andrew's expression darkens, and for a fleeting second, I see defensiveness flash across his features. But just as quickly, he recomposes himself and gives a chuckle. "Well, I can see why that might be a red flag, but I'm sure it's just a coincidence."

I smile at him so that he doesn't feel like he's being interrogated but say nothing to keep him talking.

He switches back to his original seat, leans back in the supple leather booth, and throws his right arm over the back cushion. He glances over my shoulder at one of the oversize gold-framed paintings of horses hanging from the walls.

"My father's a big softy and, like my great-grandfather, has a passion for charitable causes; always has. My grandfather, on the other hand, was a real penny-pincher who thought charity was a waste of money. He used to say 'The only things you should ever give to a man are a job and a swift kick in the ass.' He was sort of an Uncle Scrooge type."

Andrew laughs to himself at the thought of his grandfather and takes a sip of his martini. "Anyway, about twenty-five years ago, my grandfather passed away, which gave my dad full control of the trust. Which then gave him the ability to increase our family donations substantially. Which he did, and he's been in love with Saint Agnes ever since. I'm sure my grandfather is rolling over in his grave. He was actually in Paris when Mia went missing. You can check the police report. I believe they questioned him."

"Why did they question him?"

"He's on the board at Saint Agnes, and I think they were just trying to get background information. They questioned all the board members."

"Got it. Will you excuse me a moment? I just need to run to the restroom."

"Of course."

I slide out of the booth and make my way to the bathroom. I grab a stall, shut the door, and pull out my phone. I text

Bobby Riether. I hate to do this, but when you're a private investigator, you have to verify everything. Everything.

Hey, did you interview Preston DuPont?

I tap my foot on the floor, waiting for his response. "Please be there," I say to myself. A totally normal thing to hear someone say to themselves in a bathroom stall. Thankfully, Bobby's available.

Hey. Yeah I interviewed him. Why?

Just verifying some information. Was he in Paris the night of Mia's disappearance?

Yeah.

Is that confirmed?

Confirmed.

Anything suspicious in the interview?

Nope.

I put my phone back in my bag. A wave of relief washes over me. Andrew's father being a serial kidnapper would have been a real thorn in our relationship. Obviously, Preston being out of town doesn't mean he couldn't still be involved in this somehow, but it definitely means he didn't take Mia. I make a mental note to strangle Kenny when I get home.

I return to our booth and let out a sigh.

Andrew's looking at the menu, oblivious to my concerns. "Should we order some food?" he says. "I promise, I have nothing to do with the cooking here."

I laugh and reach across the table and grab his hand. "I appreciate you answering my questions. I know it's not the best dinner conversation."

He smiles, waving off my comment. "Please, don't give it another thought. Given the circumstances, I would have done the same thing. You can always ask me anything, Hazel. I'm an open book. We DuPonts may have our faults, but abducting young girls certainly isn't one of them."

I nod, lacing my fingers through his. The lingering doubts that have been plaguing me all day are finally subsiding. I take a sip of my champagne to calm myself down.

"I know that. It's this job, you can never turn it off..." I trail off, shaking my head.

Andrew squeezes my hand. "I know. But I'm glad you talked to me about it. I'm sure I speak for my father when I say we'll do anything we can to help."

"I believe you."

We continue chatting over dinner, the conversation flowing easily now that the elephant in the room has been addressed. I tell Andrew about my love for EDM and '80s music. He tells me about his love of golf, tennis, squash, and other obscure sports rich people play. We tease each other, and I revel in the fact that not only is he handsome but he's funny as well. He knows who he is and is confident enough to laugh at himself. I'm even getting used to people staring as they walk by, unable to take their eyes off him. I can't blame them. I can't take my eyes off him either. Normally, being ignored by others might bother me, but Andrew gives you such full attention that you don't need anyone else's validation. It's like having a permanent spotlight shining on you. With him, I'm the most important person in the world.

As we leave the restaurant, Andrew pulls me into a warm embrace. I want to lose myself in this moment, but I can't ignore the gnawing unease that lingers in the back of my mind.

Mia is still out there somewhere.

Chapter 32

We head back to Andrew's apartment on the Upper East Side. When we arrive, the doorman throws us a cheery greeting, and we head upstairs. The elevator door pops open into Andrew's apartment. I'll never get used to that.

"Make yourself at home," he says with a warm smile, gesturing to the plush sectional sofa. The comfiest sofa in Manhattan. He takes off his jacket and throws it on one of the kitchen stools. He rolls up his sleeves, giving me a view of his tanned, rippled forearms. The scent of sandalwood fills my nostrils as I make my way across the room. His coffee table overflows with books, mostly biographies of captains of industry, like Vanderbilt, Rockefeller, and Carnegie. I wonder how often Andrew thinks about the Roman empire.

I grab a book about Rockefeller called *Titan* before I collapse onto the soft cushions. I've never been a big biography fan. As I flip through the pages, I sneak glances at Andrew. He pours us both glasses of red wine, his movements fluid and confident. I aspire to be that cool. He hands me a glass and sits down beside me, close enough that our thighs brush together. I feel a tingle run up my leg. I'm in trouble.

We sip our wine in silence for a moment. We've covered a

lot of ground tonight: my history, his family, death, violence. I think both of us just want to enjoy being with each other in peace. After a moment, Andrew leans in, and our lips meet. The kiss is tender at first, then grows more passionate, our bodies instinctively moving closer together. My mind quiets as I get lost in the sensation, momentarily forgetting about the case and my worries. Our lips part, and we lie on the sofa, wrapped in each other's arms.

"Stay the night?" he asks, his voice a gentle whisper. I nod, unable to resist the allure of his embrace. We move to the bedroom, and Andrew takes his shirt and pants off, revealing a sinewed body that makes me self-conscious about taking off my dress. I try not to stare, but I feel like I've been dropped into a Versace ad. If he's expecting my body to match that, he's going to be sorely disappointed. But once again, he surprises me. He grabs a T-shirt and shorts from his dresser and hands them to me. I change, and we slip into his buttery sheets together. I expect him to make a move on me—I'm half hoping he makes a move on me. But he doesn't; he just holds me, sensing that the time isn't right, given tonight's conversation. I guess when every woman wants you, you can afford to take your time.

As we drift off to sleep, Andrew's breathing slows and deepens, but my thoughts refuse to rest. Even though he had a perfectly good explanation for his father's donations tonight, Kenny's words echo through my mind: "Andrew's dad might be involved." That's the curse of being a private investigator. You don't feel at peace until you verify and reverify everything.

Against my better judgment, I slide out of Andrew's arms, doing my best not to wake him. I tiptoe out of the room and ease the bedroom door closed behind me. Guilt accompanies me. I hate to break his trust and invade his privacy, but I have to know for certain that his family isn't involved in this. First, I search the living room, rifling through drawers and bookshelves. Nothing catches my eye. I venture deeper into the apartment, creeping into his home office.

I pull up a seat at his desk, which looks like something the Kennedys would use. I slide open the ancient wood drawers and grab the manila file folders that rest inside. I see car titles, property surveys, tax returns with numbers so big I get dizzy, but nothing about Saint Agnes. I grab the mouse and click to rouse the computer out of sleep mode. It plays a three-note tune as it awakes.

I freeze.

The last thing I need is Andrew waking to find me fiddling with his computer. My mind fires with excuses for why I'm on his laptop. I'm doing research for work. I needed to check my email. I'm paying a bill.

But the house remains silent.

Fortunately, he's left his computer open, so no need for passwords. I scan through Andrew's disturbingly organized folders, looking for any mention of Preston or Saint Agnes. Still nothing. Family photos, movies, and games are all I find. I check his browser history, but even that's mundane. News websites, sports blogs, typical guy stuff. I'm always astonished at the sheer volume of sports information some men can consume. But I guess if you don't have a job, why not? I don't know why that bothers me, but it does.

I squint at the computer screen and ponder. My fingers tense as I grip the mouse. In one last-ditch effort, I search for any information on the Dionysus Theater. If there's a connection between it and the missing girls, it could be the key to solving this nightmare. The clock on the wall ticks louder in my ears with each passing second, a reminder that time is slipping away.

The search returns no results. I spin his desk chair and stare into the dark of the apartment. There's nothing here except my own paranoia. It's a dead end, just like every other lead I've pursued. I sigh, pleased that Andrew and his father are indeed what they seem but resigned to the notion that this case might be slipping through my fingers. A weight sits in my chest. What will I tell Madeline?

I shut down the computer and return to the bedroom, making sure not to wake Andrew. I don't want him thinking I'm some kind of stalker girl digging through his medicine cabinet. Should I dig through his medicine cabinet? *All right, Hazel, that's enough.* I slide back into bed, and on reflex, Andrew rolls over, puts his arm around me, and pulls me close to him.

What is wrong with me? I have this incredible guy sitting next to me, and I'm wandering around, digging through his apartment. I guess that's what you do when you're desperate. I can still hear the clock in Andrew's office clicking away. Starting tomorrow morning, I have two days left to find Mia, or Madeline will take her money and run. But it's not just the money. Something about that little girl struck a chord with me. Again, I play Mia's voice in my mind as I fall asleep, hoping it will stir something in me.

Lying in bed, I hear the clock tick and think of her.

Chapter 33

wo days left

I wake up in the morning with a big smile. I've been alone so long that I'd forgotten how good it feels to sleep with a man's arm around me. I've been poor so long that I'd forgotten the feel of a king-size bed and one-thousand-thread-count sheets. I've been scared so long that I'd forgotten what it was like to feel safe. I could stay here forever.

Nothing kills motivation like happiness.

Sun slips through the hunter green curtains, casting a glow on Andrew's penthouse, and I curse myself. I was hoping to get up and out early so that Andrew didn't have to see the train wreck of staticky hair and clown-show makeup that is me at first light. Ah well, if this is going to work, he's going to have to see it sometime.

I roll over, expecting to see Andrew's handsome face next to me, but find myself staring at an empty bed. For a moment I wonder if once again I'm the victim of a one-night stand, the man slinking out in the middle of the night and me left with emptiness. Then I remember that this is Andrew's apartment, so he's not slinking out anywhere. Then something worse occurs to me. Did something happen to him? Have Jaw Scar and Zombie Eyes crawled out of that ravine and found me?

"Andrew," I call out, softly at first, then louder. No response comes.

Okay, now I'm worried. It's nothing, I tell myself. He probably went out to get bagels or coffee or something.

The crashing of pots and pans jolts me from my thoughts. I flinch, and my breath stops. Who the hell is here, and where is Andrew? I spring out of bed and tiptoe across the plush cream carpet toward the kitchen, ready to face an intruder.

Fear pulses through me.

I peek my head around the corner, and the fear vanishes. A grin creeps across my face.

Andrew is sitting on the kitchen floor in a white T-shirt that hugs his biceps, hair askew and lips screwed sideways, earbuds in, retrieving and organizing pots and pans that have tumbled out of the cupboard. The scent of fresh coffee and frying bacon wafts through the air, and my stomach growls.

"Would you keep the racket down? Some of us are trying to sleep," I say.

Andrew glances up at me and busts out laughing. I love his laugh. It's a deep, throaty chuckle devoid of self-consciousness.

"Good morning," he says, removing his earbuds and scratching his five o'clock shadow. Is it possible he looks even more gorgeous in the morning? It's like when Hollywood stars go out to grab coffee, pretending like they just rolled out of bed, but you know they've spent hours prepping to look that way. Except he does it naturally.

"Apologies. This was meant to be a surprise breakfast, not an orchestra of pots and pans," he says.

I look over at the kitchen island. It's what I imagine a

five-star bed-and-breakfast would set for their guests. Two porcelain plates with green trim sit on the white-and-gray marble surface with monogrammed napkins and silverware. A bowl of chopped fruit in a rainbow of colors sits at the center, surrounded by croissants, blueberry pancakes, bacon, and sausages. My mouth waters at the blend of savory and sweet aromas.

"This is incredible. You didn't need to do this."

Andrew puts away the last of the pans he sent crashing around the floor and returns to the stove, where eggs are frying in a pan. I can't help but stare at his cute, perky butt in his gray designer sweatpants.

"I know, but I thought it would be nice for me to do something for you, since you've been working so hard on this case. How do you like your eggs?"

"Over easy, please."

He attempts to flip the eggs, but they land off kilter, and the yolk runs around the pan. He slaps his forehead with his free hand. "C'mon, I was doing so well," he says.

It's official. He's not going to make it as a chef. I walk over and give him a big hug and a kiss.

Andrew's eyes twinkle.

"What was that for?"

"For trying."

His face reddens, and he looks down at the ground—his way of accepting a compliment.

"Here, have a seat," he says, gesturing to one of the tan leather barstools at the kitchen island.

I perch myself on the barstool and try to disguise the fact that I'm so hungry I could probably consume this whole spread by myself. He places the mangled eggs on my plate, gives me a kiss on the cheek, and sidles up beside me. He grabs a sterling-silver coffeepot and offers it to me.

"Would you like some coffee?"

"Ah, I actually don't drink coffee. The orange juice is fine, thanks." I decide to keep my sugar-free Red Bull addiction to myself for now. I think my morning dishevelment is enough truth for one day.

"All right then, dig in," he says and takes a bite of bacon.

We plunge into the breakfast, and it's not quite as incredible as it looks. The pancakes are dense and dry. The bacon is burned. Still, sitting in this beautiful kitchen with him is amazing. Again, I wonder if I should live this life forever and become a dilettante like Andrew, leaving my brutal job and shitty little apartment behind. But the thought of Mia still nags at me.

"Are you okay?" he asks.

"Yeah, I'm fine. Just thinking about the case."

"Is that what you were working on in my office last night?"

My insides lurch at the question. I thought Andrew was asleep.

"Um," I stammer, feeling my cheeks flush. "My bad, I thought you were sleeping, otherwise I would have asked."

Andrew places a gentle hand on my wrist and shakes his head, a dimpled grin rising on his face.

"No, it's no problem. Mi casa es su casa. I was just curious what you were doing. I'm a lot lazier than you are. If I'm in bed, I'm in bed. There's no work happening after that."

I sigh and look at the ceiling, embarrassed by my snooping and my lack of progress in this investigation. Then I think of having to face Madeline Hemsley again with nothing to report.

"Oh, it's nothing," I lie. "I was searching the internet

for information on this underground club that might have some tenuous relationship with Mia's disappearance, but it's probably a dead end that will suck the life out of me, like everything else in this stupid case."

Andrew raises an eyebrow and bites into a piece of bacon.

"Sounds interesting. What's the name of the club?"

"The Dionysus Theater." It feels even more ridiculous when I say it out loud.

"Oh, I've heard of that place," he says casually, while buttering his rock-hard croissant.

My eyes bulge, and I grab his shoulder, startling him.

"What? You know what the Dionysus Theater is?"

Andrew takes a bite of his croissant and chews slowly. I'm so eager to hear how he knows about the Dionysus Theater that I'm tempted to slap it out of his mouth. After an interminable five seconds, he finishes chewing.

"I'm not totally sure, but I think it's one of those pop-up clubs that finance douchebags and gold diggers go to. Sadly, many of my friends are finance douchebags, so they've probably been there. I think they do an event every weekend at different spots around the city. It's pretty exclusive, from what I understand. But what does that have to do with your case?"

"I don't know exactly, but I think Mia wanted to go."

"Hmm," he says and takes another bite of his croissant.

"Have you been before?" I ask.

His eyes shift left and then right, like he's trying to recall.

"No, I've never been. That's not exactly my scene. I'm more of a stay-at-home-and-watch-movies kind of guy. Why? Do you want to go?"

"Really? Yes, I would definitely like to go. This could be a real game changer."

My leg is shaking back and forth. Finally, a break in this case. And of course it comes from Andrew, the only good thing to emerge from this mess.

"Okay. Let me text my friend," he says with an amused look on his face. I think he's still having trouble wrapping his head around how an obscure nightclub could tie back to a missing girl from a children's home upstate.

While Andrew fires off a text message, I look down at the cracked screen of my phone. It's already nine thirty, and I've got three missed calls from Madeline Hemsley and one from Bobby Riether. At least I've got some good news to give Madeline this time.

I need to head to the office.

Andrew's phone dings, and he looks at the screen.

"Bam, we're in. Tomorrow night, at the Dionysus Theater. You ask and I deliver." He takes a triumphant bite of bacon.

I give Andrew a big hug and a squeeze.

"Thank you so much. This could be exactly what I need to track down Mia."

"It's my pleasure. I'm just glad I could help. I was feeling a bit useless."

"Not at all. Just having somebody to talk to about this besides my nosy roommate has been incredibly useful."

Of course, none of this is going to work if Madeline gets pissed at me again for ignoring her calls and cuts me off. I force down a few more bites of rubbery eggs, chug some freshly squeezed orange juice, and then grab a croissant.

Andrew looks at me in confusion.

"Where are you going?"

"I'm sorry. I wish I could stay here all day, but I need to get to work. We're on for tomorrow night, though."

I lean in and give him a big kiss, his soft lips sending a tingle up my neck.

"You're just using me for a free breakfast, aren't you?"

"Guilty as charged," I say, and give him another kiss. I run back to his bedroom, throw on last night's dress, grab my bag, and rush in my heels to the elevator in the foyer. I feel like a college girl doing the walk of shame, except in this case there's absolutely nothing to be ashamed of.

"Thank you so much for breakfast and for everything, Andrew," I yell back to him.

"You're welcome," he shouts from the kitchen. "I'll pick you up tomorrow night."

Chapter 34

I step onto Sixty-Eighth Street, and the bright-blue sky and cool, dry air shake me from my Andrew-induced trance. I swear, being in that apartment with him is like being in some type of vortex where the outside world ceases to exist. I was so immersed I nearly forgot that I have less than forty-eight hours to solve this case and get paid, according to Madeline.

As I start walking toward the subway station, reality invades my consciousness. If my time with Andrew is a dream, then my real life is a nightmare. My bills and credit cards come due in two weeks, and if I don't solve this case, my income will be exactly zero. I've pushed the anxiety down for a while now, but as the deadline approaches, it creeps back up my stomach and into my chest. I can't ask my friends or family for money. That would be humiliating. I can't show anyone I've failed. It would confirm everything my parents predicted when I became a private investigator. I have no choice but to solve this case. But how? There are too many moving pieces and not enough time.

I get on the subway at Hunter College and head south, back toward my office. I can't break the habit of checking behind me to see if I'm being followed. I almost expect Jaw Scar and

Zombie Eyes to be there. I look around at the commuters dressed in their office gear, broken expressions hanging from their faces. It reminds me why I chose this life despite the danger involved. I don't think I can go back to the regular world.

When I arrive at my office, all my excitement wilts under the gaze of Madeline, who is standing in the alley outside the entrance of my building. She's wearing a black pencil skirt and a white blouse that looks like ten thousand silkworms had to die to make it. She stands perfectly straight with her tangerine Birkin bag resting in the crook of her arm. Disappointment drips from her face.

Just once I'd like Madeline to catch me on a good day.

"Another late night, Hazel?" she asks as I walk past her and open the door to my office building.

Apparently, Madeline's chosen to forget about our hug-it-out moment from her previous visit and settled back into her more comfortable role of condescending bitch.

"That joke never gets old, Madeline. I'm sorry, did we have an appointment?"

She mutters something under her breath, but I ignore it.

We walk up the stairs, Madeline sidestepping upward in her heels as dramatically as possible, like she's climbing Kilimanjaro.

"No, but I figured since your contract terminates end of day tomorrow and you weren't returning my calls, I would stop in to see what progress you've made. Frankly, I was shocked you weren't here, given that I won't be paying you a dime unless you locate Mia by the end of the day tomorrow."

We reach the top of the steps, and I open the door to my office. What I'm about to say to her is not meant for public consumption. I sit down at my desk and offer her a seat but say nothing. I watch as her self-satisfied grin fades and she fidgets in her chair. One of the great things about being a PI is you learn how to get comfortable with silence as the normals squirm.

"Did you hear what I said?" says Madeline, attempting to gain back control.

I nod, still saying nothing.

"Well, what do you say to that?"

I steeple my fingers, lean forward in my chair, and stare into her eyes. For the first time, I notice how the grass green of her irises serves to distract from the fear lying beneath.

"I don't have to say anything, Madeline. I believe it's you who have something to say."

Madeline stiffens in her chair.

"What on earth are you talking about?"

"You've lied to me since the beginning, Madeline. First, you told me you were Mia's godmother. Then you tell me you're her mother. Then you tell me you just want to find her. Then I find out that you'll come into a great deal of money if Mia's found dead."

Madeline crosses her legs, and her smug smile returns. But now rage replaces fear in her eyes. I've misplayed my hand.

"Ah, so that's it. You think I'm in this to prove that Mia's dead so I can inherit the money? You probably think I killed her as well."

I sit back in my chair.

"The thought had occurred to me. Well, did you?"

Madeline leans forward in her seat and extends her bony pointer finger in my direction. I'm tempted to smack it out of my way, but I'm too curious to hear what she has to say.

She speaks slowly, savoring every word.

"How dare you? After I shared my darkest secrets with you, how dare you use that against me? You should get your facts straight before you accuse me of anything. You think I would kill my daughter for money? Check again."

"I did check. And that's why I asked."

"It's true that my trust documents state that funds would go to me in the event of Mia's death. But if you had done your research, you'd know that we have an additional provision that states that we will donate any funds to the Saint Agnes endowment in the event of Mia's death."

I flinch forward.

"So, what are you saying? If Mia dies, the institution inherits her portion of the trust?"

"Ah, so now you're listening. That's exactly what I'm saying. My father felt it would help ensure...discretion."

"I'm going to need to see that document."

"I don't have it on me."

"That's okay. I'll wait."

Madeline harrumphs and pulls out her phone. She taps at it, evidently texting her attorney.

I assess her face. She appears genuine, but her face is lined with embarrassment. Madeline has fooled me before. I take a moment to ponder what this new information means. Would Mackenzie kill Mia to fund his cherished Saint Agnes? It doesn't seem plausible. Judging from the crowd at that fundraiser, I don't think money's a problem. And we don't even know for sure she's dead. And that wouldn't explain the other missing girls.

Madeline interrupts my thoughts.

"Check your inbox."

I open my email and click on the newest message, from Madeline's attorney. I peruse the legalese, and sure enough, there it is, the donation to Saint Agnes in the event of Mia's demise.

"I would suggest you spend a little more time tracking down this mysterious Dionysus Theater you keep telling me about and a little less time investigating the woman who's paying your bills," says Madeline.

Now it's my turn to correct the record. I close my email with an angry click of my mouse and stand up from my desk, prepared to throw her out.

"First of all, you're not paying my bills. You're holding a prize over my head like I'm a goddamn dog. Second, this may shock you, but I'm able to investigate both you and the Dionysus Theater at the same time. It's called multitasking."

That sounded more badass in my head. A warm smile crosses Madeline's face.

"Are you saying that you've found out what the Dionysus Theater is?"

It's astounding how quickly she can go from haughtiness to anger to sweetness. I feel like I'm being gaslit. I sit back down and remind myself: *One more day with this woman. One more day.*

"Yes, as a matter of fact I did. It's a pop-up nightclub. I'm going tomorrow night. Maybe we'll get lucky and someone will know something about Mia."

Madeline's eyes crinkle with hope. "It appears I've underestimated you."

I straighten the papers on my desk. "It wouldn't be the first time. So, now can we get rid of this ridiculous deadline and let me do my job?"

"Absolutely not."

The second the door to Madeline's humanity opens a crack, she slams it closed.

"Why?"

"Because, Hazel. The only reason you've gotten as far as you have is because of this 'ridiculous deadline,' as you call it. My father was an investment banker, and I always remember him saying 'Time kills deals.' And I can't afford for this deal to fall through. I need you to close it."

She rises from her chair again, places her oversize sunglasses on her head, and glides to the door. Apparently, Madeline has decided that our impromptu meeting is over. When she gets to the doorway, she rests a hand on the wood frame and taps on it with her professionally painted fingernails. She turns to me.

"Find Mia by the end of the night tomorrow, and the money is yours. Otherwise, I move on to someone who can find her."

She wants this to be the last word, but I won't give it to her. I throw my feet up on my desk and place a pen in my mouth like a cigar.

"Okay, Madeline. But you should know, you're not off the hook. I will go where this investigation leads, even if it leads me back to you."

She nods and swallows as she exits.

"I would expect nothing less."

Chapter 35

The last day

The following evening, I get ready for my big night out at the Dionysus Theater. I'm not nearly cool enough to know what to wear to a pop-up club, but even if I was, I'm almost certain I wouldn't have it. The best I've got is a skintight electric-blue dress that got me through a few bachelorette parties when I was a little younger and skinnier. As I slide it on, I feel like I'm stuffing a sausage into its casing. But miracle of miracles, it fits. And I look damn good, if I do say so myself. The tightness of the dress smooths out the lumps on my body, and my boobs get a lift because they've got nowhere else to go. If I don't move or breathe for the rest of the evening, I should be in great shape.

I look at my watch. It's nine forty-five. Andrew picks me up at ten. I've got fifteen minutes for makeup. I can hear Kenny out in the living room playing *Call of Duty*. Fortunately, he's not cooking tonight, so I won't have to hang my dress in our nonexistent garage. I'm not looking forward to him seeing me like this, in full club gear. He's either going to fall in love all over again or be jealous that I'm leaving with Andrew or both.

I walk into our dilapidated bathroom to apply my makeup. It's a real challenge trying to look glamorous when you live in a space that is the opposite of glamorous. We have two mismatching towels. The tile lining the wall is postwar faded pink. And here I am applying eye shadow and eyeliner like I'm Paris Hilton. It hits me that if I don't find something on Mia tonight at this club, I may not even be able to afford this dump. The thought of moving back in with my parents at age thirty shakes me to my core.

It seems like every day the pressure builds. Will I be able to pay the bills? Will I find Mia? Will another set of cops come after me? Is Bobby one of them? Is Mackenzie in on it? Will I ever be safe? My throat catches.

Not now.

When my makeup is complete, I look at myself in the mirror. My black hair and black eyes pop against the electric blue of my dress and my blue eyeshadow. If nothing else, I should make an impression on Andrew tonight.

I throw on my black heels and do my best to rub the scuff marks off the sides and then walk into the living room.

"Ta-da," I say to Kenny, with my arms out.

Kenny looks up from his *Call of Duty*, sees me, and then does a double take. I couldn't have asked for a better reaction. There's such a schoolboy innocence in his eyes that for a moment, I forget the guillotine hanging over my head.

"Oh my god, Hazel. You look so, so beautiful."

I can't stop the flush rushing into my cheeks.

"Thanks, Kenny. That's sweet of you."

"No, I mean it. I've never seen someone so pretty."

He's probably overdoing it a little, but I'm lapping it up. His lips sink into a frown, and he taps his video game controller on his leg.

"What's wrong?" I ask. I regret the question the second I

say it.

"I'm worried about your safety."

I roll my eyes and move to the kitchen table to grab my purse. I throw my keys in my bag and turn to look at him.

"I know. But you got to understand that this is my job. I can't back away just because it could be dangerous."

Kenny pauses his game and gets up from his chair.

"I understand. I just don't want you to get hurt. And Andrew seems like a nice guy, but I don't know if he's going to be able to do much if something goes down."

I can't argue with that. Bobby would probably be a better date for tonight.

Our intercom buzzes. Andrew's here.

"I gotta go, Kenny."

"Hazel, I'm serious."

His voice carries a depth and urgency I've never heard before. I throw my purse over my shoulder.

"Okay, I'll make you a deal. Call me in an hour, and if I don't answer, you can call the cops. Does that make you happy?"

He shrugs.

"I guess. Do you have the knife I gave you?"

I check my purse. The hazel-wood switchblade rests comfortably at the bottom.

"Yes. Little Hazel is ready for battle." I open the door to our apartment. "Now I have to go. Don't worry about me."

"All right. Have a good night."

He gives me a wave as I shut the door behind me.

The juxtaposition between Kenny moping around in my apartment and Andrew standing outside could not be more striking. Right outside my front door, Andrew poses in front of a black SUV, waiting to whisk us away. When I see him, my mouth falls open. He's somehow taken his looks to another level of handsomeness. He's wearing a formfitting black suit with a black shirt, a couple of open buttons revealing a defined collarbone and muscular chest. His hair is gelled and pulled back, and his blue eyes glow like my dress. A charming hint of red shows on his cheeks from the cool evening air. I start to speak, but he beats me to it.

"You look positively breathtaking," he says as he grabs my hands and places a gentle kiss on my lips. The way our lips feel together, I never want to stop kissing him.

"No, you look breathtaking. I literally think I had the wind knocked out of me just by looking at you," I say.

Andrew smiles at the compliment but says nothing. I'm sure he's heard the same thing from a hundred different women.

He opens the door and ushers me into the back seat of the Lincoln Navigator. He introduces me to Charles, his driver, who gives me a polite wave and a head nod. I could get used to having my own personal driver.

"So, are you ready for the Dionysus Theater?" Andrew says, rubbing his hands together in excitement.

"I don't know if I'll ever be ready, but we're going anyway."

Andrew laughs, and I notice his leg shaking back and forth.

"You seem excited."

He pauses his leg, and a touch more red surfaces on his cheeks.

"Yeah, I've never been a part of an investigation before. I feel like Hercule Poirot or something. Should I have brought a trench coat and a magnifying glass?"

I laugh, shake my head, and tap his leg. If he only knew how boring actual detective work was. Most likely I'm going to spend the entire night talking to surly bouncers and distracted bartenders, showing them pictures of Mia, and getting nothing out of them. But it's my only option at this point.

We arrive at the club, which looks nothing like a club and very much like an abandoned brick warehouse by the seaport near the southern tip of Manhattan. There's faded paint marking whatever was here before. As I get out, I smell a faint scent of fish in the air. I wonder if this used to be a fish market. I'll never understand rich people.

A lone bouncer stands outside dressed in a black T-shirt, muscles bulging. He eyes me up and down and smirks to himself. It rattles my confidence. Maybe I don't look quite as good as I thought I did.

"IDs and bags, please," he says.

Andrew and I hand him our IDs, which he scans into some type of computer that's clearly recording our information. I side-eye Andrew, and he rolls his eyes. I hand the bouncer my bag, and he rifles through it and pulls out the Taser.

"Sorry, no Tasers in here."

I look at Andrew, and now it's my turn to shrug. "Comes with the job." I tell the bouncer: "You can take it."

The bouncer nods and grabs my cell phone out of the bag.

"No cell phones either."

Andrew frowns. "Seriously, man? Is this really necessary?"

"Yeah. Club policy. They get a lot of celebrities in here, so we don't want people taking pictures and videos. Don't worry. We'll give them back at the end of the night."

I don't like anything about this, especially when I think of the unexplained bloodstain I found at the last club. But we've come too far to turn back. I put a hand on Andrew's shoulder.

"It's fine. Let's just go in."

The bouncer puts our phones in a secure pouch and cracks

open the steel door.

"Go straight back and follow the red light."

Andrew heaves open the ancient steel door wider, and we step inside the empty structure. The warehouse is dark except for a stunning path made of leaves resting on the concrete, lit by white candles on each side. The effect is both beautiful and eerie, like an enchanted path through a dark forest. The candlelight casts shadows on the worn brick walls, and a cold wind pours through the broken windows. Pigeons flap their wings as they move along the rafters, thirty feet above us. It feels as though we're standing in a ruin.

Andrew raises one eyebrow and gives me side-eye.

"I'm not sure I like detective work. Are you sure you don't want to go home and watch *The Proposal* again? I've got some good wine."

My first instinct is to say yes and turn around. Andrew's cozy couch seems a lot more appealing than spending another minute in this bizarre playground for the elite. But then I remember why I came here.

For Mia.

For all the other girls who don't have anyone looking out for them.

I stifle a shiver and grab Andrew's hand.

"No, we have to see this through."

Andrew holds my hand as we continue walking through the leaves. The clicking of my high heels echoes around the space, and the floor vibrates from distant music. One hundred feet in front of me, I can see a doorway glowing red. It looks like the entrance to hell. Andrew senses my nervousness and gives me a reassuring look and squeeze of the hand.

We reach the end of the path of leaves, which reveals a

staircase leading down to another door. Above glows a solitary, oversize red light bulb. This must be it. I'll finally get to see what secrets the Dionysus Theater holds. I hear the faraway echo of a woman's voice from below.

My heart drops into my stomach.

"Time after Time."

Mia's song. Could it be? She's here. She's performing.

As we descend the staircase, I take a deep breath to steady myself. I don't know what I'm going to find in here. I have to be prepared.

But as I open the door and take in the scene before me, I realize I'm not prepared.

I'll never be prepared.

Chapter 36

T he club resembles a lounge more than a modern electronic club. To the left stands an old cherrywood bar stocked with backlit bottles of expensive booze. To the right, a recessed main room with round tables draped with crimson tablecloths. The lighting is low. Cheap perfume and thick cigar smoke poison the air.

But it's who's inside the club that freezes the blood in my veins. The customers gathered around the bar and sitting at the tables are all men, older men, self-satisfied, drinking and laughing. Drifting among these men are girls, none older than sixteen, dressed in lingerie, faces caked in makeup, every one of them flirting like prostitutes at an Old West brothel.

The sight sickens me, but my eyes keep moving, searching the room for that voice, searching for Mia.

And then I see her.

At the center of a dimly lit stage in the right corner of the room.

Mia.

My mouth falls open, and I freeze.

I can't believe what I'm seeing.

This beautiful girl that I've been searching for is here.

The girl with the brightest smile you ever saw and a voice

like honey, standing in front of me.

I've done it. I've found her. This is why I became a private investigator.

All this time, all the doubts, all the asshole clients, all the obstacles, all the fear. It was all worth it for this moment.

But my excitement at finding Mia is crushed in an instant when I look closer at her.

She's dressed in nothing but underwear and a black corset that hangs loose on her prepubescent body. Her beautiful springy hair has been straightened and matted down, and I can see bruises on the soft skin of her arms. Her face is pallid, and her eyes rest in a drug-induced fog. She's singing "Time after Time," and her voice is as rich and haunting as it was in the video. But this time, no one is listening. The drunk, self-absorbed older men ignore her, too focused on grabbing and slobbering over the girls that trickle past their tables.

I have to get her out of here.

I spin on my heels and look at Andrew, horror blanketing my face.

"We need to get the police, now," I say, expecting to see matching disgust on his face.

But I see the opposite.

Andrew's face shows delight. Pure, maniacal delight.

His smile—broad and high—reveals his canines. The twinkle in his eyes has morphed into a demonic glare.

While holding his gaze on me, he rotates his body toward the door of the club and slowly turns the lock. The sound of the bolt locking, and the realization that comes with it, feels like a gunshot. He puts his body between me and the exit and holds out his arms in pride.

"So, what do you think of the place, Hazel? I designed it

myself."

The truth hits me like a sledgehammer.

Andrew kidnapped Mia.

Who knows how many more?

He's behind all of this.

How could I have been so blind?

I reach into my bag for the Taser, but it's gone. I think back to the bouncer taking it from me with a smirk as we walk in. I curse myself.

Two figures emerge from a side door. It's the two cops that followed me, DeGrom and Hanley. They're both banged up from their tumble into the ravine the other night. A gash sinks into Jaw Scar's forehead, and Zombie Eyes is missing a tooth. The hate in their eyes cuts through me. They're both smiling, knowing that this is their chance for payback.

I turn back to Andrew.

"Why? Why would you do this?"

He takes a few steps toward me and flashes his million-dollar smile. He attempts to place a hand on my shoulder, but I shrug it off, every hair on my body standing on end.

"Call it a family tradition. But you haven't even seen the best part yet. Follow me."

The two cops stand behind me, clarifying that following Andrew is not a choice.

We trail Andrew as he skips down the steps into the sunken main room. He's the mayor of the place, stopping at tables to shake hands. One of the men sits with a girl who can't be more than twelve on his lap. Andrew grabs a bottle from one of the ice buckets and tops off the man's lowball. These men look up to him. As we wade through the tables, they don't even notice me. They're too absorbed in satisfying their pedophiliac urges.

Mia's singing in the background is like a cruel joke.

Beauty drowned in sin.

Bile rises to my throat, and I have to swallow it to keep from vomiting.

On the other side of the showroom, stairs rise, leading into a dark hallway of padded velvet behind the stage. We walk by Mia, and I look at her, hoping to make contact, to somehow tell her that things will be okay. But she has no idea who I am. She just keeps singing, staring off into space.

We reach the hallway. Two red light bulbs hang from the ceiling, one near and one far, providing the only light. But I can see door after door of rooms. We march forward, and I can hear the squeak of steel and the groans of men. My heart pounds, and sweat pours from every inch of me. I think back to the spot of blood I saw before.

Never in my wildest nightmares could I imagine the horror of this place.

We reach the end of the hallway, and Andrew opens the last door on the left. I tell myself that I should scream, that I should run, that I should fight, but I'm paralyzed. I keep thinking this must be a nightmare and any second I'll wake up and be safe in my bed. I follow Andrew into the room, and the two crooked cops shut the door behind me and wait outside, blocking the exit.

I'm going to die here.

Chapter 37

I look around the space and realize that I'm never getting out of this room. We're in a basement. The ceiling is concrete. The walls are cinder block. It must have been a storage room at one time.

Now it's a cell.

A king-size bed sits in the middle of the room on a white metal frame, like a 1950s psychiatric-ward bed. Two manacles hang from the wrought iron headboard. Beside the bed stands a lone side table and a lamp. The walls are bare. The floor is bare. No warmth, no humanity. The room itself reveals the perversion of its designer.

Andrew stands in the middle of the room, grinning. On the surface, he looks the same: the ocean-blue eyes, the smattering of freckles across the nose and cheeks, the plush chestnut hair. But now, instead of being beautiful, his features seem distorted, like those Halloween masks of dead presidents. My eyes meet his, and I see the sickness revealed. It's as though something primal and violent in him has awakened: a shark smelling the chum.

"Here, let me take your bag," he says with faux sweetness.

He grabs my purse and hurls it against the wall. The bag slams and falls to the floor next to the bed. My mind races, trying to calculate a way out of here, but there's only one way out, and I'd have to go through Andrew and two cops. I could scream, but nobody would hear me. And even if they did, these girls are surely all too used to hearing screams and too scared themselves to help me.

The terror takes hold.

Andrew walks toward me, his cheeks flushed.

"We call this room the dungeon. Each of our rooms has a theme. There's the dungeon, the Wild West room, the medieval room—you get the gist."

I backpedal toward the wall. I can barely speak.

"Andrew, this isn't you."

His eyes spark with rage.

"Oh, that's where you're wrong. This is very much me. That guy out there in the real world—polite, simpering Andrew? That's the fake me. I'd rather walk on broken glass than cook you breakfast again."

I know I've got much bigger problems, but his comment still cuts. I would cry, but the horror freezes my tear ducts, along with everything else in my body.

"I just don't understand. Why me?"

Andrew paces the room, savoring my ignorance. My vulnerability makes him feel powerful.

"You should be flattered, Hazel. You want to know why you? It's because you were the only one in that shitstorm of private investigators that Madeline Hemsley threw at us that got close. You were too smart for your own good."

"Our meeting at the gala. It wasn't an unfortunate coincidence, I take it?"

I'm trying to keep him talking as long as I can. I tell myself that this will buy me time to come up with a plan, but the reality is I'm just stalling the inevitable.

"Ha! No, that was not a coincidence. You think I'd be interested in a girl like you? Don't make me laugh. I mean, you're cute, but look at me. I could tell that you had a brain on you, though. The other investigators were hacks. Too old, too slow to see the genius of what we've built. They didn't even put together Mia's disappearance with the other girls. Each time we sent one of those bozos away, I thought we were in the clear. But then that damn Madeline would dig up a new has-been PI, finally landing on you."

"But why spend so much time on me? The dinners, the dates?"

"You know the old saying: keep your friends close and your enemies closer. Or my favorite: I'd rather have 'em inside the tent, pissin' out, than outside the tent, pissin' in. I needed to know what you knew. Of course, I would have preferred not to have you involved. I've got better things to do than spend time with a six out of ten. But the second you mentioned the Dionysus Theater at breakfast, I knew the fun was over. If you think about it, you did this to yourself. Curiosity killed the cat. Literally."

A bitter smirk crosses my face. Yes, this is clearly my fault.

"So, how did you do it? How did you take Mia and the others?"

He snarls and undoes the first couple of buttons on his shirt.

"It's quite an elegant little system, if I do say so myself. Every year, I attend the stupid little concerts the girls put on for the community. There's usually a Christmas, spring, and fall concert. I spot the ones who I think would appeal to our clientele: pretty, but with a nice diversity of styles and looks."

Vomit rises in my throat. I can't believe I liked this monster.

"Then after the concert I go up to them and tell them I'm a theater producer and that they are the most talented girl I've ever seen, blah, blah, blah. Of course, they eat it up. But when you look like me, you can tell anybody anything, and they eat it up."

He points to me and laughs. "Case in point. Anyhoo...then I tell them I have this incredible underground theater where we only invite celebrities and billionaires and I'd like to show it to them." He adjusts his voice to a high, soft pitch. "But it's very exclusive, so they can't tell anyone. They love that shit. I make a date to pick them up in my boat and then meet them after lights-out down by the lake."

He's feeling very proud of himself now. I need to lean in to the mansplaining.

"And you have a house on the lake. So, no hotels, no gas stations, no cameras. Am I right?"

"Exactly. Or at least that's how it was until that old fool Mackenzie finally insisted on a camera on the lake. We'll figure out a way around that, though. Carve a path through the woods or something. That Paver guy's a moron. All we have to do is get them to my house and we're good. I have a lovely little basement where we keep the girls for a couple of months, get them hooked on our love medicine, and break them down into compliance. Once they're ready, we bring them to the theater."

"Who is this 'we' you keep talking about? I have a hard time believing that you, DeGrom, and Hanley run this entire show."

Before I can think, Andrew lunges at me, grabs me by the shoulders, and throws me onto the bed. My head slams against the headboard, dizzying me. His strength surprises me, but the sudden act of violence shakes me loose of my paralysis. My fight-or-flight instinct lands firmly on fight. I start to push myself off the bed, but he shoves me down.

He leaps on top of me and straddles me. I reach for his arm and twist, but he rips away from my grip before I can get hold. He snatches my wrists and pins them down, taking away my leverage.

He's practiced at this.

I'm not the first woman he's raped.

I squirm and flail with all my power, but his body weight is too much. He presses my wrists together and clutches them in one hand. The next thing I hear is the sound of him pulling down his zipper and his hands moving the dress up my thighs.

"Don't worry about who 'we' is, Hazel. And don't you dare disparage me. Right now, all you need to know is that I'm in charge."

He strokes the hair from my face with the back of his hand, tracing his hauntingly delicate fingers along my cheek. I snap my head away from his touch.

"You know, I thought you were one of the orphans at first. You wore that cheap red dress at the gala, the same one the orphan girls wear. I knew there was a private investigator I was supposed to intercept, but I didn't know it was you on the dance floor. That's why I caught you when you tripped. If I had known what I know now, I would have let you hit the floor." He lifts my dress above my waist. "Imagine my disappointment when I found out you weren't a pretty little orphan but a shitty PI trying to tear down everything we've built. I see now why that other guy raped you."

The memory of the rape, of waking up in that bed, dried blood on my leg, tears through me. I can't go back there. I scream and spasm as hard as I can, attempting to throw him off me. I push my pelvis skyward, but he weighs too much. I twist my wrists, but his grip is like iron. I scream with every ounce of oxygen in my chest, but no one hears. His fist slams against my cheek, and I can feel my lip split open and taste the blood in my mouth. He grabs my neck, and his fingers close around my windpipe.

"Shut up, you wh—"

Voices shouting outside the door interrupt his threat.

He releases his grip from my neck and pauses but continues to hold me down. The only sound is our panting. My gaze darts around the room. If I could just get a hand free, maybe I could grab something.

The door opens, and I hear a familiar woman's voice say "What the hell is going on here?"

Andrew's blocking me, so I can't see who it is. My mind churns, trying to place the voice. The accent.

He jumps off me and lifts himself up from the bed.

My heart leaps when I see who's in front of me.

It's Sonia.

Chapter 38

Excitement fills me at the sight of my friend. But it quickly evaporates when my gaze meets Sonia's rich brown eyes. I expect to see kind eyes, concerned eyes, eyes that say "I will help you." Instead, I see disgust and irritation.

Then the truth crashes down on me.

"We" are Andrew and Sonia.

Sonia's the puppet master.

The girls started disappearing from Saint Agnes shortly after Mackenzie took the job as headmaster, but Sonia got there at the same time, right after her divorce left her penniless.

It all adds up.

Her vow never to be poor. Her frequent trips to New York. Goolsbee's hesitance to speak in front of her. Her beautiful clothing. Her secretive meetings with male patrons at the gala. Naming the club after Dionysus to implicate Goolsbee and Mackenzie. She's been manipulating everyone from the beginning.

My eyes squint at Sonia as if I'm seeing her for the first time. She's her typically elegant self. Thick, shimmering black hair against tan skin. A red silk dress clings to her curvaceous body, and the red lipstick on her lips matches perfectly. Her sharp floral perfume spreads through the air like a poison. She looks and smells like what she is: a madam.

Zombie Eyes and Jaw Scar tromp into the room behind her. She feels my judging eyes and looks away from me to Andrew.

"You were supposed to dispose of her, not have a night with her," she says.

I note how she uses the phrase *have a night*, not *kidnap and rape*. The things people can rationalize and euphemize.

Andrew zips up his pants and heaves himself out of the bed with a groan, granting me a reprieve. I can tell from the chastened look on his face that he is merely a lieutenant. Sonia is the general. I wonder if I can reason with her.

"I know, Sonia," he says. "Trust me, I'm going to get rid of her, but I figured, Why not have a little fun first?"

Andrew throws a wink at Zombie Eyes and Jaw Scar, and they chuckle.

Sonia sighs and looks at me. I search her dark eyes for any connection, any sign that she cares about me, but there's nothing. She raises her stubborn cleft chin in the air and looks at me with the same dispassionate assessment that she would give to an old piece of furniture she needs to get rid of. She crosses her arms, bangles sliding up her wrists, and looks back at Andrew.

I seize the moment.

"Sonia, please, help—"

"Shut up," she says, her voice flat and cold. Just from her tone, I know it's over. There's nothing left inside her but vanity and greed. Her past humiliations have convinced her that the world owes her something. She ignores me and turns to Andrew.

"This isn't a time for fun or freelancing, Andrew. This is

business. The stakes are too high to mess around here. She's the only person who knows us, and we need to be rid of her. We've come too far for this nonsense. We have a plan. Now let's stick to it."

As the two of them bicker about what to do with me, my eyes search for something, anything, I can use as a weapon. The handcuffs hang from the bed frame but are locked, and I don't have the key. The lamp is too light to do any damage. The table is bolted to the floor. Then I spot a glint of light from the floor next to the bed.

My switchblade.

My hazel-wood switchblade.

The bouncer was so focused on my Taser that he missed it.

God bless Kenny and his crazy knife collection. My purse lies on its side—half spilled out on the floor—and there's the knife resting on the top zipper. I look back at Andrew, at Sonia, at Jaw Scar and Zombie Eyes. None of them have noticed. My right hand is hanging off the bed about six inches from it. If I can reach a few more inches, I should be able to grab it without them noticing. I slide my body to the right along the stiff sheets.

There's a slight groan of the mattress spring.

Andrew doesn't notice. He's too preoccupied with charming Sonia.

"Sonia, how long have we been working together? When have I ever asked for anything from you?"

Sonia paces the room, and, per usual, all eyes are on her. She has a gravity that pulls everyone toward her. That's how she's built her empire of filth.

"I never should have let your father talk me into bringing you into this, Andrew," says Sonia.

His father? That explains it. I wrote Andrew off because of his age, but if Preston DuPont is involved in this, he probably raised Andrew into this pedophiliac cult. Now I wonder if his mother really committed suicide. Andrew's face turns purple, like he's a boy about to throw a tantrum. He's used to getting what he wants.

"Are you kidding me? If my father were here, he'd want to take a shot at her too."

Take a shot at her. These people see me as cattle. Maybe I can use that to my advantage.

I use their distraction to grab the switchblade with the tips of my pointer and index fingers. I slide it up along the side of the mattress and under my thigh.

Sonia stops pacing. The room falls silent, and for a moment, I think she's spotted me. I look up, but her eyes are elsewhere.

"Fine, Andrew. You have five minutes. Have your way with her, but then I want her dumped in a river so far from here that no one will find her."

The matter-of-fact way Sonia says it breaks my heart. I admired this woman. She was beautiful, strong, independent, and self-assured. I thought she was the woman I wanted to be. I thought she might be my mentor, my friend. And she was merely using me. Now she wants me dead.

Sonia floats out of the room, followed by the two cops, malevolent smiles drawn to their faces.

"Five minutes," she shouts as she walks out.

Andrew slams the door shut behind them and locks it.

"Now, where were we?" he says, rubbing his hands together.

I remain lying on the bed. My temples pound, and sweat beads in my palms. Every ounce of me wants to get up from this foul mattress and run or charge Andrew with the switchblade in my hand. But I can't. He's too big and too strong to attack directly. I have to be patient. I'll wait until he's absorbed in his sick fantasies and then strike.

Andrew turns to me, his bright-white teeth glinting.

"Ah, yes, I was just about to give you what you deserve."

He takes his black sport coat off slowly, savoring the moment. He folds it neatly on the end of the bed and then rolls up his sleeves, almost daring me to run.

I look at him and play the role he wants me to play. Passive. Terrified.

"Please, Andrew, don't do this."

As I suspected, this only turns him on more.

He leaps on the bed and straddles me. In one swift, practiced move he rips the back of my dress open, tears it off me, and tosses it on the floor like a piece of trash, grunting like a wild animal with every move. Then he uses his legs to pin my hands to my sides. I keep them there, so he thinks I'm too terrified to fight him. He runs his tongue along my shoulder and neck.

I gag.

"I haven't had a grown woman in a long time," he says.

Goose bumps crawl up my skin. His sick sweat stinks in my nostrils.

He begins to unzip his pants again, and I feel the pressure on my wrist from his legs give way. For a second, the zipper gets stuck.

This is my moment.

I flip open the switchblade with my thumb and rip my right arm out from under his legs. I drive it deep into his neck. I feel the blade slice through skin, then muscle, hitting bone. Blood spurts on me and pours from his wound instantly. The smell of copper floats in the air. I must have severed an artery.

I look at Andrew. At first, his face shows only shock. Then he reaches for his neck, and I watch as the realization of what has happened creeps over him. His eyes swim in fear, and as much as I hate to admit it, I find pleasure in watching his life drain away, and he knows it.

He lurches backward, loses his balance, and topples off the bed to the floor with a bang. A whimper limps from his lips as he presses his hand around the knife, trying to stanch the bleeding, but it's too late. He writhes on the floor, choking and gurgling sounds bubbling from his throat. His pants fill with urine as the rest of his body fails.

Within seconds, he's gone. The only sound is my pulse ringing in my ears.

Death is so much less than what he deserves.

I only have a moment to savor killing this psychopath before I hear voices from outside. DeGrom and Hanley. They're still out there. They heard Andrew's body hit the floor. They'll want to know what's going on.

I throw on my torn electric-blue dress and Andrew's blazer for warmth but skip the heels. I consider using them as weapons but think better of it.

Fists slam against the door.

"Everything all right in there, buddy?" shouts a voice from outside.

I groan deeply and try to shake the bed to simulate sex noises, but it's a pretty weak attempt. I can tell from their silence they're not buying it.

The doorknob shakes.

"Andrew? Let us in, man. Your five minutes are almost up. I don't want the boss lady to get pissed."

The pounding grows louder. I scan the room, looking for any

way out of this concrete and cinder block cell, but it is what Andrew said it was: a dungeon.

The door rattles on its hinges. It's old, and I can see the rust around the edges.

It won't be long before they knock it down.

I rip the switchblade out of Andrew's neck. The sensation of the knife through the flesh sickens me. My hand can barely hang on to it. It's trembling so violently.

The fists bang louder.

I tiptoe toward the door.

They're coming, but I won't go down without a fight.

Chapter 39

The lock snaps and the door bangs open.

It's Jaw Scar and Zombie Eyes.

The two men guard the door as Sonia blows by them and enters the room.

She spots Andrew on the floor, and I watch as her brow shifts from confusion to rage.

"You little bitch. What did you do?" says Sonia, her lip curling into a sneer.

I raise the switchblade.

"The same thing I'm going to do to you if you come near me."

It would be more convincing if my hand wasn't wobbling like Jell-O.

Sonia looks at my hand, and her mouth parts into a sinister grin. She laughs and points to Zombie Eyes. He opens his jacket and removes a pistol from his holster and flips off the safety. She points a talon to the floor.

"Drop the knife."

The trembling spreads from my hands to my entire body, but I don't move.

"Shoot her," says Sonia.

Zombie Eyes raises the gun, and I see that this man has no

feelings of uncertainty about pulling that trigger.

The knife falls from my hand.

"Get on the bed," says Sonia.

I close my eyes. Every part of my body is shaking, overtaken by fear and the damp chill of the basement. I can't go back to that bed. I barely escaped Andrew. I'll never escape this. Nausea reaches up from my stomach to my throat. I debate whether it would be better to charge Sonia and take a bullet in the head or submit to whatever she has planned for me. I can't move. I hate that I'm frozen right now, but it's an involuntary reaction to looking death in the face.

"Now!" she barks.

My instinct for self-preservation takes over, and I sit down on the bed.

Zombie Eyes holsters his pistol, smiles, and licks his lips. He looks over at Jaw Scar. Sonia tosses him the handcuffs.

"Put the handcuffs on her."

He marches over and grabs my wrists. I don't even resist. I gave everything I had resisting Andrew. I float outside myself now, resigned to the fact that I'm not leaving this room alive and there's nothing I can do about it.

The cold steel cuts into my skin as he secures the cuffs. Every part of my body is shaking, but my mind is somewhere else, incapable of absorbing the violence that is about to be done to me.

I just pray it will end soon.

I should have chosen the bullet.

Jaw Scar and Zombie Eyes resume their post at the door, one on each side. Now that I'm cuffed to the bed, Sonia pauses for a moment and releases a long breath. She rubs her palms together and steps toward Andrew's body, which now rests in a pool of blood. She examines the wound on his neck and clicks her tongue against the roof of her mouth. She stops and points at him.

"You did this?"

I nod, too scared to speak. I'm quivering so hard the manacle on my arm clinks against the steel bed frame.

"Impressive. Such a shame, though. He was my best man. I don't know what I'm going to tell Preston." Jaw Scar and Zombie Eyes nod along solemnly as though we lost a true American hero today.

The terror inside me shifts to anger. I swallow hard and muster my courage. "How could you do this?" A part of me still hopes there's a human inside her.

Sonia picks my hazel-wood switchblade off the floor and runs her finger along the blade. She grabs the chair, pulls it next to the bed, and sits down beside me. She strokes the hair that's fallen down in my face and tucks it behind my ear. The act is gentle, but the meaning behind it is violent.

"How could I do this? A better question is, How could I not do this? I told you before, I came to Saint Agnes with nothing. I started out cleaning toilets, for God's sake. Do you think I wanted to spend my days cleaning up after these little bitches? Day after day of watching them make a mess, knowing that I'll clean up after them. Hearing them mock me because they assumed I didn't speak English."

"But you got promoted. You were practically running that place," I say.

"Yes, when Thomas promoted me, I thought things might change. But it was the same thing, just cleaning up different messes for the same pathetic amount of money. Just a little less pathetic than before. And you saw how Thomas treated me. Like his glorified assistant. At first, I figured he'd retire soon—or better yet, die—but no, he just kept going, stuck in that past and making sure I was stuck there with him."

"And you thought kidnapping little girls was the best way to solve your problem?"

"Kidnapping? Who said anything about kidnapping? That's what you don't understand, mi amor. All the girls here chose to be here. Nobody forced them to get on that boat with Andrew. They all chose to be on that boat. You remember what Thomas said about Saint Agnes? How we teach these girls to be Apollos? To be kind, selfless, and humble. Some of the girls are. And those girls graduate from Saint Agnes and lead good lives. The girls that are here chose another path: the path of Dionysus. They were selfish, they were greedy, they wanted to be famous. You reap what you sow."

"So you're saying this is their fault?"

"Yes, just like it's your fault that you're here." She points to Jaw Scar and Zombie Eyes. "They told you to stay away from the Dionysus Theater, did they not? And did you listen? No."

I start to speak, but Sonia puts her long-nailed finger on my mouth. "Shhhh." She places her hand on my knee and then slides my dress up my thigh. My leg quakes. "Enough of your questions. Now I have a question for you. Who have you told about our operation?"

I try to keep my mind from imagining what she'll do to me if I don't answer. I think of Madeline, of Bobby, of Kenny. "No one," I say, maintaining eye contact as best I can.

Sonia peers deep into my eyes, searching for the truth. Then one of her eyelids twitches, and I see the knife blade cut through the air and plunge into my thigh. I feel the steel rip through me and hit my femur. I scream in agony, but Sonia covers my mouth with her hand. A hot pain tremors up and down my leg, throbbing and fading as shock takes over my body.

"Shhhhh," Sonia whispers again. She rips the blade out of my leg, and a new torture explodes through my thigh. I watch as blood seeps from the wound. It's slow, so I know that I'm not dead yet. Still, sweat beads down my face, and my chest heaves as I prepare for what's next.

Sonia leans closer and whispers. "Who have you told about our operation?"

I clench my teeth and try to swallow, but my mouth is so dry my spit catches in my throat. Groans escape from my chest. Bobby's face flashes in my mind. Then Kenny's. If I talk, they're dead. I'm dead either way.

Sonia lifts the bloodstained blade to my face and traces the edge along the skin under my eye. I feel a damp line run across my cheek. A sneer snakes across her face.

"Hazelita. I wish I had known you in another life. You have heart. We could have been friends." I strain my neck and turn my head to keep the edge of the knife from cutting into my skin, but Sonia keeps pressing. "Ah, you are tough when I cut your leg, but maybe you're not so tough when I cut your cheek. You tell me who knows about us, or I filet your pretty little face."

I keep my jaw clenched and remind myself that whatever I do, I'm dead. The least I can do is protect the people I care about.

Sonia shakes her head in disbelief and shifts the blade in her hand, ready to cut. My blood drips from the handle and runs down her wrist. She pulls her hand back, preparing to strike. I close my eyes and drift off to another place where these horrors don't exist.

The swing of the door and the shout of a steely voice bring me back.

"Police. Drop the knife and step away from the girl."

I open my eyes.

Two men dressed in black with *SWAT* in white across their chests stand at the doorway, guns trained on Sonia, Zombie Eyes, and Jaw Scar.

The two thugs immediately raise their hands to their heads and step aside, but Sonia remains still. Time freezes as I watch her calculate her options, the knifepoint inches from my eye.

One of the officers takes a cautious step closer and points his pistol at Sonia's chest.

"Ma'am, put your weapon down, now."

A lifetime of buried fury crosses Sonia's face. A vein bulges beneath her left eye, all her perceived slights bubbling to the surface. My initial relief is replaced by panic that she might stab me in one final farewell shot. But then the anger on her face recedes when she realizes that she doesn't want to die tonight either. She drops the knife and puts her hands behind her head. For a moment, I wonder if I'm dreaming.

"Get down on the ground now," shouts the officer.

The trio drop to the floor, and in a flash, the other police are on them, pinning and handcuffing them. As the cops drag them out of the room, Sonia hurls obscenities in Spanish, while Jaw Scar and Zombie Eyes curse and spit.

I watch them leave in cuffs, and a wave of relief bursts through my chest, so strong I can barely breathe. I look to the ceiling, searching for someone to thank for this miracle.

Then I hear a familiar voice.

"Hazel?"

I look up and see Kenny standing in the doorway.

"Oh my God, Haze."

He runs over to me, past the other cops and Andrew's dead body, and hugs me. He holds me tight, and his body heat feels so good against the chill that I don't want him to let go.

I cry.

I cry so hard my body spasms and I think I might throw up. But I still can't believe he's here and I'm handcuffed to a bed. Through the tears, I muster two words.

"Kenny, how?"

He sits up in the bed, grabs the handcuff key from the nightstand, and uncuffs me. I look into his eyes and see that he's crying too.

"You told me to call you and if you didn't answer, to call the police, so I did."

My mind searches for the memory. I barely remember saying that. I'm still in a fog.

I sniff the blood and snot from my nose and clutch at my wounded leg.

"I can't believe you actually did that. I was sort of joking."

Kenny shrugs and grabs a tissue from his pocket. He wipes the blood from my face and then puts pressure on my leg.

"I didn't think you were joking."

"But how did you know where I was? I didn't tell you the address."

He pulls his phone out of his pocket and shows me a map with a little circle with my face on it.

"Find My Friends. My stalkerishness finally paid off."

I give him another big hug and sit up in the bed while police pour into the room. A paramedic tends to my leg wound, which has gone completely numb. It's as though my body has pain in

295

so many places it doesn't know where to hurt. One of the cops throws one of those funny silver blankets on me and gives me a bag of ice for my lip. I place it to my face and groan. The cool feels incredible against the heat of my swelling cheek.

"But how did you get the police to get here so fast?"

A mischievous grin creeps across Kenny's face.

"Well, in my police academy training, they taught me that if there's an active shooter situation, the police have to respond immediately, so I may have said that there was an active shooter. It probably didn't hurt that I know a couple of these guys from training."

Kenny winks, and I hug him as hard as I can. I squeeze him so hard a little grunt escapes from him as the air pushes out of his lungs.

One of the guys from the SWAT team walks over to us.

"I'm sorry to interrupt, ma'am, but we need to get you to a hospital and clear the scene."

They bring in a stretcher for me, but I wave it off. Before I go anywhere, I have to find Mia. Kenny and I stand up and limp our way out of the room, me walking shoeless, with my thigh bandaged, a silver blanket around my shoulders, and the ice pack to my face. I'm still shivering, so Kenny puts his arm around me and guides me as I stumble through the now-empty club. Cops pat Kenny on the shoulder as we pass. I look at my watch. It's eleven thirty. I made it. Just before my Friday deadline.

Take that, Madeline.

Chapter 40

We step outside, and I take a deep breath of the cool night air, overjoyed to be free of the sickening perfume and cigar smoke. A police officer escorts us through the maze of people. As Kenny and I limp away from the warehouse, a gentle river breeze blows over my swollen cheek and reminds me how my mom used to blow on my face to calm me down when I was a little kid. I wish she were here right now. I wish my whole family were here right now. I squeeze Kenny's shoulder tighter as we walk.

A smattering of stars peeks through the Manhattan glow, and my throat clenches.

In that basement I didn't think I'd see them or anyone or anything ever again.

Sirens echo through the Seaport. Cop cars, fire engines, and ambulances scream up FDR Drive. Red and blue lights bounce off the buildings. Police put up caution tape, and pedestrians crowd around to see what all the fuss is about.

To my right I see the degenerate men from the club, the "customers," being loaded into the police wagon in handcuffs like the criminals they are. They squint and squirm as camera flashes capture their deviance for posterity. Every one of them shouts and protests their innocence. Saying they didn't know the girls were underaged, that they've never done this before, that they were drunk. The standard playbook for men behaving badly.

Fortunately, the cops aren't listening. There's not a prison dark enough for these men. At the back of the police wagon, I glimpse red. It's Sonia. She stares at me, her jaw set and dark eyes smoldering. The hate runs deep in that woman. She's spent so much time telling herself that these girls deserve what they get that she can't fathom she'd be punished for it. I wonder if she'll ever realize what she did was wrong. My guess is she won't.

To my left, I spot the girls from Saint Agnes—and God knows where else—huddled in a group, crying and hugging each other. Terrified at what they've just seen but happy that their nightmare is over. You can tell from their sunken faces and pale skin that they've been drugged for a long time, but the thrill of the moment seems to bring them out of the trance. Mia stands at the center of the group, shining like a beacon. She's one of those people you can't take your eyes off.

"Kenny, can you give me a minute?" I say.

"Of course," he says and walks off to be congratulated by more cops. Talk about making an entrance into the police force.

I limp over to the group of girls, who all eye me as I approach, wary of anyone from the outside.

I wave to Mia and give her my blanket to show I mean no harm.

The girls part and give us space.

"Hi, Mia. You don't know me, but my name is Hazel Cho. I'm the private investigator who your godmother hired to find you."

Mia looks me up and down, probably as surprised as everyone else is to see a five-foot-tall Asian woman PI. Let alone one who's got a torn dress, a bruised face, and a bloody bandage on her thigh.

"Hello," she says.

Her voice is so innocent and sweet that my heart drops to the floor. How anyone could harm such a beautiful thing as this is beyond me.

"How are you doing?"

"I'm okay," she says, but I can see that she's not. Her lips quiver and her shoulders shudder.

I give her a big hug, and she sobs into my shoulder. I can feel the tears on my bare skin. I hear onlookers behind the caution tape mumbling and murmuring, attempting to glean what happened here.

"I'm so sorry," she says.

I pull her away so I can look her in the eyes.

"Hey, you have nothing to be sorry for. You did nothing wrong."

She nods, but the sobs keep coming.

"I know, I know. I just never meant to cause this much trouble. Andrew said after one of my concerts that I had a pretty voice, and that he had this theater I could perform at, and he'd make me famous."

I think back to how easily I fell under Andrew's sway. Mia didn't stand a chance. He was a seller of dreams. I flash back to his lifeless body. Fortunately, he won't be able to sell any more dreams ever again. I give her another hug, and her sobs resume. I know what it's like to be in her shoes: to be victimized yet made to feel you deserved it. For years, I blamed myself. I won't let that happen to Mia.

"It's not your fault, Mia. It's not your fault. You did nothing wrong. You understand?"

She sniffles and nods. "Are those men going to jail?"

I place my arm on her shoulder. "Yes, all of them are going to jail. Those men won't ever be able to hurt you again." I wish I could tell her no man would ever hurt her again.

Her forehead scrunches. "Am I going to go to jail?"

I stifle my frustration that she even has to ask that question. "No, of course not. You've done nothing wrong."

"Where will I go?"

"We're going to find you a nice safe place to live, okay?"

"Where?"

"I'm not sure yet, but worse-case scenario, you can live with me. My roommate's a great cook. How's that sound?"

I give her the best smile I can through my swollen cheek, and she returns a close-mouthed grin.

A female officer with round cheeks and kind eyes approaches us and points to Mia.

"Ma'am, we're going to need to take her and the rest of the girls in now." She points at the bloody bandage on my leg. "And you need to go to the hospital."

I put my hand on Mia's shoulder.

"This nice lady is going to take care of you now, but I'll check on you in the morning. Here's my card. You can call me if you need anything. Anything at all."

"Thanks, Hazel," she says and starts walking away with the officer. In her limping walk, I can see the toll that this torture has taken on her.

"Oh, Mia, one more thing," I say.

She turns to look at me.

"You have a beautiful voice."

For the first time, I see that bright-white smile from the video cross her face. There's still some joy in her.

I just hope she can hang on to it.

Epilogue

Two weeks later

It's a gorgeous fall day in New York. I sit at a bench in Washington Square Park, drinking a sugar-free Red Bull (someday I'll quit) and soak in the scene. A pianist has dragged a baby grand into the park and is tinkling away at a song I've never heard but that captures the light, breezy air of the day. The sun moseys through the treetops, trying not to intrude. A faint smell of roasted nuts floats in the air as street-cart vendors prepare their food for the day. Couples roll strollers around, looking tired but content and going nowhere in particular.

It's been two weeks since the night at the Dionysus Theater. Thinking back to it still sickens me and probably always will. The smell of sweat and perfume. The little girls in makeup and lingerie. The lascivious, slobbering men groping them. The sadistic look in Andrew's eyes when he locked that door behind me. The sound of life escaping his throat when I stabbed him. I'm glad I was there, glad I could save those girls, but now I wish I could just ball it up and throw it in a trash bin and never look back. Of course, I can't. And I guess that's okay. I'm stronger now, harder now. I've been to places I never thought I'd go, and I have a better sense now of what I'm truly capable of.

I'm a survivor.

I shake the memories from my mind and force a smile onto my face. Some good things came from this case as well. Mia is safe now. It turns out that Madeline was telling the truth and she didn't have anything to do with Mia's kidnapping. She even stepped up and fulfilled her responsibilities as a mother, although I'm not sure how good she'll be. Mia will live with her from here on out, which makes me a little nervous but is probably better than the alternative. I went up to visit them last week at Madeline's "cabin" in Lake George, which is actually a ten-bedroom mansion. Madeline was true to her word and paid me one hundred grand on the spot. So I guess I don't have to worry about money for a little while. She let me keep the Tesla, too, although I don't know where I'm going to park it. It was pretty funny watching Madeline trying to be a mother—so stiff and awkward—but I can tell she cares and is trying, and I think that's probably what matters.

Mia's still having nightmares but slowly returning to physical health. She even invited her old roommate, Penny Besser, and a couple of other friends from Saint Agnes over for a sleepover, and the girls promptly forgot that Madeline and I even existed. As it should be.

The Manhattan DA has assured me she will prosecute Sonia, Andrew's father, and the rest of their associates and customers to the fullest extent of the law. That includes the murder of Gregory Goolsbee. It turns out Goolsbee suspected Sonia's scheme, so she set him up as the fall guy. They are also reopening the investigations into the "suicide" of Andrew's mother as well as the missing persons investigations of Olivia Blankenship, Brooke Anthony, Malika Washington, and the other girls that went missing from Saint Agnes. And the New York AG's office is investigating the Warren County Sheriff's Office to weed out any other remaining bad apples.

Fortunately, Bobby Riether is clean as well. Just a good cop in a bad police department. He's taking a leave of absence to figure out if he still wants to be a police officer. Believe it or not, he called me the other day and asked me out. I was flattered but told him now isn't the right time. I'm not a psychologist, but I'm pretty sure after your last boyfriend tries to rape and murder you, it's not a great idea to jump right back in the dating pool.

As for Saint Agnes, the New York State Office of Children and Family Services has temporarily taken over management. Sonia's poison spread to all parts of the institution, including staff and board members, so the state figured it would be better to start fresh. Thomas Mackenzie resigned from his post as headmaster, too heartbroken at what had happened under his watch to continue. While I never liked the man, part of me worries for Saint Agnes and the girls there. Thomas loved that place and loved those girls. He had strange methods, but he truly cared, and I wonder if that will get lost when it's managed by the state. But I guess the state plan is only temporary, and the hope is to appoint a new board and a new headmaster who can bring Saint Agnes into the future. Maybe there's a younger, kinder—maybe female—Thomas Mackenzie out there waiting in the wings.

We'll see.

"Whatchya thinking about?" says Kenny as he walks up to my bench with a paper bag full of bagels in his hand. He and I have a little tradition now of going to the park and eating bagels on Sunday. There's a place right by here that makes the best bagels and is extremely liberal with the cream cheese. He likes cinnamon raisin; I like Asiago with chives. I can smell the mix of flour and herbs coming from the bag as he opens it.

I snatch my bagel and unwrap it.

"I'm not thinking about anything in particular. Just what a whirlwind the past two weeks have been."

Kenny nods and sits down next to me. I think he's finally accepted the fact that we're just friends. He rubs his hands through his tennis ball hair.

"Yeah, about that, I've been thinking."

His legs bounce up and down.

"Have you now?" I say, taking a massive bite of my bagel. Cream cheese bursts out of the bagel and onto the corners of my lips, but I don't care. It's just that good.

"Yeah, I was wondering if you'd like to have an assistant?"

I nearly spit out my bagel chunk but eventually force it down.

"What do you mean? You just passed the police entry exam, and you're sort of hot shit given that you helped bust a sex trafficking ring. Not a lot of cops have that under their belt before they even start."

Kenny's eyes and nose crinkle.

"Thanks, Hazel. Yeah, I was excited about being a cop at first, but having watched you work for the past few months, I feel like I'd enjoy it more on the private side. Plus, I'd have a lot more fun working with you than a bunch of guys I don't know. And you need the help. I mean, since the news broke about the Dionysus Theater, your phone has been ringing off the hook. I'm already your personal messaging service. You can't take on these cases by yourself. Think about it. You can be Sherlock Holmes, and I can be Dr. Watson."

I've always worked alone, so at first, Kenny's idea seems

crazy to me. But the more he talks, the more I warm to the idea. He's right that business has been booming since Mia's case. And he's also right that I can't handle all those inquiries and still do my job well. And he saved my life. I owe him one. Although working with me will be more punishment than gift.

"You make a compelling case, Watson," I say, smiling.

"Really?"

"Yeah, why not? Let's give it a shot. We can try it, and if we end up hating each other, we'll just stop. *Cho and Shum* doesn't have the same ring as *Holmes and Watson*, but we'll make it work."

I raise my bagel up to Kenny like I'm toasting with a champagne glass.

"To Cho and Shum."

Kenny taps his bagel against mine.

"To Cho and Shum."

The two of us sit back in silence on our park bench with contented smiles glued to our faces. The pianist plays a merry tune, and pigeons flap by overhead. It will be a long time before I recover from what I've seen these past few months, but with a sidekick like Kenny, I'm ready to face whatever comes next.

Thank You

Thank you for reading *The Orphanage By The Lake*. I hope you had as much fun reading it as I did writing it.

You can find out what happens next to Hazel and Kenny by downloading *The Red Letter*, Book 2 in the Hazel Cho Series.

If you enjoyed the book, I encourage you to leave a review on my Goodreads and Amazon pages. Reviews from readers like you are the fuel that keeps authors like me going, so even a one-sentence review can make all the difference. Thank you so much for your support!

Check out my Amazon author page and follow me to see the full catalog of my novels and get updates on new releases. You can also find out about my upcoming projects and get access to deals on future books by visiting danielmillerbooks.com and signing up for my newsletter.

I love hearing from readers, so feel free to email me anytime with your thoughts at dan@danielmillerbooks.com. Lastly, in the rare event that you find a typo that has slipped through the cracks, please don't hesitate to message me and I'll get it fixed.

Thank you for your support.

About the Author

Daniel G. Miller is a bestselling author of the Tree of Knowledge and Hazel Cho Series. When he's not writing, he enjoys contemplating the "what-ifs" of the world, traveling and celebrating with his wife, and sitting on the couch like an ogre watching NBA basketball. He currently lives in Florida with his wife, Lexi.

You can connect with me on:

- https://danielmillerbooks.com
- https://twitter.com/danmillerauthor
- https://www.facebook.com/DanielGMillerAuthor
- https://www.instagram.com/danielgmillerauthor

Also by Daniel G. Miller

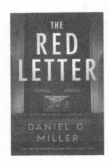

The Red Letter
A MYSTERIOUS LETTER

A SECRET FROM THE PAST

Hazel has everything she wants.

Business is booming at her boutique private investigation firm.

She's dating the man of her dreams.

Even her always skeptical mother seems impressed.

But when Hazel receives a red envelope containing a letter from a man from her past, haunting memories from an earlier time come roaring back to reality. **One by one the red letters continue to arrive, each one more mysterious and threatening than the last**, and Hazel realizes that to find the truth she must confront a sociopath that she locked away years ago. Her investigation leads her to question everything she thought she knew about herself and her past. Even worse, Hazel discovers that the only way to find the truth is to open one more...

RED LETTER

The Tree of Knowledge
Albert can see the future...

He just doesn't know it yet.

It is said that chess Grandmasters can envision a match's outcome ten moves before it occurs. Imagine a person who can visualize ten steps ahead, not simply in the game of chess, but in every human interaction.

Imagine a person who could anticipate what you would say before you said it, who could see a punch before it was thrown.

Imagine a secret that could make all of this possible.

Albert, a Princeton mathematics professor, is such a person, and as he is thrust into a murder and burglary investigation on campus he finds that the secret is buried in an obscure cipher. The discovery leads Albert to team up with an aging mentor, a curious graduate assistant, and an unusual "book club" on a frantic chase across the country to recover the secret and clear his name.

Through this adventure, he rediscovers a woman from his past and is forced to confront his own understanding of love, rationality, power, and the limits of the human mind.

Of Good & Evil: Book 2 in The Tree of Knowledge Series
Albert has seen the future...

Does he have the power to change it?

An unstoppable force is sweeping the United States. Powered by a secret ability to predict and manipulate events, Cristina Culebra and her RED Army relentlessly accumulate followers with one goal in mind: Absolute Power.

While Cristina and her movement captivate the country, the one man who knows their next move— who knows their every move—Mathematics Professor Albert Puddles, hides, grief-stricken from the loss of his one and only mentor. Hoping that Albert holds the key to solving the secrets of the RED Army, his comrades in arms, known as the "Book Club", recruit friends and foes alike to bring him back from exile.

But they may be too late, for a new enemy has risen to challenge Cristina and disrupt the Book Club's plans, a mysterious terrorist known only as "The Cipher".

Faced with twin threats to everything he holds dear, Albert is forced to use his singular power to decode the riddles of a dead man while reckoning with the ghosts of his past.

The Tree of Life: Book 3 in The Tree of Knowledge Series
Albert can see the future...

Does he have time to change it?

Albert, a Princeton mathematics professor, has discovered a secret known as The Tree of Knowledge—a method of predicting and manipulating the future with mathematical precision.

But he's not the only one.

Cristina Culebra, and her insurgent RED movement, seek to harness this same power to gain control of the United States and eventually the world.

Albert's only hope to stop Cristina's victory lies in a secretive global network dedicated to toppling tyrants the world over. But as Albert and his friends grow more enmeshed, they begin to question whether they've chosen the wrong side.

Or if there is a right side?

Faced with a frightening new world order, Albert races to save his friends and family and searches for the key to the cipher that may hold the secret to the Tree of Knowledge and possibly to life itself.